# A HERO DREAMS

**A NOVEL**

Linda,

So lovely meeting you! I'm looking forward to embarking on this journey with you... the hero's journey...

*[signature]*

# A HERO DREAMS

## A NOVEL

## MARK RISTAU

— Beaver's Pond Press —
*Minneapolis, MN*

**I Still Can't Say Goodbye**
By Bob Blinn and Jim Moore
Copyright © 1987 Athens Music and Captain Kidd Music
All Rights on behalf of Athens Music Administered by Sony/ATV Music Publishing LLC, 424 Church Street, Suite 1200, Nashville, TN 37219
International Copyright Secured All Rights Reserved
*Reprinted by Permission of Hal Leonard LLC*

This book is a work of fiction. Any references to historical events, real people, or real places are used fictitiously. Other names, characters, and events are products of the author's imagination.

Book Design by C. Tramell
Cover photograph by Matt Benson

ISBN: 978-1-59298-803-7
Library of Congress Catalog Number: 2017907379
Printed in Canada
First Printing: 2017
21 20 19 18 17     5 4 3 2 1

Beaver's Pond Press, Inc.
7108 Ohms Lane
Edina, MN 55439–2129

To order, visit www.ItascaBooks.com or call 1-800-901-3480 ext. 118.
Reseller discounts available.
For more information, visit www.MarkRistau.com

*For Dad*

*1938–1974*

# LIFE

FRAID? NO WAY. RICKY WASN'T AFRAID. How hard
could swimming be? It seemed to come so naturally
to the older boys. But still . . .

Behind him, an old banyan tree looked on with keen
interest but remained silent. What else could it do? After all, it
was just a tree.

At four years old, Ricky was ordinarily very good about
following instructions. On this day, however, his azure eyes
turned green with envy as the two older boys twisted and
bobbed in the far end of the pool—the deep end. Unaware of
Ricky's presence and displaying the exuberance of adolescent
porpoises, they splashed each other with tidal waves tinted
blue and sharp with the scent of chlorine. Their voices rang
out in a spirited duet of yelps that carried across the length of
the pool and throughout the gulf-side resort.

The midday sun shone brightly—so brightly that Ricky
had to squint against the glare rising up from the pool's rippled

surface. Turning his little head away, he spied the gulf. Except for the occasional dwarf-sized wave rolling lazily toward the sandy coastline, it was calm. A gentle whisper arose from the surf and encouraged him to move forward.

His mother had told him to stay away from the water, but when he found an unattended Donald Duck inner tube lying on the deck, it was too tempting.

With the grinning mallard now wrapped snuggly around his waist, he stepped forward, pushed himself away from the stairs, and floated into the pool. His tiny feet dangled freely beneath him. His chest swelled with exhilaration. He started to kick.

*This is fun!*

"Dougy! Gordy! It's time for lunch!"

"Coming!" they cried before climbing out of the pool and following their parents back to the condominium.

Ricky was alone now. *All alone.* He felt a shiver of apprehension. Then suddenly and without any apparent cause, he slipped through the middle of the tube and down into the water.

*It's cold!*

He grabbed for the tube but succeeded only in knocking it away. Rising to the surface, he watched helplessly as Donald floated out of reach. Like a wounded duckling, Ricky flapped his arms and kicked his legs but couldn't prevent himself from sinking.

Through seemingly infinite layers of pale-blue water and a swirling multitude of bubbles, the distorted outline of a washed-out sun looked down at Ricky with cool detachment.

Stretching his hands toward the distant sphere, he rose to the surface . . . and down again . . . up and down . . . up and down . . . over and over and over until, coming up for one last breath, he spotted a group of grown-ups lounging under a cluster of palm trees. Daddy wasn't among them. Frantically, Ricky looked for Mommy, but she, too, was nowhere to be seen.

The last droplet of fight drained from his body.

It was over.

Then his eyes met with and melded into the eyes of a young woman. *An angel!* Time stopped. Weightless now and hanging in suspended animation over the water, he gazed deeply into those eyes—each a swirling river of chocolate—where there were no rules to follow, no harsh words, and no punishments. Just pure love.

Still floating in midair, he disappeared more deeply into those eyes and discovered another world—a hidden world filled with pain and sadness, one spinning desperately out of control. A lump rose into his throat.

In spite of her inner turmoil, Ricky's angel spoke tenderly to him, her words embracing him and filling him with a sense of calm and boundless wonder.

*Something's wrong here, my love . . . and together, we're going to make it right.*

The moment ended as quickly and unexpectedly as it had begun. The young woman's eyes widened. A look of alarm spread across her face. In one graceful motion, she leaped up from her chair and dived into the pool as the boy disappeared into the water for the last time.

The next thing he knew, Ricky was sitting hunched over by the side of the pool, coughing up a lungful of water and shivering under the warm midday sun. He was surrounded by grown-ups.

"Oh my God!"

"What happened?"

"Is he okay?"

"Ricky, you scared me half to death!"

He closed his eyes and willed the voices to stop. If only he could swim—but no, it was too late. The damage was done. He had messed everything up. Again. His face and ears turned hot. Tears streamed down his cheeks. He hated being the center of attention.

He thought of his angel—her kind face; those sweet, chocolatey eyes; and the sadness hidden deep within.

*I can help. I can take her sadness away. I know I can!*

Opening his eyes, he scanned the growing swarm of worried faces, but she wasn't there. He stood up, bolted through the crowd, and ran to the beach. She wasn't there either. She was gone! He looked back at the pool and, for the first time, noticed the old banyan tree. A strong breeze blew in from the gulf, raising goose bumps on the back of his neck.

There was something familiar about that tree. He almost thought he could see an image of some kind woven into its mysterious web of twisting and interconnecting roots. *A message?* But no matter how hard he squinted against the intense Floridian sun, he couldn't make it out.

With a deep sigh, he forgot all about the tree, turned away from the pool area, and looked out over the Gulf of Mexico.

*There's something wrong with me—very wrong. I can't do anything right. I can't even swim.*

*Yes, my love. Something's wrong. And together, we're going to make it right.*

# LOSS

*No matter how hard I try*
*No matter how many tears I cry*
*No matter how many years go by*
*I still can't say goodbye*

—Bob Blinn and Jim Moore

# CHAPTER ONE

SOMEWHERE, *SOMEWHERE* IN THIS OVERSIZED DESK, there's a sheet of paper—yellowing, frayed along the edges, and embossed with the seal of the State of New York—a *single* sheet of paper that insists upon referring to me as Richard Atticus Williamson. Yet I've always been known as simply Ricky. Haven't I? If I could just find the damned thing, it would prove once and for all I was born in Brooklyn.

Brooklyn. I have no memories of Brooklyn.

You see, Stanley, before I reached my first birthday, my father accepted a teaching position at Seton Hall University and moved our fledgling family of three across the Upper Bay and into a redbrick house kitty-corner from the elementary school in South Orange, New Jersey. A few months later, my mother gave birth to my brother, Danny.

Other than almost drowning in a swimming pool at the age of four, I had a fairly normal and carefree childhood until

February 11, 1974, when my father died suddenly from an aortic aneurysm. He was thirty-five. I was eight.

I loved both my parents, but I was especially close to my father. As far as I was concerned, his word and the word of God were one and the same.

When I was almost five, I decided to ask my father about my rather unusual middle name. Phonetically, *Atticus* sounded weird to me—more like what one might say in response to a sneeze than a name—and I wanted to know what it meant before setting off for my first day of preschool.

Sitting me down in the kitchen nook, my father first tied my shoelaces and then looked me squarely in the eyes. I shivered with anticipation. He smiled and, in his usual tone of unquestionable mastery of all things in heaven and earth, he explained that my middle name belonged to a fictional character who represented the principle of standing up for what you know in your heart is true, *no matter what.*

"No matter what?" I asked in a breathy whisper that escaped through the comically wide gap separating my two front teeth. I was enthralled. Without really having any idea what he was talking about, I was enthralled.

"No matter what," he assured me. "No matter what anyone else thinks, says, or does, you must always be true to yourself and what you know is right. One of the greatest challenges—" He stopped short to correct himself, as he often did when making an important point. "*The* greatest challenge in life is to have complete and utter faith in yourself and to listen to the voice deep inside you, regardless of what's going on in the outside world."

Without releasing me from his hypnotic gaze, he leaned in close and touched me lightly on the shoulder before continuing.

"You'll be exposed to a lot of nonsense as you grow up. Don't listen to it, Ricky. I want you to promise me that when things are difficult and you're confused and don't know what to do, you'll follow your heart."

"I promise, Daddy."

My father was everything to me. With him gone, life as I knew it was over. Yet as the oldest son, I had to be strong. I had to be responsible.

After my mother broke the news to me, I wandered into the kitchen with the wooden shaft of a broom gripped tightly in my hands and began sweeping the floor. My heart had just been shattered beyond repair, yet somehow I had to find it within myself to continue—continue living, continue breathing, and continue sweeping, sweeping, sweeping. Clenching my teeth so hard my jaw ached, I swept that floor with every living fiber of my being. I swept every square inch of its surface, every corner, every nook and cranny, over and over again. Sweeping, sweeping, sweeping . . .

At the tender age of eight, I had become head of the household. Of course, I was nowhere near up to the task. Unfortunately, neither was my mother. She promised me we would survive by living our lives one day at a time. As it turned out, my mother "survived" by drinking. I survived by looking after my mother.

After the funeral and an unbearably long weekend of tears, hugs, and heartfelt condolences, I plodded home from my first day back at school in a zombielike funk to find my mother passed out in bed with a lowball glass in one hand and the smoldering remains of a cigarette in the other. On the night-stand, a cracked porcelain ashtray overflowed with at least a dozen lipstick-smeared butts. An empty bottle of Smirnoff lay label-side up on the carpet. Exercising painstaking care so as not to wake her, I removed the cigarette from her fingers and stubbed it out in the ashtray before cleaning up the mess. When I was done, I pulled the sheets up to my mother's chin, kissed her cheek, and tiptoed out of the room, closing the door behind me.

In my bedroom, I stood at the window facing our muddy backyard, which was bordered with a sparse row of naked shrubs. Directly below, a long and winding driveway slith-ered past the house before turning toward the garage in the far back corner of our lot. Gazing vacantly through the swirl-ing clouds of fingerprints that smudged the windowpane, I waited for my father to appear in our powder-blue Pontiac LeMans.

*Fiery-red taillights pierce the gray afternoon. Daddy parks the car and within seconds emerges from the garage. He looks up at me with a big smile. He waves. "How you doin', sport?"*

I waved back, but he was no longer there. In his place was nothing but a patch of dirty snow successfully eluding a springtime I believed would never arrive. Still I contin-ued my vigil. The gray afternoon darkened into evening. Just before midnight, a menagerie of wet snowflakes and rain-drops streaked the windowpane. I lowered my face into my skinny arms and wept.

The passage of time had come to a screeching halt for me. But like a freight train leaving the station, its wheels creeping sluggishly along the rails and its engines wailing in mighty protest, time resumed its journey. It lurched forward slowly, very slowly at first, each day surrendering itself grudgingly to the next and each week disappearing quietly over the horizon. As the train's momentum increased, a year passed, and then two.

*Friday, June 11–Saturday, July 3, 1976*

The last day of school fell on a Friday in early June. That morning we attended classes—a mere formality, perhaps, yet a necessary prelude to the beginning of summer, we were told. At noon, the annual end-of-year picnic commenced. Swarms of hooting and hollering kids stormed the school's front lawn. Beaming parents and teachers looked on. I stood off to one side with my hands buried in my pockets, torn between staying for the cookout and going straight home.

Hamburgers and hot dogs sizzled on a grill that opened up toward a cloudless sky like a small fishing boat filled not with the day's catch but with mounds of glowing charcoal briquettes. Tables adorned with red-and-white-checkered cloths were jam-packed with plastic containers of baked beans, coleslaw, potato salad, and the like. Waves of popcorn poured from a machine on wooden-spoked wagon wheels.

Pink webs of cotton candy spun out of another. Lines formed. The celebration had begun.

Next to the popcorn and cotton candy machines stood a dunk tank with a sign that read: "Dunk Your Favorite (Or Not-So-Favorite) Teacher, 3 Chances: 25 Cents." My brother, Danny, stepped up and took aim, intent upon dunking his third-grade teacher, Mr. Garrison. Throwing the ball in one fluid motion, he hit the target dead center. Down went Mr. Garrison into the water. Up jumped Danny into the air, squealing with delight. I smiled. My little brother had become quite an athlete.

The broken sound of the first few bars of "Kung Fu Fighting" filled the air. Principal McFadden had hired an exceptionally untalented cover band to entertain us with the previous year's pop hits. We'd already been treated to barely recognizable versions of "Listen to What the Man Said," "Some Kind of Wonderful," and "You Ain't Seen Nothing Yet." I was more in the mood for Queen's "Bohemian Rhapsody," but they didn't appear to be taking requests.

"Why do you spend so much time alone, Ricky?" asked Principal McFadden. He had appeared out of nowhere.

I removed my hands from my pockets and crossed my arms. "I dunno. I'm just thinking, I guess."

A cool breeze blew in from the hills that overlooked the village. It ruffled my hair, which had grown long, more from neglect than an attempt to be fashionable. My mother didn't seem to care one way or the other, and neither did I. Then I felt a presence—an utterly palpable presence that gathered me in an unexpected embrace. A shiver traveled up and down my spine.

*Daddy?*

It was almost, *almost* as if my father were there with us, listening to "Kung Fu Fighting" and watching Danny take another shot at dunking Mr. Garrison. Just as suddenly as the feeling came, it disappeared.

"Why don't you get yourself a hot dog, my boy? Have some fun." With that, Principal McFadden receded into the crowd.

I slipped my hands back into my pockets, looked down at the thick green grass, and chewed on my lower lip. As of eleven forty-five that morning, fourth grade was behind me. Somehow the winter of '74 had become the summer of '76, yet the memory of my father's death remained as fresh as ever.

My mother had promised me we would survive by living our lives one day at a time.

"Yes, but when will I start to feel better?" I demanded after she had repeated that promise for the hundredth time.

She just smiled sadly and made me another promise—that I would feel better "in time."

But it had been over two years now, and I felt worse, not better. The adage that "time heals all wounds" was a lie.

Coming out of my thoughts, I gazed out into the crowd of teachers, parents, and students celebrating on the sun-drenched front lawn of Marshall Elementary. Danny had moved on from the dunk tank to Jacob's Ladder. I had no doubt he would reach the top and ring the bell with no difficulty whatsoever. My tummy rumbled. Ignoring my hunger, I turned away from the festivities and plodded home with my hands still in my pockets.

"I have a big surprise for the two of you!" my mother exclaimed as we sat down that evening to a specially prepared meal of baked chicken, instant mashed potatoes, and peas, which I had been eyeing suspiciously. "Two spots just opened up for the second session at Camp Abenaki Valley, and I enrolled you both. You boys are going to summer camp!"

"When?" I asked, stunned by the news.

"In July."

"For how long?"

"Five weeks."

*Five weeks?*

My mother had made an executive decision to send Danny and me away. We had no say in the matter. Her friends the Underwoods had two sons who had attended Camp Abenaki Valley for the past several summers and loved it. Camp Abenaki Valley was located in southern Maine, a forty-five-minute drive from Portland and a six-hour drive from South Orange. A six-hour drive!

"It'll be an amazing experience for you boys. They have so many activities to choose from."

"But, Mom—"

"And the camp overlooks the prettiest little pond. See?" Holding up a glossy brochure and showing all her teeth, she looked just like one of Barker's Beauties from *The Price Is Right*. "And there are mountains nearby. You boys can go hiking in the mountains!"

"Sounds fun," Danny said with his usual enthusiasm.

With another summer upon us and no improvement in my emotional state, my mother probably thought that sending me to camp was just what I needed—a change in scenery to snap me out of my melancholic funk. Or maybe she wanted us out of the way for five weeks so she could go on her all-night cocktail-drinking binges with our next-door neighbor, Mrs. Payne, without having to face us the next day. Whatever her reasons, I wanted no part of it.

"I don't want to go."

"Ricky—"

"No! Danny can go if he wants, but I'm not going!" I jumped up from the table and ran upstairs to my bedroom, leaving my chicken and mashed potatoes untouched.

My mother followed me into my room, where I was lying facedown in bed with my head buried in the pillow. She sat on the edge of the mattress and ran her fingers through my hair a few times. It felt good.

"Ricky . . ."

Even though I was having difficulty breathing, I didn't look up.

"Ricky, darling, it's only five weeks. It'll be good for you. It'll be good for us."

"How will it be good for *us*?" I demanded, raising my head from the pillow.

"It'll be a great experience. You might even have some fun. As for me, I need some time—"

"Away from us."

"No, that's not what I meant. I just need some time to myself for a few weeks."

"Mom, it's *five* weeks. That's forever!"

"Nonsense, Ricky. It'll be over before you know it. Besides, you'll have a wonderful time. I promise. They have archery, baseball, canoeing, swimming . . ."

*Swimming?*

I swallowed hard. A knot formed in my stomach. After almost drowning, I had taken swimming lessons. My parents had insisted. But I never got past the fear. It was like a poison I carried wherever I went. Most of the time, it lay dormant in the cells of my body. But it didn't take much to trigger a response, which was either to become hysterical or shut down. On this particular occasion, I shut down and complied with my mother's wishes.

"Okay. Maybe five weeks isn't so long after all." I reached for my stomach. The poison was hard at work, attacking vital organs and wreaking havoc on my bodily functions. "Mom, I have a tummy ache. Mind if I skip dinner tonight?"

"A tummy ache? Hmm . . . Do you have a fever?" She placed an open palm on my forehead.

"I don't think so. It's just my tummy."

"Well . . . okay. But let me know if you're feeling better. I'll keep your plate warm, just in case."

Danny and I were due to report at camp on July 17—just over a month away. In the meantime, we had little league baseball to keep us occupied. It was Danny's first year, my second. In my first year, I had earned the title of Strikeout

King. In his first year, he was leading the league in batting average and home runs. In fact, according to the local buzz, my little brother was the best pure hitter ever to come through the South Orange little league system. In the field—when he wasn't pitching complete-game shutouts—he sparkled at shortstop, never once making an error, and turning double plays in a league where the rest of us were happy to get one out at a time. Danny was a natural.

After a game in which he had thrown a no-hitter and gone four-for-four at the plate, including two singles, a double, and a grand slam, the local paper interviewed his coach, who went on record saying, "Amazing. Simply amazing. Never seen nothin' like it. That Williamson boy is gonna play professional ball one day."

Danny led his team to an undefeated regular season, followed by a relentless march through the playoffs that set up a July 3 championship game between his team and mine. In our semifinal, my team won 3–2 on a wild pitch in the bottom of the tenth. I scored the winning run from third base and allowed myself a brief moment of joy as my teammates mobbed me at home plate. But the moment was tempered by what I knew lay ahead—a showdown with my brother on the following Saturday.

That week, the townspeople talked of little else. With each passing day, excitement grew. It seemed everyone wanted to watch the two Williamson boys go head-to-head in the biggest game of the season. Many families, including our next-door neighbors on both sides, canceled their plans to go to the shore for the holiday weekend. We became instant and somewhat reluctant celebrities. There were phone calls from old friends and impromptu visits from neighbors. Baked goods appeared at our doorstep with greeting cards wishing us well. Even the reporter who had interviewed Danny's coach came to our house. He convinced my mother to allow him to visit on the promise that he would interview both of us. When he arrived, however, he spent the entire hour asking Danny about his accomplishments and prospects for the future.

The day of the big game arrived. Sunshine flooded the sky. Lines formed around a Good Humor truck camped out in the Cameron Field parking lot. Parking spaces became scarce. A light breeze carried the *pop* of a Black Cat firecracker over the treetops and across the well-manicured field. A whistling bottle rocket painted a smoky arc across the sky's impossibly blue canvas.

As my team took infield practice, I did my best not to be distracted by the gathering hordes, but I couldn't help feeling overwhelmed by the commotion. Just before game time, I heard that almost a thousand spectators were in attendance, many of whom were from neighboring towns and had come to catch a glimpse of my brother, "the young Williamson phenom." My mouth was dry as sandpaper. My stomach churned. My hands shook. I grabbed a bat and held it until my knuckles turned white. On other side of the diamond, Danny sat calmly on his bench, apparently oblivious to it all.

The Knights of Columbus Pipes and Drums Band took the field to perform "The Star-Spangled Banner." A woman in a feathery white dress stepped up to a microphone. A hush fell over the crowd.

"O-oh, say can you see, by the dawn's early light . . ."

There was something about that woman's voice. It was smooth as silk yet powerful beyond measure. I imagined she was singing for me—only me. An emotion striking the midpoint between sadness and exhilaration rose up and filled my chest. My heart raced. As her voice soared, I held on for dear life but felt myself being swept away by an emotional crescendo.

"O'er the la-and of the free and the home of the brave."

Whipped into a patriotic fervor, the crowd cheered wildly. Danny's team took the field. My heart steadied itself. I was ready to play ball.

The final result was predictably anticlimactic. It went badly for my team from the start. With Danny pitching, we were held scoreless while his team posted nine runs in the first three innings. Then the bases were loaded when he came to bat in the bottom of the fourth and promptly slugged the first pitch over the left field fence, making the score thirteen to nothing and invoking the ten-run rule. The umpire stepped forward from behind home plate, waved his arms in the air, and put the contest to a merciful end.

"That's it, folks," he announced. "Have a happy and safe Fourth of July."

That was it, indeed. I wanted to curl up under the bleachers and disappear. Instead I trudged off the field and joined my teammates on the visitors' bench. No one spoke. For the first time ever, the ten-run rule had been invoked in a championship game. Our loss would be remembered as one of the worst in town history. In addition to his game-ending grand slam, Danny had hit two doubles while leading his team to the lopsided victory. I had been hitless in my team's losing effort. Sitting on the bench with my shoulders hunched forward over my knees, I overheard a departing fan exclaim, "That Williamson kid sure can play ball!" These words were salt in my wounds, for it was painfully obvious to which "Williamson kid" he was referring.

After celebrating with his teammates, Danny crossed the diamond and offered me his hand. He smiled brightly. His eyes twinkled. There wasn't a speck of sympathy in those eyes, just the pure joy that came from playing a game he loved. Winning was never the object for him; it was simply a natural by-product of his passion for the game. I believed he would have been just as happy if his team had lost. For me, on the other hand, winning meant a great deal, for I had something to prove—that I was worthy of being Danny Williamson's older brother.

In spite of our father's death, Danny was a happy kid. He had grieved for a short while, put the unpleasant past behind him, and moved on, taking our mother's advice and living "one day at a time." Later, when we were adults, I asked him to share his secret with me. He shrugged and replied simply, "That's easy, Ricky. I have a short memory."

Still extending his hand, Danny said, "Good game, Ricky. Great season."

I hated him in that moment. How could he stand there smiling like that and offer to shake my hand after single-handedly inflicting such a crushing defeat on me and my team? Was he mocking me? No, of course not. I knew he was sincere, but still I hated him. I hated his smile. I hated that he was acting as if he were the older brother approaching me with congratulations. As the older brother, I should have been the one taking the high road and approaching him instead of sitting on my bench, wallowing in self-pity. I hated that he was a better sport than I was. I hated that he was a better athlete than I was. Most of all, I hated myself for hating my own brother. I was so ashamed and envious I could barely stand it, but I somehow found it within myself to shake his hand anyway.

I smiled weakly and said, "Thanks, Danny. You too."

That evening, my mother took Danny and me back to the baseball field—the scene of the crime. Whose crime? Mine, of course. I was the guilty one.

Staying together, we navigated the crowd and laid our picnic blanket on the outfield grass alongside a cluster of some other players and their parents, who were waiting eagerly for the fireworks to begin. Thoughts of the afternoon's game began to fade. Joining our friends, Danny and I devoured two large bags of popcorn and watched in wonder as hundreds of lightning bugs appeared in the purplish twilight sky.

"Look, Danny!" I whispered. "One of them just landed on your shoulder."

"Where?" He twisted his head in both directions but couldn't locate the insect. "I can't see it."

"Be careful. It's right there," I said, pointing at his shoulder. "Don't swipe at it. You might hurt it."

"I'm sorry. I'll be careful."

"Okay, good. Hold still. Watch this."

I reached for his shoulder and rested my hand, palm side up, next to the tiny creature. Without a moment's hesitation, the fearless lightning bug crawled into my palm, while Danny, trying not to move, giggled with delight. I raised my hand toward the sky. The insect's tail turned incandescent gold. Then it spread its wings and disappeared into the night. We looked at each other and smiled.

"That was neat," said Danny.

My smile broadened into a wide grin, but I said nothing. There was nothing to say. For the first time in a long while, I was simply enjoying my brother's company. It reminded me of how good it used to feel when we would take walks with Mom and Dad along the leaf-carpeted trails winding through South Mountain Reservation's cedar-scented forests. Or collect shells on a beach in Florida. Or just watch a sunset together. The simplest things always brought us the most happiness.

Of course, that precious moment couldn't last forever. Soon, *too* soon, it was interrupted by an endless stream of people descending upon us to congratulate Danny on a great game and phenomenal season. As one person after another showered him with praise, I felt myself becoming invisible. He didn't seem affected one way or the other, but I was bewildered. What had he done to deserve this outpouring of public adoration? Sure, he was a good baseball player. But did that make him a town hero? Had this nine-year-old boy given the people of South Orange something to believe in?

As the procession of Danny's doting fans continued, I sat there on the blanket, picking at the tiny pieces of popcorn stuck between my teeth and watching him hold court. My mother made a few halfhearted attempts to persuade them to respect our privacy, but it was like trying to hold back a tsunami with a single sandbag. On and on they came, one wave after another. She soon surrendered. I couldn't decide which irritated me more—the wanton disregard of our privacy or the intractable pieces of popcorn lodged in my mouth. I closed my eyes and prayed for the fireworks to begin.

Finally, a thunderous *boom* brought the procession to a halt. Everyone scurried back to their spots in the outfield. The oohs and aahs began. A brilliant medley of colors exploded across the sky. I fell into a trance and watched breathlessly as they turned to ash and trickled down to earth.

When we got home, I went straight to the bathroom and spent the next twenty minutes flossing and brushing my teeth. As with sweeping the floor, I would be satisfied with nothing short of perfection. When I was finished, I went into my bedroom, put on my pajamas, and crawled into bed. A knock came at the door. Mom poked her head in.

"Too old to be tucked in?"

As soon as I saw her face, the tears began to flow. "Why do things always work out for Danny?" I sobbed.

She pulled the blanket over my chest and up to my chin, where she knew I liked it.

"You have magnificent days ahead of you, Ricky. You do. You're a very special boy, and you're going to have a wonderful life. Someday, today's baseball game will seem unimportant. You might even forget all about it."

"It's not just the game. It's everything. Why does he have to·
be the best at *everything* he does? It's not fair. I hate him."

"You don't mean that."

"Yes, I do!"

"Ricky . . ."

"No, I don't mean it."

Smiling now, she tried to cheer me up with promises
of how much fun we would have the following day in New
York, where we would be celebrating the bicentennial with the
Andersons and the Walkers—friends of ours who had stayed
close and looked after us since my father's death. Each family
had children about the same ages as Danny and me. They were
really nice kids, and I always enjoyed our outings together.

For the past two years, we had gathered to celebrate
Independence Day on Long Island, in a little town called
Bridgehampton. During our last visit, there was quite a commotion when, just after release of the movie *Jaws*, we saw
the fin of a great white shark bobbing in the waves just off
the shore of Sagg Main Beach. Everyone was ordered out of
the water while the lifeguards monitored the situation. After
much discussion, it was determined the shark was either sick
or dying and not a threat. Besides, the fin had disappeared.
Satisfied with this reasoning, the lifeguards announced it
was safe to go back into the water. *Safe?* Were they insane?
Wasn't it obvious that a sick shark was just as great a threat
to human life as a healthy shark? Not that I needed a reason
to avoid the water, but our shark sighting provided me with
a convenient excuse for staying safely on the beach for the
remainder of the trip.

This year we would go into the city to walk the international street festival and see the parade of tall ships in New York Harbor. It sounded fun. I started to feel a little better.

Mom kissed me on the forehead and stood up. "Good night, darling. Keep the faith."

"That's what Dad would say."

"I know."

"Mom?"

"Yes, Ricky?"

"I wish he was here."

"Me too, honey." She moved quietly to the door, hesitated for a moment, then turned out the light and was gone.

# CHAPTER TWO

*Sunday, July 4, 1976*

THE NEXT MORNING, WE MET the Andersons and Walkers on the street level of the sixty-year-old train station that crossed over South Orange Avenue. Mr. Anderson emerged from the shadows of the underpass, followed by a flock of pigeons escaping into daylight. Flashing an endearing smile that made me think of Herman Munster, he greeted my mother with a hug and a peck on the cheek.

"Hi, boys. We enjoyed yesterday's game," he said, adding diplomatically, "you both had great seasons."

Very tall and lean, Mr. Anderson walked with a subtle but noticeable limp caused by a congenital discrepancy in the length of his legs. Yet with his boundless supply of energy, it didn't slow him down. In fact, his kids often admonished him: "Wait up, Daddy! You're going too fast . . . *again!*"

Mom touted Mr. Anderson as a "big-time New York City lawyer." Using his privileges as a partner with one of the city's most prestigious firms, he had arranged for us to view the Fourth of July street parade from the firm's office building overlooking Fifth Avenue. Later in the day, we would watch the parade of tall ships from the shoreline along Battery Park.

Mrs. Anderson came next with hugs and kisses for us all. She was one of the sweetest and most loving people I had ever known. After my father's death, she was at our house daily for at least two weeks, preparing meals and looking after Danny and me. When we needed one most, she had become a second mother to us.

The Andersons had two daughters, Marsha and Linda, ages eleven and nine, and a son, Gary, the baby of the family at age six.

"Hi, Danny!" cried Gary, overjoyed to see his new hero. Immediately, he began to pepper Danny with questions. "How many home runs didja hit this year? When ya gonna turn pro? Who's ya favorite Yankee? D'ya think the Yankees are gonna win the World Series?"

"Give Danny some breathing room, honey," said Mrs. Anderson.

The Walkers were more reserved than the Andersons but every bit as friendly. Mrs. Walker approached my mother and embraced her warmly. Mr. Walker stepped forward with their children, twelve-year-old Christopher and nine-year-old Claire. Mr. Walker, an architect, was a rather stout fellow with a thick but well-groomed beard that had just begun to turn gray. Christopher and Claire referred to him affectionately as Papa Bear.

When all greetings had been exchanged, Mr. Anderson assumed command and marshaled us up two flights of stairs to the east platform, where all trains departed for New York. The Erie Lackawanna approached from the south and lurched to a stop. We climbed aboard. Falling into a state of disorder, the children competed with each other for the best seats, while the adults took care of purchasing tickets from the conductor. When our game of musical chairs was over, I was sitting alone, one row in front of Mom and Mrs. Walker and one row behind Danny and Gary.

As we pulled out of the station, I gazed down at the platform and thought of the terrible accident that had occurred back in late December, a couple of days before New Year's Eve: Well after sunset, four teenaged boys had been walking on these very same tracks, within sight of the station, when three of them were hit from behind. News of their deaths spread quickly throughout South Orange over the next few days, dampening the town's spirits as we prepared to welcome the new year.

Pondering the tragedy, I disappeared into my head. The accelerating *clippety-clop* of the train's wheels faded into the background. My imagination—*my imagination?*—conjured dreadful images. In one, the boys made impact with the front of the locomotive before being launched like human projectiles into the air. In another, one of the lifeless bodies hung in a nearby evergreen tree, like some kind of macabre Christmas ornament. In an alternative scenario, I pictured the three boys being ripped to shreds under the train's steely wheels, their blood painting the tracks bright red. I thought of the surviving boy and tried to imagine how being witness to such images might affect the rest of his life. *If only there were something I could do to help . . .*

Although I didn't know the boys personally, news of their deaths distressed me so much that I slept only fitfully in the weeks following the accident. Bathed in pools of sweat, I would wake in the middle of the night from nightmares filled with ear-piercing cries of train whistles and gruesome images of body parts flying in silhouette across a sky illuminated by a bloodred moon. Often I would wake screaming, "My angel! Where are you, my angel?" before urgently scanning the darkness for something, *anything* familiar. Only then would I be comforted by the warm glow of a light reaching out to me from the far corner of my bedroom. It was my nightlight—a miniature replica of a colonial American lighthouse that served me throughout my childhood years as a loyal and faithful beacon of hope.

Throughout those first few wintry months of 1976, South Orange reverberated from the emotional aftershocks of the incident. Then, as spring approached, people returned to their daily concerns, and the reverberations subsided. My nightmares of train whistles and flying body parts became less frequent. But they were replaced by a different type of nightmare—of being trapped deep underneath the surface of a chillingly familiar pale-blue body of water with the distorted outline of a cold and distant sun staring down at me from above.

The world was not a safe place. I had reached this all-too-logical conclusion long before the three boys were killed on the train tracks. Disaster lurked in every corner. Every twist and turn in the road needed to be negotiated with the utmost care to ensure survival.

My greatest fear was that my mother would follow my father's path and die, leaving Danny and me alone in the world. When I expressed this fear to her, she stated in no uncertain terms that she was *not* going to die. But I was inconsolable. I knew better than to be comforted by her words, for that was all they were—words, mere words, nothing more than meaningless utterances swirling around in the space between us like powdery snowflakes in the wind before coming to rest and melting into the sidewalk.

*Clippety-clop . . . clippety-clop . . . clippety-clop . . .*

Still looking out the train's window, I turned my gaze upward. Although the skies were cloudy, my mood lightened—lightened ever so incrementally—as we approached the city, leaving one bedroom community after another in our wake. My intuition told me disaster wouldn't be striking. Not today.

At quarter to eleven, we disembarked at Penn Station. Making sure we stayed together, Mr. Anderson led our troop through the bustling concourse to the Thirty-Second Street exit, where we climbed the stairs into the open air of the city. A light haze blanketed the sky. It was pleasantly warm. The streets buzzed with the energy of an occasion that comes only once in a lifetime.

A horn blared. And another. Soon a grand ensemble of car horns filled the air, not with the sound of anger and frustration one might expect, but with music—music of goodwill and celebration. A fleet of convertibles painted red, white, and blue and decorated with fluttering streamers pulled up beside us. At the wheel of the one closest to me sat a man dressed up as none other than General George Washington. He beeped his horn and waved at the crowd. I caught his eye and, not knowing what else to do, saluted him. Producing a brilliant smile, he returned the salute. The fleet moved on.

Falling into formation behind Mr. Anderson, we marched toward his Fifth Avenue office at an upbeat tempo we would maintain for the rest of the day.

We had Mr. Anderson's twentieth-floor conference room all to ourselves. Lined up with our faces pressed against the window, we watched marching bands, decorative floats, and huge bundles of red, white, and blue balloons advance up Fifth Avenue. About a dozen Uncle Sams filtered through the crowd, passing out miniature American flags to onlookers, who shook them in a collective wave of patriotic fervor as the parade passed by. I wanted one of those flags.

"Can we—"

Cutting me off, Gary complained he was hungry, and immediately this sentiment was echoed by the others. Acting quickly to avert a mutiny, Mr. Anderson pulled out a copy of the *New York Times*, which included a special bicentennial insert with a complete schedule of events for the day. He laid the insert flat on the conference room table, and we formed a huddle around him. The parade of tall ships was to begin at one thirty, so there was plenty of time for lunch.

On Fifth Avenue, we were promptly assimilated into a swarming multitude of parade goers. I spotted a mini flag lying on the sidewalk and snatched it up.

"Come on, Ricky!" Danny shouted above the thunderous music reverberating between the buildings that lined the street.

With Mr. Anderson once again leading us, we disappeared into a crisscrossing maze of city streets that had been closed to traffic for the international festival. From endless rows of booths, vendors served foods from countries all over the world—Japan, China, Korea, Thailand, France, Italy, Greece, India, Mexico, and many others. Grills produced clouds of smoke that hovered overhead and infused the city with an intoxicating scent that made my head spin. In the midst of this exotic mélange of edibles, there was a two-wheeled push-cart sporting a red-and-yellow umbrella and serving plain old American hot dogs. Danny and Gary made a beeline for the cart. Feeling adventurous, I approached a Korean stand and ordered something called bulgogi. At home, I was used to such delicacies as peanut butter and jelly on white bread, mac and cheese, Shake 'n Bake, Hamburger Helper, and pigs in a blanket. So when the vendor handed me a paper plate filled with a conglomeration of grilled marinated beef and vegetables, I eyed it with a healthy level of suspicion. Taking my first bite, however, I discovered it was absolutely delicious!

After an uneventful subway ride and a short walk from the Bowling Green stop, we found ourselves—all twelve present and accounted for—on a crowded dock just north of Battery Park. Shoulder to shoulder and hip to hip, we gazed out into New York Harbor and waited for the first tall ships to come into view. Behind us, the Twin Towers of the World Trade

Center ascended into the afternoon haze and kept dutiful watch over the proceedings. Their presence comforted me but also made me feel small and insignificant—a tiny soldier in a vast army of ants congregating at the foot of the Tower of Babel. Above us, the Goodyear Blimp circled the harbor, humming gently.

*The roar of a jet airplane overcomes me. It's so loud my skull cracks down the middle and my head splits in two. I reach for my ears and fall forward into a black cloud of smoke, choking and coughing as I go . . . It smells and tastes like burning rubber, like our laundry room when the dryer went crazy and the fire department had to come . . . My knees strike the dock with a smack. I look up and the towers are gone . . . they're gone . . .*

"Ricky!" exclaimed my mother. "Are you okay?"

Uninjured but embarrassed, I picked myself up from the dock and muttered, "I'm fine. Someone must have bumped into me, that's all."

"Are you sure you're all right?"

"Yes, Mom. I'm sure."

"Well, it's awfully crowded. Try to be more careful, okay?"

I returned my gaze to the sky. The blimp was making another circle around the harbor. There were no other aircraft of any kind. And no smoke. Behind me, the Twin Towers still kept watch over the proceedings.

"Here they come!" shouted Mr. Anderson.

"Where?" Danny and Gary pushed their way to the front of the crowd and scanned the harbor for signs of the first tall ships.

"There!" Mr. Anderson pointed them in the right direction. "See, kids? The first ship is just about to pass Lady Liberty!"

I consulted the Operation Sail program Mom had purchased for me when we exited the subway. The tall ships were very large, multiple-masted, nineteenth-century-style sailing ships. There were sixteen tall ships in the parade, but at least a hundred smaller ships filled the harbor, including a fleet of fireboats, one of which was leading the way and spraying jets of foamy harbor water into the air.

The first tall ship was the US Coast Guard Cutter *Eagle*, a vessel whose white hull bore a thick red stripe across the bow. Its numerous ivory sails fluttered in the breeze as it approached. Next came the *Danmark* from Denmark and the *Christian Radich* from Norway. The Argentine ship *Libertad* followed.

As each tall ship passed our dock, a tremendous cheer rose from the crowd and soared across the harbor toward New Jersey. Everyone around me seemed so happy, so proud to be an American. I wanted to share in their happiness, but I couldn't. I didn't know how. My mind drifted off to thoughts of my father. I wondered what he would have thought of this display. I wondered what he would have thought of the state of our country on this, her two hundredth birthday.

In 1976, the United States faced significant political and economic challenges, including a slow recovery from a three-year recession, during which we had witnessed the collapse of the international monetary system, learned the term *stagflation*, and suffered through an oil embargo and gas rationing.

I remember making trips to the gas station with my parents in the fall of 1973 and sitting in the back seat of the LeMans while we waited in line, sometimes for hours. Inevitably, a border skirmish would break out between Danny and me before we were banished to opposite sides of the car. It seemed we were forever making trips to the gas station in those days.

On one occasion, it was just my father and I. Pulling the car up to a pump in Newark after a particularly long wait, he instructed me to stay put while he made a trip to the men's room. Before he could return, an attendant with a grizzled beard and hands covered with black smudges approached the LeMans and motioned for me to roll down the window. "What can I do for you, young man?" he asked sourly.

This was it—a golden opportunity to practice acting like a responsible adult and help out my father at the same time. "Fill it up with regular!" I said enthusiastically, borrowing the phrase my parents had always used when purchasing gas.

"Young man, don't you know we're in the middle of an oil crisis? I can sell you five gallons and no more."

"Okay, five gallons, then," I said sheepishly.

So much for acting like a grown-up. Obviously, I had a great deal to learn about life in the real world—and not much time in which to learn it, as my father would be gone in just a few short months. That Christmas would be our last together.

Meanwhile, the stock market was in the middle of a two-year nosedive. By December of 1974, less than ten months after my father's death, the Dow Jones Industrial Average lost almost half its value. Even at the age of nine, I was acutely aware that this financial crisis threatened the very survival of our beleaguered family. Without my father to take care of us, I was certain we were doomed to become a homeless family dressed in foul-smelling rags and begging for handouts. I imagined pushing an old, rusty shopping cart filled with all our worldly possessions down the street, its wheels clattering against the hard pavement and sending an awful racket into the cold night air that warned the entire village of our approach. Every once in a while, we would encounter a group of classmates from school, who would either laugh disdainfully or turn away in disgust, leaving us to wallow in our shame.

As of July 4, 1976, the country still suffered from the effects of the recession. Unemployment was high and economic growth was low, yet it was an election year, and both presidential candidates were offering hope for improvement. To many, the choice was clear. Jimmy Carter, a peanut farmer from Plains, Georgia, represented a fresh approach to politics after the Vietnam and Watergate fiascos. Campaigning on the appealing promise to restore trust to politics, Carter was beginning to get people's attention.

Spain's *Juan Sebastián de Elcano* sailed majestically by and made its way upriver against a strong northerly wind. According to the program, it was the third-largest tall ship in the world. A Romanian ship came next, followed by two ships from the Soviet Union.

The sixteenth and final tall ship of the day, Italy's *Amerigo Vespucci*, was a menacingly elegant ship with dark sails and a black-and-white striped hull. It seemed ready for battle. I closed my eyes and saw cannons firing from its gun decks. Dark clouds of smoke infused the harbor with the sharp scent of gunpowder.

When I opened my eyes, the *Amerigo Vespucci* had moved on. In its place, a lone fireboat signaled the end of the parade by spraying fountains of water into the air in front of a hazy silhouette of the Statue of Liberty. The crowd cheered. I slipped both hands into my pockets and remained silent. The water arched skyward in a colorless rainbow before surrendering to gravity and descending back into the Hudson.

"Ricky!" Danny's voice pierced through the deafening rumble produced by the herd of men, women, and children stampeding off the dock. "Come on! The show's over. We're gonna see the beheading of King George in the park!"

According to Mr. Anderson's copy of the *New York Times*, the beheading was about to begin, so we entered Battery Park with a sense of urgency. Asking passersby if they could direct us to the beheading, we received some very strange looks but no assistance. After twenty minutes of wandering around the park without any luck, we found an information booth and learned there had been a reenactment of the July 9, 1776 beheading of the statue of King George III in Bowling Green Park earlier in the day. We had missed it. Disappointed by this news but eager to get home, we agreed it was time to return to South Orange.

We entered Penn Station at quarter to five, exactly six hours after our arrival that morning. I looked forward to getting off my sore feet and sleeping on the ride home. As we approached the platform, an unusual sound rose above the screeching of the oncoming train's brakes and echoed throughout the station. The train stopped, the doors flew open, and there stood a chorus of young people, probably high school students, dressed in colonial costumes. They were singing, "My Country, 'Tis of Thee."

*Land where my fathers died,*
*Land of the pilgrims' pride,*
*From every mountainside, let freedom ring!*

And freedom did ring. It rang into the concourse and throughout Penn Station as we stood there in front of those open doors, contemplating our next move. Hesitating for only a few seconds, we climbed aboard the train. The song came to an end. Then, after a brief moment of silence, something remarkable happened—*everyone* in that compartment spontaneously joined in as the chorus launched into a jubilant rendition of "You're a Grand Old Flag."

The train's doors remained open while we stood huddled together with our arms around each other, singing our hearts out. Without missing a beat, we transitioned into "This Land Is Your Land." Some newcomers accepted the premise of the song and joined us in the compartment. Others remained on the platform, staring at us as if we were crazy. Oh, well. Their loss.

The doors slammed shut, and off we sped, still singing and still holding on to each other. Approaching the North River Tunnels, we sang "God Bless America." Then, crossing under the Hudson to New Jersey, our voices grew stronger as we flung ourselves into an impassioned version of "America the Beautiful."

Our voices merged together as one. I looked up at my mother, my eyes filling with tears of both joy and sadness. I struggled to understand the nature of the emotion I was experiencing. I wanted to label it so I could categorize it, remember it, and hold on to it. I asked myself, *Why am I feeling this way? What does it mean? Is this what it feels like to be free?* Stymied, my little brain gave up asking such questions. Surrendering to the moment, I opened my mouth and simply sang.

*America! America! God shed his grace on thee,*
*And crown thy good with brotherhood*
*From sea to shining sea!*

At the first stop in New Jersey, the singing came to an abrupt halt. Hasty goodbyes were exchanged, and the chorus exited the train. A few new passengers boarded. Through the window, I watched the young colonials say their farewells and go their separate ways.

I was beginning to learn a valuable lesson: sooner or later, all things pass and all experiences come to an end. Our holy alliance had been broken, but a new one would one day rise and take its place—or so I hoped. Grappling with a new emotion that was attempting to bubble to the surface, I closed my eyes and asked, *Am I right? Please let me be right.*

As we pulled out of the station, everybody in our compartment retreated into their own little worlds. Smiles faded. Tired eyes replaced twinkling ones. I looked down at my feet and felt overwhelmed by a horrible sense of loss. But then a voice whispered softly in my ear, *Keep the faith, Ricky, and the joy will return . . .*
     *Keep the faith?*
     *Keep the faith.*

Monday, July 5–Friday, July 16, 1976

Using the official Camp Abenaki Valley packing list as our guide, Danny and I visited one store after another in search of headgear, clothing, footwear, bedding, toiletries, and other miscellaneous items—everything we needed for our upcoming five-week adventure, including "a large footlocker or heavy-duty trunk" and "a duffel bag" in which to pack our newly purchased belongings. As I acquired my gear, I added each item to the assembly line in my bedroom, attached a label with my name using a laundry-proof pen, checked the item off the list, and packed it away. I was almost completely packed well in advance of our departure date.

As the seventeenth approached, my anxiety level skyrocketed. I worried. I worried about packing enough gear. I worried about packing the right gear. I worried about entrusting my footlocker to the delivery service Mom had hired. I worried about moving my oversized duffel bag from my bedroom to the car. I worried about the six-hour drive. I worried about sleeping in a cabin filled with strangers—would I even be able to sleep? I worried about hiding my fear of the water—what would the other campers think when they discovered I could barely swim? Most of all, I worried about making friends.

Making new friends had always been difficult for me. The previous summer, just before the school year started, a family moved into the neighborhood, two houses from ours. Without a moment's hesitation, Danny ran down the street to meet the new boy and asked him to play. Soon the two were engaged in a fierce but good-natured game of one-on-one stickball. I wanted desperately to befriend the new boy, who was my age, not Danny's, but I was much too shy to approach him on my own. Besides, it was too late. Danny had beaten me to the punch.

When my mother found me at my bedroom window in tears, she guessed what had happened and took immediate action. First she called Danny back home. Next she took me by the hand, walked me to the new boy's house, and introduced us. It was a painfully embarrassing way to begin a friendship, but to Mom's credit, it worked. Ken Hamilton and I became good friends.

On the evening before we left for Camp Abenaki Valley, we gathered in the kitchen nook for our last supper together. The odor of burned fish sticks filled the air. No one spoke. I planted an elbow firmly on the table and thrust my chin into the palm of my hand. Then, eyeing my plate, I poked at a blackened fish stick as my fear of being away from the safety of home for five weeks—*five whole weeks!*—simmered into anger. *How can she send us away? It's not fair!*

"What the hell's wrong with you, Ricky?" Mom snapped. "You know better than to put your elbow on the table!"

There was a glass of vodka in front of her. She'd been drinking all day. Her face was so red it was purple.

"Why are you sending us away?" I snapped back. "Five weeks is forever. It's a prison sentence. I don't want to go!"

"Ricky, for God's sake, stop whining. You're not a baby anymore. We already discussed this. You're going, and that's all there is to it."

"You just want to get rid of us." My voice quivered with equal measures of anger and fear. "You never wanted us in the first place, did you? Dad wanted us. Dad loved us, but you never did."

"You know that isn't true."

"You'd be happier if we went away and never came back."

"Ricky—"

"You don't care about us. If you cared about us, you wouldn't be sending us away. You care more about your cocktail parties with Mrs. Payne than us."

"Ricky, that's enough!"

"You're not even a good mother. Look at these lousy fish sticks—they're burned to hell!"

"Ricky! How . . . how can you be so hateful and mean?"

Danny started crying. "Shut up, Ricky!" he yelled. "Just shut up! I think she's a good mom—the best!"

"You shut up, Danny. You're just saying that because you're her little favorite."

"Stop it, Ricky!" Mom screamed.

"No!" I knew I was about to go too far but couldn't stop myself. "I hate you! I wish *you* were dead! You're nothing but a mean . . . a mean . . . a mean old bitch!"

*Slap!*

My face turned red-hot from the sheer impact of the blow. Her glass fell to the floor and shattered. And then . . . dead silence. Cautiously, I peered up at her. There was a look of shock on her face that must have mirrored my own. Without a word, we stared at each other for what seemed an eternity. Finally, I leaped from my chair and ran out of the kitchen. In close pursuit, she tackled me on the staircase and held on tight.

"Let me go!" I demanded, struggling to wiggle free.

"No!" She tightened her grip. "Listen to me, Ricky. We need to talk."

Realizing there was no escape, I surrendered into her embrace and cried until I was too tired to cry anymore. Then I allowed her to cradle me and rock me like a little baby. This went on for some time before she spoke.

"Ricky, I'm sorry for snapping at you. But most of all, I'm sorry for hitting you. I let my anger get the best of me, and that was inexcusable."

Chewing my lower lip like a wad of bubble gum, I gave her words time to sink in. Then I took a deep breath and looked down at my hands, which were clasped together in a white-knuckled grip.

"I deserved it, Mom."

"No, you didn't."

"Yes, I did. I'm a rotten son."

"Ricky . . ."

"I'm sorry for what I said in the kitchen. I didn't mean it. I didn't mean any of it."

"I know."

A moment of silence ballooned in the space between us before being interrupted by the thumping of my heart against the inside of my bony rib cage.

"Mom, I'm scared."

Drawing me close, she gently ran her fingers through my hair.

"I . . . I don't think I'm gonna fit in at camp. I'm not like Danny. It's not that easy for me to make friends."

Her warm lips grazed my forehead. "I know, honey, but you'll be fine. You're a great kid, and the other kids will see that when they meet you."

"But, Mom, there's something wrong with me—*really* wrong. I'm . . . I'm messed up inside."

"There's nothing wrong—"

"At school, they think I'm weird. The other kids . . ."

"What about the other kids?"

"They . . . I dunno . . . they, they tease me."

"You never told me this."

"I didn't want to worry you."

"Ricky, you can tell me anything."

After a long pause, I said, "Mom . . ."

"Yes, honey?"

"Nothing."

"What is it, Ricky?"

"Maybe . . . maybe if I was a better kid, if I did more around the house, you would love me more."

"Stop—"

"Or maybe if I was more like Danny—"

"Stop right there. You're perfect exactly the way you are. I love you with all my heart. I love you more than my own life. You are my firstborn child. You will always be my firstborn child. Got it?"

Fidgeting, I bit into my thumbnail. It was salty, like a pretzel.

"Got it?"

"Got it," I said, although I wasn't fully convinced. "Mom?"

"Yes, dear?"

"I love you."

She smiled, stood up, and took me by the hand. "Come on. It's time for bed." Raising her voice a little, she added, "You too, Danny."

Danny, who had been hiding in the dining room the entire time, poked his head out from around the corner. His face was puffy; his eyes were red.

Mom held out her other hand to him. "C'mon." Her fingers trembled . . .

# CHAPTER THREE

*Saturday, July 17, 1976*

After a late start and a grueling six-hour car ride, we arrived at the front entrance to Camp Abenaki Valley. It was the seventeenth of July. I was already counting the days of my prison sentence. This was day one of thirty-six.

My "prison" was located just outside a little town called Waterboro, about thirty miles southwest of Portland, as the crow flies. The Abenaki Indians called the area Massabesic, meaning "the place of much water." But we hadn't yet seen any water—not so much as a lake, a river, or even a stream since crossing the Maine-New Hampshire border.

A weathered hand-painted sign stood at the intersection of Maine State Route 4 and a dirt road leading into the camp. It read: "Welcome to Camp Abenaki Valley—Where Abenaki Honor Reigns!"

"That's it, Mom. Right there!" I exclaimed, desperate to get out of the car and find something cold to drink.

By now, my mother was sick and tired of my backseat driving. She slowed the car down to a crawl and glared at me in the rearview mirror before turning off the highway and onto the dirt road. The red dashboard light indicated the Pontiac's engine was on the verge of overheating. We'd been without air-conditioning for the last three hours of the journey. We were hot, sticky, dehydrated, and irritable.

Coming out of the turn, Mom stepped on the accelerator and churned up a large cloud of dust that poured in through the car windows. I jumped from one side of the back seat to the other, grabbing the handles of the window cranks and spinning them as fast as I could, while Mom and Danny rolled up the windows in front. This left us with little air to breathe and made the last few minutes of the trip virtually intolerable. I was so hot I almost passed out. And to make matters worse, my stomach was in turmoil. With each passing minute, I became more certain I was going to throw up.

Our only saving grace was the thick canopy of tangled branches and overgrown foliage that stretched overhead from one side of the road to the other. The canopy was so thick, in fact, it blocked out almost all sunlight. Hallelujah! We were in a tunnel—a tunnel so dark that Mom was forced to turn on the headlights.

After ten minutes of negotiating twists and turns and bumps in the road, Mom was ready to turn around, certain we had gone too far. Just then, however, we came around a sharp bend and arrived abruptly at the camp's main gate, which consisted of two tall wooden posts painted to resemble totem poles and surmounted by a sign that read simply: "Camp Abenaki Valley, est. 1947." We had learned in school that totem poles were a tradition of Indians from the Pacific Northwest, not the Atlantic Northeast, but these totem poles had been carved and painted with such great care and exquisite attention to detail that I forgave the obvious geographic blunder.

As we rolled into the visitor parking area, a middle-aged woman wearing bright orange horn-rimmed eyeglasses and an outdated bouffant hairstyle scurried out of a nearby building with a sign over the door that read "Camp Administration." A multicolored beaded chain hung loosely around her neck. As she approached the Pontiac, the chain swung rapidly back and forth to the time of her hurried gait, chafing the pasty skin just below her neckline and dotting it with a pink rash. I would have laughed if I hadn't been so exhausted and felt so sick. She reminded me of a cartoon character—Sweet Polly Purebred on speed.

We crawled out of the car and into the fresh air, which was laced with a sweet evergreen scent. Mercifully, my stomach began to feel a little better. The woman approached us with a big smile.

"Hello! So nice to meet you. I'm Miss Howard. Virginia Howard. My given name is Virginia, but you can call me Ginny. You must be the Willises."

She extended a hand to my mother, who shook it, probably thankful for adult company after six hours in the car with her nine- and ten-year-old boys.

"I'm Mr. Gordon's administrative assistant. I help him manage the day-to-day aspects of the camp."

"It's Williamson," Danny said.

"I'm sorry?"

"Our last name is Williamson. You called us the Willises."

"Williamson. Of course. Yes, here it is. It's right here," she said, looking at her clipboard as her face turned crimson. "I'm so sorry, sweetie."

I liked Miss Howard immediately. It had probably been a hectic day for her, with first-term campers moving out and new campers arriving throughout the afternoon. She was a little scatterbrained and perhaps too eager to please, but I liked her just the same. There was something very sweet and genuine about Miss Howard.

"It's quite all right," Mom assured her. "We've all had a long day," she added, giving Danny the evil eye. "We must be the last ones to arrive."

"You are, but don't worry, dear." Miss Howard glanced at her wristwatch. "Three thirty. There's plenty of time before dinner for the tour. We'll start here and come back for your things afterward."

"What about our footlockers?" I asked, worried the delivery service had lost them.

"Let's see." She referred again to her clipboard. "Oh, good. We received your footlockers just yesterday. They're in storage. After our tour, I'll ask a couple of junior counselors to move them into your cabins."

She adjusted her horn-rims and flashed me a reassuring smile. *Both happy and sad. Lonely?* I began to relax.

"Okay. Let's get started. This is the welcome area, and behind me is the administration building, where the camp director and his staff have offices. The camp director's cabin is just over the hill. He stays there all summer—oh, and wouldn't you know it? Here comes Mr. Gordon now."

Appearing from the other side of the hill, a tall (six-foot-five or six-foot-six) and lanky man with a Ping-Pong ball for a head approached us and lumbered by, his eyes glued to the ground in front of him. He was in his late forties, I guessed, and wearing spectacles. It was hot, over ninety degrees, yet he wore a plaid shirt and a pair of khaki trousers with white sneakers.

Later I would learn that to those few who knew him well, Mr. Gordon was a walking paradox: awkward yet graceful, shy yet friendly, reserved yet generous, and naïve yet wise. Mr. Gordon was single—had been for as long as anyone at camp could remember. Yet no one seemed to know whether he was widowed, whether he was divorced, or whether he had simply chosen never to marry. Only one fact was abundantly clear: he was a very private man.

Reaching the door to the administration building, he looked up just long enough to acknowledge our arrival with an enigmatic smile and perfunctory wave of the hand and then disappeared.

"And there he goes," said Miss Howard. "He has a lot of work to do this afternoon." The crimson snuck back into her face. "Did you know he won the silver medal in the Olympics in swimming?"

"We heard," my mother answered impatiently. The Underwoods had made a big deal of this point in pitching the idea of Camp Abenaki Valley to her. "Can we get something cold to drink?"

"Sure! Let's head over to the mess hall."

The kitchen staff was busy preparing dinner, so Miss Howard took the initiative and treated us to sodas from the vending machine: Cokes for Mom and Danny and 7Up for me. Miss Howard handed us our drinks and asked us to meet her at the picnic table on the front deck. Pointing us in the right direction, she promised she'd be only a minute or two.

The three of us proceeded slowly down the center of the cavernous dining area and toward a pair of doors that seemed to extend beyond the cornice and into the shadows inhabiting the vaulted ceiling above. Each step sent a sonorous echo throughout the room. The late-afternoon sun filtered in through the west-facing windows and cast long, sinewy apparitions across the aging hardwood floor. *I've been here before. There's something about this place . . .* Of course, it was impossible, but my feeling of déjà vu was so powerful I couldn't dismiss it. I was absolutely certain I had been in that room before and had witnessed something remarkable take place there. I would spend much time in the coming weeks pondering this strange and tantalizing feeling when instead I should have dismissed it outright as utter nonsense. And yet I couldn't help myself . . .

The doors opened out onto an elevated deck that presented us with a spectacular vista: a distant mountain range looming in the soft haze to our left; a pond that lay straight ahead and less than a mile downhill; and to our right, beyond the camp limits, rolling forests as far as the eye could see. Mom and I sat down at the picnic table while Danny, excited as a puppy, scampered over to the railing to take in the view. I envied his enthusiasm.

Miss Howard appeared moments later, carrying three tall glasses filled with ice. Danny ran back to the table, tore the tab off his Coke can, tossed it onto the deck, and filled his glass without waiting for the foam to settle. Mesmerized, he watched the thick head of foam rise to the top and flow onto the table before he lunged for the drink with both hands and took a huge gulp.

"Danny, for Pete's sake," I said, giving him a dirty look.

"What?" he asked innocently as Mom bent down to pick up the discarded tab.

A group of boys about my age shuffled by. One of them snickered. I pretended not to notice. It was embarrassing to be seen hanging out with my mother, yet I didn't want her to leave. My stomach churned. I peered out at the mountain range and took a deep breath.

On our way to the mess hall, Miss Howard had pointed out the archery and riflery ranges as well as the athletic fields, talking fast the entire time. The facilities seemed nice. I thought it might be fun to try archery and maybe even riflery. Danny had wanted to stop and watch the lacrosse team practicing, but Miss Howard assured him there would be plenty of time later for lacrosse or any other game he wished to play.

Talking now at a more leisurely tempo, she resumed the tour.

"Below and to the left, you can see Lewis Lodge. The building is named after John Lewis, who founded the camp shortly after the end of World War II. The concept for the lodge's architectural design is based loosely on Iroquois Indian longhouses. For the most part, the Indians who lived in this area, the Abenaki, lived in wigwams, but some of them actually built longhouses. See how long and narrow the building is? On Saturday nights, we have movies in the lodge's rec center."

"Movies?" I asked. "Did you say *movies?*"

"Every Saturday night. Movie night is very popular. Almost the entire camp attends—campers, counselors, and staff. Tonight, *The Bridge on the River Kwai* is showing."

I *loved* movies. Back home, I went to the movies every chance I got. I had just seen a matinee of *The Bad News Bears* with my friend Joey, a fellow movie buff and little league teammate. Joey liked the beer-drinking coach, played by Walter Matthau. He thought he was funny. I liked Tatum O'Neal. I had a little crush on her—okay, a big one—although I never would have admitted that to Joey.

"On days like today, we have a clear view of Parson's Pond. See? It's just past that last row of trees and about a ten-minute walk from here. Parson's Pond is where all the water activities are held—for example, swimming, water-skiing, canoeing, and sailing. To get there, you take a path that begins next to that two-story cabin."

Squinting, Danny craned his neck in the direction of the cabin.

"Do you see it, honey?" asked Miss Howard. "The path is right next to that big cabin—the one that stands all by itself."

"Oh yeah. I do! I see them both—the path and the cabin. Ricky, do you see that cabin? It's really neat, don't you think? Miss Howard, is that where I'm gonna sleep tonight?"

I smiled. Danny really was a sweet boy. But of course, I could never tell him that.

"I'm afraid not, honey. That cabin is Parson's Abode. It's reserved for senior campers only. If you look to our right, you'll see Cabin Row. Your cabins are toward the very end. Yours is green, and Ricky's is the blue one, right next door."

"Okay." Danny was easy to please.

"At the end of Cabin Row is another path that leads up to Parson's Peak, where we gather for campfire every Sunday evening to sing songs, tell stories, and listen to important announcements for the upcoming week. Campfire is a very important part of the Camp Abenaki Valley experience."

Miss Howard paused and took a dramatic breath before continuing.

"Let's see . . . what else can I tell you about the camp? As you know, it's owned and run by Mr. Gordon, who you've already seen. Did I mention he's an Olympic medalist? He won silver as part of the four-by-two-hundred-meter freestyle team at the 1952 Olympic Games in Helsinki. During the school year, he's a high school teacher in a Boston suburb. He teaches math and science."

At the reference to Mr. Gordon's Olympic medal, my mother sighed and allowed her eyes to roll skyward. Apparently, she was tired of hearing this same old story.

"What else? Oh yes, of course, our cherished bell," Miss Howard said as she turned a fond gaze toward the front of the deck, where a large antique cast-iron bell was mounted on a heavy-duty floor stand. Much of the charcoal-gray bell was speckled with an uneven terrain of rust. But, all in all, it appeared to have withstood the test of time.

"Our tour wouldn't be complete without my mentioning the Governor's Bell. It weighs one hundred pounds and is estimated to be at least one hundred years old. We at Camp Abenaki Valley are very proud of this bell. It was a gift from the governor shortly after the camp opened, under the terms of a special loan arrangement from the people of Maine. Before that, the bell had been stored in the governor's mansion since at least 1919, when Harriet Blaine Beale donated the Blaine House to the State of Maine. When Governor Milliken moved into the Blaine House in 1920, the bell was found in storage. There it stayed until Governor Hildreth—who was good friends with our founder, John Lewis—transferred possession of the bell to Camp Abenaki Valley. The bell can be heard for miles. Each week, a senior camper is assigned the task of ringing it for breakfast, lunch, dinner, and lights-out."

"Hello, Miss Howard." A rather large boy with an amiable smile sauntered over to the picnic table. "Regaling your friends with the story of the Governor's Bell?" He extended his hand to my mother and looked her straight in the eyes. "Hi, my name is Neil Kennedy."

Neil Kennedy had a round face, a button nose, a double chin, and an ample tummy. By any commonly accepted standard, he would have been considered obese, yet he was light-footed and carried himself with the poise and elegance of a dancer trained in the fine art of classical ballet. His auburn hair was cut short, parted on the left, and impeccably well groomed. His hazel eyes gleamed when he smiled. In spite of the hot weather, he didn't perspire. He wore a clean white T-shirt that looked as if it had been pressed. The T-shirt had a pocket with a picture of a donkey and a caption that read: "Young Democrats of America."

"Very nice to meet you, Neil," replied my mother, taking his hand. She was obviously impressed by his good manners. "I'm Anne Williamson, and these are my sons, Ricky and Danny."

"It's very nice to meet you both," he said, turning to us. "Welcome to Camp Abenaki Valley."

Danny stuck out his hand. "It's nice meeting you!"

I felt a little overwhelmed by the force of Neil's personality, but I smiled and managed a hello.

"Neil is one of our senior campers," Miss Howard interjected. "This will be his last year here, unless he decides to come back as a junior counselor."

"You must be second-term campers," he said. "It's good to have you here with us. We'll have a great time together. Camp Abenaki Valley is the best summer camp in all of New England. We have amazing campers and the most dedicated staff you'll find anywhere. Mr. Gordon is an inspiring leader. Did you know he won a silver medal at the 1952 Olympics?"

"Why, no, we didn't. How wonderful," Mom said.

Danny and I each gave her a puzzled look.

A handsome young man with blond hair, blue eyes, and an athletic build emerged from the mess hall with a can of Dr. Pepper. Moving toward our table in a graceful trot, he displayed the confidence of a thoroughbred champion. His sharp Nordic features were chiseled into a look of determined ambition. His teeth were perfectly straight and pearly white. This was an all-American boy through and through.

Miss Howard introduced us. "Mrs. Williamson, boys— this is Ryan Lucas." She checked something on her clipboard. "Ryan is the junior counselor for Ricky's cabin."

"Hello, Ryan," said my mother, smoothing out her blouse with one hand and fixing her hair with the other.

"Ryan, this is Mrs. Williamson and her sons, Ricky and Danny. They'll be joining us for the second half of the summer."

"Great! Very pleased to meet you. Has Miss Howard given you folks the nickel tour?"

"We just finished," said Danny.

"What did you see?"

"We saw Mr. Gordon, we saw the archery and riflery ranges, and then we saw the soccer and lacrosse fields."

"Did you talk to Mr. Gordon?"

"No, he was too busy," replied Danny.

"Did Miss Howard tell you Mr. Gordon is a former Olympian?"

"Yeah, she told us."

Miss Howard cut the chitchat short and recruited Neil and Ryan to move our footlockers from storage to our cabins. The boys said they would be happy to help. After receiving their instructions, they turned and marched away together in double time.

"Those two young men represent the very best of what Camp Abenaki Valley has to offer," said Miss Howard, her words oozing with pride.

She looked down at her watch and nearly flew out of her chair. "My goodness! Look at the time. Let's get back to the car and pick up your things, boys. It's almost time to say goodbye," she added, casting a sympathetic glance in my mother's direction.

Back at the welcome area, Danny and I went to work transferring our things from the Pontiac to a golf cart, which was now parked in front of the administration building. Removing my bulky duffel bag from the car's trunk proved to be a challenge, as it had become wedged into the back of the compartment during the trip. Mom offered to help, but I waved her off. With one last vigorous tug, the bag came loose and fell into the dust. Breathing heavily, I wiped away the beads of sweat that had seeped into my eyes.

When we finished loading the cart, there was nothing left to do but say goodbye. Danny ran into Mom's arms and showered her with hugs and kisses. I stayed put and slipped my hands into my pockets. I wanted to reach out to her but didn't know how.

When Mom and Danny had said their final goodbyes, Mom smiled sadly at me, walked over, and kissed my cheek. Embarrassed, I didn't move. My hands remained in my pockets. She kissed me on the other cheek. This time, I flinched, yet found myself yearning for more.

"Give your mother a squeeze," she whispered in my ear. "It's time for me to go."

I offered her a one-armed hug and stoically said, "Goodbye, Mom."

As we separated, I gazed into her eyes. She was hurting too. An intense longing bubbled upward from an old, abandoned wellspring buried somewhere deep within me.

Returning my gaze, she held a hand to my cheek.

*Please, Mommy, take me in your arms and cradle me . . . you know, like when I was a little baby . . .*

Still gazing into my eyes, she took a step backward.

*Don't go! Please, don't go . . .*

"I love you, Ricky."

Her words pierced my heart.

She turned away and took a step toward the car. And another . . .

Then, remembering the red light on the Pontiac's dashboard, I shouted, "Mom!"

She turned around and looked at me expectantly.

"Are you going to be okay? I mean, is the car going to be okay?"

Her face burst into a smile. "Thanks, dear. I'm staying at a hotel tonight. I'll bring the car to a mechanic in the morning to check the radiator before driving home."

"And the air-conditioning!" added Danny.

"And the air-conditioning," she confirmed. "If I have to, I'll stay an extra night at the hotel. Goodbye, boys. Have fun! I love you both." With blown kisses to each of us and a final wave goodbye, she got into the Pontiac, successfully started the engine, backed out of the parking space, and was gone.

With Miss Howard in the driver's seat, we rode the golf cart along Cabin Row, passing one stilted, single-story structure after another. All cabins were to our right, facing downhill. To our left, an open field sloped gently away from us. A few boys were scattered about the field, playing Frisbee in the late-afternoon sun and listening to a tinny version of "Dream Weaver"

on a portable AM radio. Farther downhill, a thickly wooded area stretched along the field's eastern border. I knew from our tour that Parson's Pond was beyond the wooded area but couldn't see it from here.

Miss Howard stopped the golf cart in front of a cabin painted blue. The door was bloodred. "This is your stop, Ricky," she said cheerfully. "Danny's cabin is the green one right next door."

Danny was fine. He was always fine. I was scared—*really scared*—and already feeling the first pangs of homesickness. I stumbled out of the cart and onto my twiggy legs, which by now were shaking badly. The cabin's bloodred door stared down at me from the top of a staircase of perhaps five or six steps. *Is that real blood?*

"Ricky . . ."

The door's stare increased in intensity. *Come on in . . . I dare ya . . .*

"Ricky, dear . . ."

I peeled my eyes away from the door and glanced up and down Cabin Row. Each cabin was painted a different color, yet all the doors were that same menacing color of blood. I felt a chill.

"Ricky, don't forget your bag."

I turned back to the cart, grabbed the duffel bag by the strap, and, with all my might, hoisted it onto my shoulders. Teetering, I was trying to find my balance when Ryan Lucas, his white teeth flashing, appeared at the top of the stairs.

"Come on in, Ricky!"

I looked at Danny and then at Miss Howard.

"It's okay, hon," she said. "Go on."

Danny grinned. "Don't worry about me. I'll be fine. I'll see you later, big brother."

Trembling from head to toe, I peered up at Ryan and began my ascent. When I was halfway up the stairs, the bag started to slip, but I made a quick adjustment and continued on. Ryan held the screen door for me. I muttered a thanks and turned sideways to maneuver the bag through the doorframe without bumping into him.

I stepped into the room, feeling nervous and awkward with my duffel bag balanced precariously across my shoulder blades. At first I could make out only shadowy images in the dimly lit cabin. But then my eyes adjusted, revealing my new cabinmates in an eerily silent tableau, lying around the room, reading, playing cards, and napping.

A lethargic voice interrupted the silence. "I'm hungry."

"You're always hungry," said another.

"What's for dinner tonight?"

"Shepherd's pie."

"Shepherd's pie? Nah. That doesn't sound right. I think it's cottage pie."

Ryan tried to interrupt. "Guys—"

"Same diff."

"Guys, this is Ricky. He'll be taking Teddy's spot."

"Hey," said a kid without looking up from his card game.

"What's happenin'?" said his opponent with an ambiguous smirk on his face.

"Hey, what's up?" mumbled a boy who appeared to be waking from a long winter's nap.

"Hello."

The hello came from a boy whose bed was situated in the far left-hand corner of the room. He sat Indian-style on the bed's bottom bunk, as if in a cave. An open comic book lay in his lap. His face was partially covered by a shadow. He had dark hair and sad eyes.

Ryan turned to me. "Wayne's the senior counselor. He isn't here right now, but he'll be back before dinner. Your footlocker's over there, next to your bed."

I looked around the room, bewildered by my new surroundings.

"There," he said, pointing to the middle of three bunk beds on the left side of the room. "You've got the top bunk. Go ahead and get settled. I need to help Neil with Danny's footlocker. I'll be back before the dinner bell rings."

"Ryan!" I blurted with an urgency I hadn't intended.

"Yeah?"

I lowered my voice to a whisper. "I . . . I think I might've left a few things in the golf cart."

"Don't worry. I'll get them for you," he said before darting out the door.

I stood very still and surveyed the room. Including me, there were eight boys in the cabin. *All campers present and accounted for*, I thought. Three bunk beds, including mine, stood lined up along the left wall. Along the right wall, there was only one bunk bed. Next to it was an ordinary bed—not a bunk bed—which I guessed belonged to Ryan. In the back right-hand corner of the cabin, there was a bed much larger and more comfortable looking than the others. Beside this bed sat a nightstand with a digital alarm clock and a lava lamp perched on top. A guitar case leaned against the wall, adjacent to the nightstand. I deduced that this was the senior counselor's living area.

Just past the bed belonging to the boy with sad eyes was an open entrance into the bathroom. From where I stood, I could see three stalls. A single word was scribbled on each of the doors: *Dudes.* Someone had an exceptional flair for the obvious. I couldn't see into the rest of the bathroom from my vantage point, but there seemed to be room for at least two sinks and a couple of showers, perhaps along the back wall.

I hobbled over to my assigned living area and placed my duffel bag on top of my footlocker, careful not to drop it and attract attention to myself. What a relief! I rubbed my shoulder to restore the circulation. The footlocker sat on the floor along the wall and next to the bunk bed I was to share with a boy who had long blond hair cut into the shape of a salad bowl. He seemed to be napping, but then he suddenly flicked his eyes open and peered up at me suspiciously. A drop of drool appeared at the corner of his mouth. Without a word, he shrugged, turned away, and rolled onto his side.

I sighed and glanced up at the top bunk. Someone else's duffel bag lay there, open and only half-full. A few dozen assorted things were scattered about it. Under the debris was a nicely made bed with cleanly folded sheets, a lightweight blanket, and a pillow. Perhaps Ryan was mistaken. Perhaps this wasn't my bunk. Perhaps this wasn't even my cabin. I looked around the room, but no help was forthcoming.

As I contemplated the situation, the second door labeled *Dudes* flew open, and a boy with golden hair and a military-style crew cut emerged. He looked at me, and his eyes grew large. I had miscalculated. There were nine boys in the cabin—eight in the main living area and one in the toilet.

"Oops!" he exclaimed as he disappeared into another part of the bathroom. "I'll get that stuff out of your way in just a minute."

I could hear a faucet running. The water stopped after only a second or two.

"You must be the new guy," he said, springing from the bathroom. "My name's Theodore, but you can call me Teddy. Everybody calls me Teddy—like Teddy Roosevelt." His eyes sparkling, he waltzed up to me and offered his hand. "What's your name?" he asked.

"Ricky."

"Ricky? That's a decent name. Yeah. A very decent name. I like it!"

"My real name is Richard, like Richard the Lionheart . . . well . . . no, not really." I realized immediately how silly the comparison sounded coming from me, a skinny little boy afraid of his own shadow. Embarrassed, I threw my hands into my pockets and shuffled my feet while smiling nervously at the floor. *He must think I'm an idiot.*

Without missing a beat, he asked, "Well, what shall it be— Richard or Ricky?" If he noticed my embarrassment, he didn't show it.

"Ricky's fine."

"Good! Ricky it is. I'll get those things out of your way in a jiff." In one quick motion, he grabbed the back end of the bed, vaulted onto the top bunk, and resumed packing. "This'll be your bunk, Ricky. I'm outta here. My folks'll be here any minute now. They're taking my sister and me to Europe for two weeks. Have you ever been to Europe?"

"No, I haven't." My father had talked about taking our family to Europe someday, but of course, someday never came.

"Me neither. It's gonna be such an awesome trip!"

He threw the last few remaining items into his duffel bag, fastened it closed, and dropped it over the edge of the bunk. When the bag hit the floor, it made a loud thump that woke the boy with the salad bowl haircut.

"What the—" yelped Salad Bowl, jolting upright.

"Sorry, sport." Teddy flashed a winning smile and hopped down from the bunk. "Ricky, this is Timothy. Timothy, this is your new bunkmate, Ricky."

"Just call me Tim," grumbled an irritated Salad Bowl. "No one calls me Timothy." Rolling to his side, he returned to his slumber.

Teddy chuckled. "Some people were just born to be sour-pusses. Well, my friend, she's all yours now." With that, he picked up his bag, slung it over his shoulder, and gave me a military salute. A shadow passed over his face. Then, just before he marched out the door, his features softened into an affectionate smile. "Catch you later, Ricky. Keep it real, dude."

When Teddy was gone, I peered over at the boy with sad eyes. He was engrossed in his comic book, an *Archie*. He was small—even smaller than I was—and rather pathetic looking, I thought, with shiny brown hair and dark circles that looked like mascara smeared under his eyes. His clothes appeared to be at least a full size too large for him. Probably hand-me-downs. Perhaps sensing my stare, he looked up at me, but when I smiled, he returned quickly to his comic book.

*He's scared.*

*Scared? What is he scared of?*

The front door swung open. In walked Ryan with an older guy in his twenties, who I assumed was Wayne, our cabin's senior counselor. Wayne was medium-tall—just over six feet, I guessed. He had long brown hair. Scraggly. And unfathomably dark eyes. His face was unshaven with about three days of growth coming in. He wore an unbuttoned long-sleeved shirt—with the sleeves rolled up past his elbows—over an old Camp Abenaki Valley T-shirt, army green camping shorts, gray wool socks, and unlaced leather hiking boots.

Without acknowledging my presence, Wayne swaggered to the center of the room and bellowed, "Okay, listen up."

The room became still.

"We're all gonna have dinner together tonight—*all* of us, even Romano," he added, casting a frown over at the boy with sad eyes. "It's the new kid's first night, and, for once, we're gonna eat at the same table."

The cabin responded to Wayne's edict with a chorus of groans.

"This comes from the top, girls."

"From the top?" asked a boy with sandy-brown hair.

"Yes, from the top."

"The very top?"

"Yes."

"You mean from God?"

"No, not from God, you doofus. These are Director Gordon's orders."

A hand shot up from the right side of the room. It was a boy with fire-engine-red hair and freckles.

"Yeah, what is it, Willy?"

"This doesn't work for me at all, Wayne. You and Mr. Gordon are interfering with my social life. I've got a hot date tonight."

Everybody laughed, including Wayne.

"Very funny, wise guy. Okay, everybody—wash up if you haven't already. The bell is gonna ring any minute now."

A few boys scrambled to the bathroom.

Wayne took a couple of steps toward the back of the cabin before Ryan stopped him.

"Wayne," Ryan said, "this is Ricky Williamson."

Wayne narrowed his eyes into a squint and gave me a once-over. *What's the matter with him? Does he need glasses?* Addressing Ryan, he said, "He can unpack his gear after dinner." Then, with a grunt, he retreated to his private corner of the cabin.

Ryan cast me a sheepish glance. His mouth opened, but no words came out. Then, with a shrug, he headed to the bathroom.

A few seconds later, the dinner bell rang. It had a sad, hollow ring that echoed lugubriously in my head. *Dooong . . . Dooong . . . Dooong . . .*

My bedroom back home seemed a million miles away.

At dinner, all ten occupants of my cabin sat at an assigned table toward the back of the mess hall. At the front of the room, Mr. Gordon and his administrative staff congregated at an extra-large banquet table with a group of boys who, I later learned, were the residents of Parson's Abode, the cabin reserved for senior campers only. Miss Howard sat to Mr. Gordon's immediate right, beaming broadly through her horn-rims.

I sat next to Ryan. Over the din of about a hundred campers shouting greetings and playful insults at each other, he informed me that Mr. Gordon rarely made public appearances. "This is a special evening. Mr. Gordon wouldn't be here otherwise."

Leaning close to Ryan so I could hear him, I nodded. He was right. This was a special evening. I could feel the energy in the room building as the camp geared up for the second half of the summer of 1976.

Mr. Gordon stood up with a microphone in his hand. "May I have your attention, please?"

The din continued.

Mr. Gordon smiled nervously and tried again, speaking more loudly this time. "May I *please* have your attention? I know you're all just as excited as I am to welcome our new campers, but we do have a magnificent meal waiting to be served. It would be a shame for it to go to waste."

That did the trick. A hush fell over the room.

"Thank you. Thank you and welcome to the official beginning of the second half of our summer together at Camp Abenaki Valley. Most of you have been with us since early June. But twelve new campers have joined us today, and I'd like to take this opportunity to extend a warm Abenaki Valley welcome to each of them."

Mr. Gordon put down the microphone and began to clap his hands—a little too eagerly, I thought, and with forced enthusiasm.

*He's just nervous.*

*Nervous? The camp director?*

Others joined in. Soon, applause reverberated through the mess hall like a spring thunderstorm. When it died down, Mr. Gordon picked up the microphone and continued.

"We're thrilled to have the second-term campers with us, especially those of you who are new to Camp Abenaki Valley. I think you'll discover there's something very special about this place. And I know there are extraordinary experiences in store for each of you over the next five weeks. There will be opportunities to develop and improve yourselves, make new friends, and, most importantly, have fun!"

At this point, I caught a couple of boys at the next table rolling their eyes toward the ceiling. Clearly they weren't impressed with Mr. Gordon, nor were they inspired by his high-spirited and well-intended message of hope and optimism. Later I would learn that these same two boys viewed Mr. Gordon and the entire Camp Abenaki Valley experience with cynicism, intolerance, and disdain.

In hindsight, their cynicism should not have been surprising. The whole Camp Abenaki Valley philosophy—with its emphasis on optimism, loyalty, and honor—was a relic from an earlier era. It must have seemed hopelessly naïve to a generation of young people who had witnessed the assassinations of Martin Luther King Jr. and Robert Kennedy, the shootings at Kent State, and the Watergate scandal. These were kids who grew up watching the Vietnam War unfold on the six o'clock news. To them, *peace* was little more than an abstract concept. It was merely a word preached to them in church. Little wonder, then, that some campers scoffed at such notions as the one so prominently displayed on the sign at the camp's entrance: "Welcome to Camp Abenaki Valley—Where Abenaki Honor Reigns!"

"Before I wrap up, I have a couple of brief announcements to make. First, as most of you know, tonight is movie night. And this evening's movie is *The Bridge on the River Kwai*."

This announcement was met by only a smattering of applause.

"This is a great film. It won the Oscar for best picture of 1957. It's rather long, so we're going to start at exactly seven thirty. Please be on time. Second announcement: tomorrow night's campfire will be the official kickoff event for the Ultimate Race!"

This announcement was met by a much livelier round of applause.

"For those of you who are new to camp and who might not be familiar with the Ultimate Race, we will provide you with all the relevant details tomorrow night."

Mr. Gordon paused for dramatic effect before continuing. "Boys, there are five more weeks left in the summer of 1976. Let's make the very best of it. Let's make these five weeks the adventure of a lifetime!"

The response in the room was mediocre at best.

"Now, before we say grace, we need to introduce our new campers to the Abenaki Valley Creed."

Everyone in the room, it seemed, stood up, except me.

"Who are we?" Mr. Gordon shouted into the microphone. His voice burst forth from the public-address system and rose into the rafters.

"Camp Abenaki Valley!" responded the room, matching Mr. Gordon's intensity.

I was bewildered but came to my feet in spite of myself.

"What is our watchword?" Mr. Gordon cried out.

"Honor!"

"What kind of honor?"

"Abenaki honor!"

"And what is the first principle of Abenaki honor?"

"Excellence! We strive for excellence in everything we do!"

"The second principle?"

"Integrity! We speak and act with integrity to ensure justice for all!"

"The third and final principle?"

"Service! We live our lives in humble and obedient service to family, community, country, and God!"

Ryan nudged me and whispered, "Don't believe it for a minute, Ricky. It's really all about *winning* here at Camp Abenaki Valley."

"Outstanding," said Mr. Gordon. "Now, let's be seated for grace."

The sound of chairs sliding across the hardwood floor filled the hall as we took our seats and bowed our heads.

"Bless us, O Lord, and these thy gifts, which we are about to receive from thy bounty, through Christ our Lord. Amen."

Dinner was served. It was shepherd's pie, and it was delicious. Toward the end of the meal, just as a dessert of peach cobbler was being served, I overheard a boy at the next table expressing the opinion that second-session campers shouldn't be allowed at Abenaki Valley. "It's just plain wrong. It gets in the way of everything we've worked so hard to achieve during the first five weeks of camp." I could tell he was trying hard to sound grown up. Most likely, he hoped to ingratiate himself with the counselors at his table. Even so, I couldn't help but take the comment personally. His words stung.

Mr. Gordon had said twelve new campers had arrived that afternoon. The rest of the campers had been together since the second week of June, developing relationships and forging alliances. Taking my first bite of peach cobbler, I glanced around the room. *Where do I fit in?*

It was a packed house. Pushing my way through the crowd, I found a seat toward the back of the rec center and settled in. The lights dimmed; the room turned dark. I liked the dark. As long as it was dark, I could be anonymous—and being anonymous made me feel safe and secure. With the central air-conditioning system purring in the background, the room was comfortably cool. It was especially refreshing after a long day in the extreme heat. I even shivered a little.

I preferred movies to real life. When the lights went down and a film began, real life ceased to exist for me. I disappeared into the story and lived side by side with the characters, thinking their thoughts and feeling their emotions. Their hopes and fears became my hopes and fears. They became my best friends and, in some cases, my most despised enemies. Together we had great adventures and explored strange new worlds. We robbed banks. We went to jail. We escaped. We discovered gold and made vast fortunes. We fell in and out of love. We went to war. We made peace. We triumphed over evil. We sinned. We suffered. We redeemed ourselves.

Shaking with giddy anticipation, I savored those first few precious moments of darkness—a darkness filled with mystery and infinite possibilities for what was about to reveal itself on the big screen. I leaned forward in my seat, ready to be taken away to a World War II Japanese prison camp in the distant country of Thailand. The projector sputtered to life. A bright light cut like a sword through the darkness and illuminated the screen. The movie began.

As the opening credits played, the muscles in my neck and shoulders softened. My arms and legs became as limp as overcooked egg noodles. All my worries, concerns, and anxieties disappeared. A smile crept into the corners of my mouth. I was at peace.

Then there was a presence—a presence in the empty chair to my left—and the unmistakable scent of Old Spice. *Daddy . . . Daddy, is that you?* There was no answer.

Losing myself in the opening scene of the movie, I became a soldier in a unit of the British Army led by Lieutenant Colonel Nicholson, played by Alec Guinness.

*Whistling the "Colonel Bogey March," we stomp into the Japanese prison camp and come into formation before the camp commandant. Looking us over, he narrows his eyes into a fierce glare and speaks. We will be required to build a bridge across the River Kwai . . . it will be hard labor . . . we are in the jungle . . . there is no possibility of escape. Yet I'm not worried. I know*

*Lieutenant Colonel Nicholson will take care of us . . . But then he challenges the commandant's authority and is thrown into the hotbox. For days, he's cooped up inside this tiny wooden cube without food or water as the tropical sun beats down on its tin roof . . .*

Watching the lieutenant colonel suffer the oven-like conditions of the hotbox, I squirmed in my seat and thought of the car ride to camp. I thought of the suffocating air that filled the car when we rolled up the windows on that dusty dirt road that seemed to go on forever. Like the lieutenant colonel, I knew what it felt like to be locked in a torture chamber. That was how I felt in the car, and that was how I felt right then and there in my seat in that jam-packed rec center.

I broke into a sweat. My stomach gurgled. An unpleasant taste—like sour milk or moldy cheese—leaked into the back of my throat. I couldn't breathe. The room closed in on me. I had to get out of there, but it was too late. The shepherd's pie and peach cobbler rose upward. I tried to keep them down, but it was no use. My dinner exploded from my mouth in an avalanche of gooey mush that covered the back of the chair belonging to the boy sitting in front of me. Forming a Technicolor collage of chunky putrescence there, the mush began to ooze all over the floor.

The boy spun around with his face crinkled into an expression of utter disgust. "Oh, man—that is seriously nasty! You are one sick cat!" He then stamped angrily out of the lodge, muttering something about changing his shirt.

I just sat there, hunched over in a state of absolute mortification as the stench of bile and stomach acid infused the room.

There was quite a commotion. They even stopped the movie to clean up the mess. I was sent to the infirmary before being allowed to return to my cabin for the night. I never did see the rest of *The Bridge on the River Kwai*.

# CHAPTER FOUR

*Sunday, July 18, 1976*

O N MY FIRST FULL DAY AT CAMP ABENAKI VALLEY, I arose with the ringing of the Governor's Bell and plodded sleepily with my cabinmates to the mess hall. We entered the building together. But then, after going through the breakfast line and gathering up my pancakes, sausage, and bug juice, I found myself alone with my tray, staring into a vast sea of nameless campers and counselors. Countless heads with indistinguishable faces bobbed in waves across the room. My cabinmates were nowhere to be seen.

*Wait a second! There's Danny—*

Danny was at a nearby table, chatting with a group of boys as though he'd known them forever. He looked up, smiled, and waved me over. But I couldn't sit with my little brother. Doing so would only make me look ridiculous in front of the other campers. Pretending not to notice him, I scanned the cavernous hall for someone else—*anyone* else.

A raging storm of voices echoed off the ceiling and rained down on me. I sagged under its weight but continued scanning the room. My heart pounded my rib cage and filled my ears with a sound that rose above the storm. *Lub-DUB, lub-DUB, lub-DUB . . . a-LONE, a-LONE, a-LONE . . .* Taunting me, it beat louder and louder still. Soon I was on the verge of a full-fledged panic attack.

*A-LONE, a-LONE, a-LONE . . .*

Then, in what could only be described as a moment of pure grace, I spotted Tommy Underwood, the younger of the two brothers whose parents had first introduced the idea of Camp Abenaki Valley to my mother. Tommy was a blond-haired boy with pale skin and protuberant eyes that seemed incapable of missing even the minutest of details. This was his fourth year at Abenaki Valley. He was a veteran.

Tommy and a group of three boys were sitting at a table in the farthest corner of the room. I moved quickly through the maze of tables and chairs that separated us and arrived just as they were digging into their breakfast. There was an open chair next to Tommy. *What if he's saving it for someone else?*

"Oh! Hi, Ricky," said Tommy. "Have a seat. We're just getting started."

With a sigh of relief, I accepted the invitation and sat down.

Tommy introduced me to his three pals: Troy, Alex, and Bart, all of them "big-time" soccer players, all of them from New Jersey, and all of them veterans of Abenaki Valley. "Ricky's parents and my parents know each other. That's how he found out about Abenaki Valley," Tommy explained.

The reference to my "parents" smarted, but I let it pass.

"Aren't you the kid that puked last night at the movie?" asked Troy.

"Yeah, I guess that would be me," I answered.

"You're not going to puke again, are you?"

"No, I'm feeling fine now."

"Good."

The main topic of conversation at breakfast was the annual all-camp relay race, better known among the campers as the Ultimate Race. The entire room was abuzz with stories of past years' races and bursting with anticipation for this year's race, as the teams were to be announced that very evening. Tommy recounted the heroics of Ryan Lucas, who, as baton bearer, won last year's race for the Eagles in a dramatic come-from-behind victory. I must have looked confused because he then launched into an explanation of how the race worked.

Each year, the campers were divided into two teams, the Eagles and the Hawks, to compete in a daylong relay race involving every activity offered by the camp. Leading each team was a senior camper chosen for his leadership skills and organizational abilities. As captain, his most important decision was selecting a baton bearer, who was usually the team's best all-around athlete. The baton bearer's job was to run from one leg of the race to the next, surrender the baton to the official, and wait for his teammates to complete a task, such as achieving a score at the riflery range, starting a fire without a match, or scoring a certain number of goals in the soccer shootout. When the official determined that the task had been completed satisfactorily, the baton was returned to the baton bearer, who would then sprint to the next leg of the race.

The Ultimate Race culminated with a two-mile run, out and back along the winding dirt road that led into camp. As Mom, Danny, and I had discovered the previous day, the tangled branches and overgrown foliage extending from the surrounding forest created a thick canopy that gave one the illusion of traveling through a tunnel that blocked out almost all light, even on the sunniest of days. On a typical day, there was just enough light to allow the runners to successfully negotiate the numerous bends and curves in the road.

This tunnel was known to campers as the Tunnel of Doom.

Many campers believed the woods along the road were haunted. According to Abenaki Valley camp legend, a renegade clan of Mohawk warriors came from eastern New York to southern Maine in the mid-1600s to wipe out the Abenaki, who were indigenous to the area near Parson's Pond and whose population had already been decimated by infectious diseases brought into the region by Europeans. The Mohawk clan was led by Burning Sky, a fierce warrior notorious for his indiscriminate brutality.

One autumn night, Burning Sky led a raid on an Abenaki village and personally killed twelve people, including nine women and children. The following evening, his throat was slit from ear to ear while he slept. According to the story, the few surviving members of the village had plotted their revenge and executed Burning Sky's murder with the assistance of some local French settlers.

Believers in the legend were convinced that Burning Sky continued to inhabit the woods, seeking retribution against anyone he might encounter. Over the years, some runners even reported visions of a wrathful Burning Sky coming out of the darkness, his bow and arrow drawn and ready to kill. A few swore they heard a sinister voice echoing throughout the forest as they ran: "These are my woods . . . *my* woods . . . I will not rest until I have had my revenge!"

The story of Burning Sky was fascinating and even left me with a slight chill. But I was much more concerned about the Ultimate Race. Barring a valid medical excuse, all campers were required to participate. This left the captains with the unenviable task of going through their rosters and assigning each camper to a leg of the race. Often these decisions were based not so much on skill but rather on minimizing damage to the team's chances for victory. For example, a captain might place a less athletic camper in a large group event, such as the swimming competition, where the baton bearer was permitted to move on as soon as his team's first swimmer crossed the finish line, rendering the performances of the other swimmers irrelevant.

"Make no mistake about it," Tommy said, "winning the Ultimate Race is a *big* deal around here."

Although the Ultimate Race was the hot topic at breakfast, the teams wouldn't be posted until that evening and leg assignments wouldn't be announced until Wednesday. The more pressing concern was that of signing up for activities for the camp's second session, which was to begin on Monday. Sign-up was at ten o'clock. Although it wasn't quite nine, campers were already heading down to the lodge.

Tommy knew a shortcut to the sign-up table. "Follow me, guys!"

Instead of joining the mass exodus out the double doors that opened onto the front deck, he led his three pals and me through the kitchen—where we drew suspicious looks from the cook and his staff—and out the back door, past rusted Dumpsters filled with rotting food and infested with flies and swarms of yellow jackets. The smell was nauseating. A heavy, stifling heat descended upon us. The air was so thick I could barely breathe. My breakfast began to rise. *Not again*, I thought, and I willed myself not to throw up.

Moving quickly away from the Dumpsters, we came around the north side of the mess hall and were greeted by a refreshing breeze. The woods were on our left. Below us, droves of campers marched downhill toward the lodge, which was nestled in a grove of balsam fir trees. Beyond the grove and farther downhill lay Parson's Pond.

Tommy chuckled and motioned us to follow as he slipped sideways into the woods. "I'm the only one who knows about this path," he said proudly.

"Path? I'd hardly call this a path," said Troy, stepping forward over the trunk of a fallen tree. "If I don't get Advanced Riflery, I'm gonna hold you personally responsible, Underwood."

"I thought you knew, Troyster," said Alex. "Tommy never gets it wrong. He always comes through in a pinch. I tell you, man, he's a pinball wizard."

"Yeah, if you say so, *Smart* Alex," said Troy. "But that kid in the movie was deaf, dumb, and blind."

Ignoring Troy's sass, Alex broke into the chorus of "Pinball Wizard" from The Who's *Tommy*.

"That's getting really old, Alex," said Tommy. "And your singing sucks!"

Alex giggled devilishly.

Troy was right. Whatever path may have existed in the past was almost completely overgrown with brush and thorns. Nevertheless, we fell into line behind Tommy and followed him, receiving multiple scrapes on our shins and arms as a reward for our loyalty. I was just beginning to lose faith when Tommy declared that we were almost there. Seconds later, we found our-selves directly behind the lodge. Circling around to the front, we arrived at the main entrance, ahead of virtually all other campers.

"You're a miracle man, Underwood," said Troy. "I never should have doubted you."

"I told you, he's a pinball wizard." Alex patted Tommy on the back.

"Nice job, Tommy," said Bart.

Lewis Lodge was home to the counselors' lounge, meeting rooms, the post office, the infirmary (which I had already visited), and the rec center. The rec center served as the venue not only for movie night on Saturdays but also for such events as the annual dance. Each year, Camp Abenaki Valley hosted Camp Crystal, a nearby all-girls camp, for a dance on the last Saturday of July.

The lodge was a long, rectangular white-pine structure with a wide, open-air porch along the front of the building. Nine card tables had been set up on the porch, each with a placard taped to its front, indicating a range of letters. The placard on the table in front of Tommy and me read "U–Z." Underwood and Williamson. We were in perfect position. In spite of my fears and insecurities, I began to feel that things might actually work out okay for me at Camp Abenaki Valley. Troy, Alex, and Bart ran eagerly to their respective tables.

*Whack!*

An object as hard as a rock hit me in the face and knocked me back on my heels. A boy with coppery skin and a thick black mop of hair stood before me, staring me down with eyes as dark as coal. *Where did he come from?* At least two years my junior, this boy had just blindsided me with a right hook. A blazing fire spread across my face.

"You want another one?" He cocked his fist and prepared to deliver a second blow.

Too stunned to speak, I took a step backward.

Sneering, he moved to the front of the line with his three snickering companions, all with the same coppery skin and black hair. Later I learned he was Jihad, a boy of Arab descent whose family lived in New York. He and his three older brothers almost always traveled together as a pack. The brothers were clearly impressed with Jihad's audacity.

"That happens sometimes around here," Tommy said. "Are you okay, Ricky?"

I was too humiliated to answer. A younger boy had just gotten the best of me and taken our places in line while I did nothing—absolutely nothing. Withdrawing into my own little world, I slipped my hands into my pockets, looked down at the ground, and waited for registration to begin.

The man behind the table handed me a card that listed the meeting times and places for my activities. Thanking him, I tucked it into my pants pocket, pushed my way through the crowd, and sprinted back to the cabin painted blue.

"Hello?" I said upon entering.

No answer.

"Hello?"

*What luck!* I had the place to myself.

In the bathroom, I splashed water on my face and peered into the mirror. A pink welt the size of a small fist appeared on my left cheekbone. It stung, but it would be okay.

The cabin's living area was still blessedly empty. The solitude it offered was like a cool mountain breeze that wrapped its arms around my shoulders in a gentle and comforting embrace. I climbed to the top bed of the bunk I would be sharing for the next five weeks with Salad Bowl. A dispirited sigh fizzled through the gap in my front teeth. Lying on my back, I looked up and imagined the face of the boy with coppery skin materializing in the rafters.

*Bested by a younger boy. A younger boy! Slugged me and took our place in line. And I did nothing. Nothing!*

I retrieved my activity card from my pocket and held it up so it caught the streaky light seeping into the room through the thin layer of dust covering the front windows. The card was a little crumpled but still legible. I was signed up for baseball, camping, sailing, archery, riflery, and arts and crafts. I hadn't requested either arts and crafts or sailing, but, with my lack of seniority, choices were limited. I was pleased, however, with my other activities, especially baseball. The other three were a little outside my comfort zone. Still, I thought they might be fun.

I put the card down and again cast my eyes into the rafters. It was dark in the uppermost reaches of the cabin, so I placed my hands at the sides of my face to act as blinders. The ceiling came into a hazy focus. A spider lurked in the shadows. It was just beginning to spin a web at the intersection of two beams directly above my head. I wondered how long it took a spider to finish a web. Contemplating this, I fell into a trancelike state until lunch.

After lunch, Danny and I walked down to the lodge for our new-camper orientation. Sunday afternoons at Camp Abenaki Valley meant free time for the campers. Boys were coming and going at their leisure. Some loitered under the eaves of the lodge's front porch, while others sought refuge from the afternoon heat inside. As we entered the air-conditioned building, Peter Frampton serenaded the airwaves with "Baby, I Love Your Way." In the rec center, a group of boys huddled around a black-and-white TV with a crooked antenna mended with duct tape. The Olympics were on. A fourteen-year-old Romanian girl named Nadia Comaneci was practicing her routine on the uneven bars for that evening's competition. My heart fluttered.

We found Jack, the senior counselor in charge of orientation, sitting at a small round table in the snack bar with two boys. He waved us over to join them and introduced himself and the boys: Elliott from Massachusetts and Harry from New Hampshire. Elliott—tall and skinny with curly hair, pasty skin, and glasses—was a city boy. Harry was from the country. A strapping boy, he must have been quite an asset to his father on the family's dairy farm. Including Danny and me, only four of the twelve second-session campers were present for the orientation. I guessed the other eight had attended Camp Abenaki Valley in previous years and already knew the ropes. We sat down, and Jack gave us a general overview of the camp, most of which Miss Howard had covered the day before.

After the overview, Jack took us on a guided tour that began with a quick walk-through of the lodge. We passed the post office, infirmary, art studio, and the rec center. The group of boys watching the Olympics had doubled in size. Jim McKay was on screen talking about an American named Bruce Jenner and his chances for gold in the decathlon. Jack led us out onto the porch and asked if we had any questions. Hearing none, he proceeded with a tour of the grounds.

At Parson's Pond—more a lake than a pond—we watched a couple of boys practicing kayak rolls. Over and over again, they rolled their kayaks into the glassy water and disappeared below before reappearing triumphantly on the other side. A wild shout echoed back and forth across the pond. Three boys were on the floating dock. They had just thrown a fourth into the water. After a review of the camp's water safety rules, Jack led us back up the hill and past Cabin Row to the campfire site.

The site was set up like an amphitheater with tiered wooden benches forming concentric semicircles around a campfire pit that sat in a natural depression in the earth. Secluded from the rest of camp, the site was perched on a remote precipice known as Parson's Peak and surrounded by a vast array of conifers and broadleaf trees, including pines, spruces, cedars, elms, and many others. I plopped down on a top-tier bench to catch my breath. Danny and the other boys joined me. Together we admired the view. From our vantage point, Parson's Pond appeared tiny.

Again, Jack asked if we had any questions. "No? Okay, then, as far as anything we haven't covered, you'll just have to muddle through as best you can." He chuckled to himself as if he had just told the world's best inside joke, and the tour was over.

On the way back to Cabin Row, Danny lowered his voice into a covert whisper and asked, "What in the heck happened to your face, Ricky?"

"Nothin'."

"Nothin'? Are you sure? There's a red mark—"

"Yes, I'm sure."

After a short silence, he said, "I saw you at breakfast this morning. Didn't you see me? I was waving at you."

"No, I didn't see you."

"It looked like you saw me."

"I told you I didn't see you!"

His little rabbit nose twitched, as if sniffing for the truth. His brow crinkled. His eyes narrowed. I could feel their penetrating gaze.

"What? Do you think I'm lying?" Of course I was lying, and it was killing me. Danny deserved better from his older brother.

We finished the trek to Cabin Row without speaking.

Pausing in front of his cabin for no more than a second, he muttered, "See ya," and then disappeared inside.

I stared at his door for a long moment before walking over to my cabin and mounting the stairs.

I opened the front door. My cabinmates had formed a circle around the boy with sad eyes. His name, I had learned, was Miles Romano. Commanded by their ringleader—a boy named Keith with green, catlike eyes and a crooked nose— they shoved Miles's puny frame from one boy to the next, taunting him with shouts of "Bed wetter! Sissy! Homo! Thief!"

*Miles? No way. I don't believe it. I don't believe any of it!*

Two of them—Keith and a sandy-haired boy named Tony—pointed lit cigarettes at Miles and threatened to burn him if he didn't return Keith's things. "Cough 'em up, Romano, cough 'em up, or else . . ."

Tony's bunkmate, Andrew, had rolled a towel into a rattail and dipped the tip in water to improve its potency. In a display of raw power, he whipped the rattail against the floor. *sssSNAP! sssSNAP! sssSNAP!*

The door slammed behind me. "What are you guys doing?" I yelled.

"Romano kiped a comic book and a pack-a baseball cards from my care package," said Keith. "What's it to you?" Then, taking a long, deliberate drag from his cigarette, he refocused his attention on the interrogation.

At lunch, I had learned that baseball cards were a precious commodity at Camp Abenaki Valley. They were traded like currency. Any boy with a decent collection could exchange his cards for cash to finance a trip to the general store in town. Getting there was a problem, though. You had to find a counselor who would agree to take you along during his time off from camp duties. If you were so lucky, however, you could be sure all your friends would hound you with orders for candy, comic books, and more baseball cards to be circulated into the camp's economy, paying you a broker's fee for your trouble, of course. Inevitably, the counselor would require that you split the fee with him as compensation for his services. If you refused, your only other option would be to go AWOL and hitchhike your way into town. Earlier that summer, a couple of campers had attempted this option, but they were apprehended when they reentered the camp grounds. Their punishment was a week of washing dishes in the mess hall kitchen.

"Cough 'em up, Romano!" Andrew whipped his rattail at the floor—*sssSNAP!*—missing Miles's feet by inches.

"I don't have them! I didn't take them! Leave me alone!"

Andrew aimed higher and connected this time, leaving an ugly welt on Miles's thigh.

"*Ooowww!*" Miles grasped his leg with both hands and fell to the floor.

The door swung open, and three boys strode inside: an older boy, who I guessed was maybe fourteen, and, behind him, two giants, who appeared to be identical twins. The first boy was big—bigger than any of us—but the giants were well over six feet tall and built like Olympic weightlifters. What brought these three into our territory was a mystery to me. Boys their age lived clear at the other end of Cabin Row, near the mess hall. In any event, I entertained naïve hopes they would put a stop to the bullying.

The first boy stepped forward. "What's going on in here, girls?"

No one answered.

"Anyone?"

Finally, Keith spoke up. "Hey, Henry."

"You're Don Hardaway's little brother . . . Keith, right?"

"That's right."

"Okay, what's the lowdown, Keith?"

Pointing at Miles, who was still lying on the floor, Keith said, "This asswipe, Romano here, kiped a comic book and a pack-a baseball cards from a care package I got on Friday. They were in my footlocker this morning, but when I came back from lunch, they were gone. No one was here except Romano. I know it was him. He's been caught stealing before."

"Oh my, my, my . . . He took your comic book and your baseball cards. That's a serious offense." Henry grabbed Keith's cigarette out of his mouth and took a drag. Circling Miles like a hungry predator, he asked, "What comic?"

"*Batman.*"

"Any good baseball cards?"

"Yeah, there were some all-stars—Carl Yastrzemski, George Brett, Johnny Bench, Tom Seaver, and a few others."

"Okay, Romano. Where are they?" Henry pulled out a Buck knife and flipped it open with a flick of his wrist.

Miles took one look at the knife and began to shake. Little beads of sweat formed on his upper lip. "I d-d-don't know. I told these guys already—I d-d-didn't take anything."

"Romano, Romano, Romano. That is the wrong answer. I'm gonna give you one more chance. Hand over the goods—*now!*"

The word *now* was projected so forcefully I nearly jumped out of my sneakers.

From his spot on the floor, Miles looked up at Henry with a tiny gleam of defiance in his eyes and said nothing.

"Okay, Romano. Have it your way. I'm done playing games with you." Henry's face turned to stone. The cold sliver of a smile appeared. "Theodore, Thaddeus—hold him down."

The two giants lurched forward, grabbed Miles, picked him up as easily as a rag doll, and pinned him on his bed.

Henry pointed the knife at Miles. "My dad just sent me this knife. I haven't used it yet . . . for anything. You know, in ancient times, they punished thieves by cutting off their hands. We'll just take a finger . . ."

"Whoa," said Willy, the boy with red hair and freckles. "Hey, Henry, take it easy. How about we just give him a Prell booster or a wedgie?"

"Yeah, take it easy, Henry," added Miles's bunkmate, Rex. "We can handle this."

Ignoring Willy's and Rex's pleas for leniency, Henry moved closer to Miles, the knife's blade flashing in the light. Miles wriggled and thrashed in a futile attempt to escape from the giants' powerful arms. He tried to scream, but one of the giants muffled him with a pillow. The other giant grabbed a hand and held it up. Henry moved in, poised to strike.

"*Stop it!*" I shouted as loudly as I could. "*He's innocent!*"

Henry turned around, sized me up, and sneered. "Who's this dork? A newbie?"

"Isn't that the kid who puked at the movie last night?" asked one of the giants.

"Yeah, that's right, Thaddeus." Henry moved toward me with a menacing swagger in his step. "The puker. You ruined

Jesse Bloomquist's favorite shirt . . . Good job! I never liked that Bloomquist kid much anyway." He took another drag from Keith's cigarette. "So, Puke, what were you saying about your friend Romano?"

"He's innocent."

"Oh, he is! And just how do you know that?"

"Because I took the comic book and the baseball cards."

"Really. What was the comic?"

"*Batman.*"

"And the baseball cards?"

"Carl Yastrzemski, George Brett, Johnny Bench, Tom Seaver, and a few others," I said, rattling them off from memory.

"Okay. If it was you, then hand the goods over." He was getting close now.

I took a step backward. "I don't have them with me."

"That's too bad . . . for you, Puke."

I took another step backward and bumped up against the wall.

Still he kept coming—very slowly, like an animal stalking its prey. This animal had the bristling hide of a wild boar and a scowl pasted on its protruding snout. It regarded me with a cold-blooded stare, but I could sense rage simmering just below the surface.

"You're just a bully." Where was this display of courage coming from? "You don't have the guts to use that knife." The words were coming out of my mouth, but it was as if someone else were speaking them.

"You're really asking for it, aren't you, Puke?"

My heart pounded.

"I'm gonna teach you a lesson you'll never forget."

My temples throbbed.

He took one final step. I had nowhere to go. My back was pressed flat against the wall. I was trapped. He glared down at my trembling face. He was so close I could smell his breath. It stank like the jar of mustard Danny had left sitting out on the counter that spring. It sat there for days until I noticed it growing fuzzy green spores, took a whiff, and chucked it in the garbage.

We stood there face-to-face for an eternity until, without thinking and without any warning, I stepped forward and threw a fierce punch that landed square on Henry's jaw. *Where did that come from?* The punch happened without any effort on my part, but it hit its mark and landed hard.

He staggered back, clutching his jaw with both hands. "What the—" Steadying himself, he checked for blood. Seeing none, he looked at me, gaping in utter disbelief.

I braced myself for the inevitable retaliation, but then something astonishing happened. Tears welled up in his eyes. *Tears!* He was nothing but a cowardly bully after all.

Recovering his wits and shaking off the sting of the punch, he growled, "That does it. No more Mr. Nice Guy. Your ass is mine, Puke."

The door swung open so hard it rattled the whole front wall of the cabin.

"What the fuck is going on in my cabin?" roared Wayne. "You three!" He pointed at Henry and the two giants, Theodore and Thaddeus. "Get the hell out of here! Right now!"

"I'll get you for this, Puke," Henry hissed at me. "You'll pay. Believe me, you'll pay."

"I said, *right now!*"

Frightened by Wayne's thunderous voice, the three boys scurried out of the cabin.

"Next time I see that knife, I'm gonna confiscate the damn thing!" he yelled after them as they hopped down the stairs and dashed across the field toward the lodge.

"What are you guys standing around for?" he said, turning now to us. "Does anyone here have a problem?"

No one uttered a sound. Keith glanced over at Miles but said nothing.

"Keith, do you have a problem?"

"No, sir."

"No problems? Everybody's getting along? Everybody's happy? Marvy! Now get to work cleaning up this pigsty. Inspection's tonight."

With a smirk, Wayne strutted over to his corner of the room and removed his guitar from its case. He then sank into bed with his back propped up by an oversized pillow and strummed a few casual chords. Apparently satisfied that his beloved instrument was in tune, he closed his eyes and played.

My heartbeat gradually slowed, and my breath returned to normal. Unsure what to do next, I grabbed a broom and started sweeping the floor.

As I was sweeping, Willy approached me and whispered, "Next time, just mind your own business. You'd be better off not making an enemy out of Henry Hatfield. He's one mean dude, and his older buddy, Spencer Black, is even worse. Avoid *him* at all costs. But if you do run into him, be careful. That dude is C-R-A-Z-Y—*crazy*. Just some friendly advice."

"Thanks, Willy."

Nodding, he started to turn away but then stopped and flashed a warm smile that revealed a set of teeth as hopelessly crooked as a jack-o'-lantern's. "Just between you and me—nice punch, Williamson," he said with a wink before returning to his chores.

"Willy!" I called after him.

"Yeah?"

"What's a Prell booster?"

He came back over and whispered in a secretive tone, "It's when they hold you down and squeeze a tube of Prell shampoo up your ass. Trust me, *kemosabe*, you do not want one of those. You'll be leaking into your underwear for a week!"

I shivered at the thought and returned to sweeping the floor.

The Ultimate Race teams were posted shortly after dinner. Almost every camper was in a fit of agony to find out whether he would be an Eagle or Hawk, which made about as much difference to me as Jet versus Shark. Pushing and shoving, a tidal wave of boys descended upon the front porch of the lodge for a glimpse of the bulletin board. The biggest boys muscled the smaller ones out of the way. One unfortunate kid—no older than Danny—caught an elbow in the eye and ran crying into the infirmary.

Shouts of delight and groans of despair merged together into a single, undifferentiated roar of emotion that echoed through the valley as campers located their names on the double-columned list. The flaunting began. "We've got Johnny Benson. Ain't no way we're gonna lose!" exclaimed an Eagle. "Benson's a stiff! We've got Terry Boggs. We're gonna cream you guys," spouted a Hawk.

High fives were exchanged as some boys floated back to their cabins while others trudged back to theirs with hunched shoulders, disappointed perhaps to be separated from their best buddies.

I hung back until the massive crowd thinned out; only then did I approach the board and learn I was an Eagle. Neil Kennedy, the boy who had made such a favorable impression upon my mother, would lead us. I decided this was good news. If I needed to discuss my preference for a nonwater event, Neil seemed like a reasonable guy.

Danny was a Hawk. He and his buddies scampered away from the lodge, hooting and hollering like a pack of wild chimpanzees. At least one Williamson boy would be victorious come Saturday. I put my hands in my pockets and plodded across the grassy field toward my cabin to prepare for weekly inspection. Shadows cast by the trees behind Cabin Row stretched across the field and swallowed me whole. The sun sank behind the distant hills.

After a successful inspection—only a few beds needed to be remade and one toilet rescrubbed—we hiked single file along the narrow and winding path leading up to Parson's Peak. A constellation of lightning bugs illuminated our way through the heavy darkness of the thick woods that surrounded and covered us like a wool blanket on a hot night. The steady hum of at least ten thousand crickets filled our ears. Quietly, so no one else could hear, I hummed along. As we drew near the site, the campfire's glow revealed itself through the trees. Whirling clusters of sparks soared skyward.

Stepping into the clearing, I looked up and gasped, awestruck by the thousands of tiny pinpricks of flickering light that blanketed the sky—the brightest of which seemed close enough to touch, if only I could stand tall enough on my tippy-toes. A shooting star blazed across my field of vision. I was enthralled.

Lost in a state of celestial wonder, I followed my cabinmates into the amphitheater while the stars shadowed me, watching my every move. They were there for me. They had always been there for me, I suddenly realized. Without looking up, I could feel their presence. I could feel their love. As long as they were there, I would be safe.

*Safe? Safe from what?*

I sat down next to Willy, who, I had learned, was also an Eagle, and returned my gaze to the heavens.

"It's quite a sight, isn't it?" he asked.

I nodded. Parson's Peak was a special place. I was at peace here.

Behind us, Miles sat alone in the very last row, the seventh, staring down into the fire with his sad eyes.

Next to the fire, Mr. Gordon stood motionless and waited for the benches to fill up. The campers were in high spirits, chatting and laughing and razzing each other mercilessly. When everyone was seated, Mr. Gordon raised a hand, and the crowd became quiet.

"Welcome to the official kickoff event for the twentieth annual Ultimate Race!"

An avalanche of applause shook the amphitheater. When it subsided, Mr. Gordon gazed placidly into the crowd and paused. The pause stretched into a silence that seemed to have no end. The audience fidgeted and shifted in their seats. Only the stars were unperturbed. Shining down upon Mr. Gordon, they waited patiently for him to begin. They could wait forever. They had nothing but time . . .

Mr. Gordon's face suddenly lit up, and he continued.

"As most of you know, the Olympics played a significant role in my life. I'll always be grateful for my experience in Helsinki twenty-four years ago. Winning a silver medal as a member of the four-by-two-hundred-meter freestyle team was a magical moment I cannot begin to put into words. Earlier this evening in Montreal, there was another magical moment at the Olympics. A young lady, a gymnast from Romania, scored a perfect ten on the uneven bars, one of the most difficult events in all Olympic competition. A perfect ten—think about that, boys. A perfect ten is an extraordinary accomplishment. It's exactly the kind of excellence John Lewis had in mind when he founded Camp Abenaki Valley back in the summer of 1947.

"I was a seventeen-year-old camper that summer. Mr. Lewis was camp director, counselor, role model, teacher, and trusted friend to all. He taught us about these woods and the secrets that lay within. He taught us to respect nature. He shared with us his views of God, family, and the importance of loyalty and friendship. He taught us life lessons that resonated deeply and stayed with us for many years to come.

"Mr. Lewis was an accountant and a member of the Anglican Church. He lived with his wife and two children in a very modest home in the woods just outside of Portland. Above all, he valued tradition, honor, hard work, and personal achievement through an unwavering commitment to excellence. Mr. Lewis founded this camp shortly after the Second World War because he believed that developing young men with solid Christian values was the key to ensuring a strong, prosperous, and free United States of America for generations of Americans to come.

"The Ultimate Race is a symbol of the competitive spirit John Lewis believed made America great. All campers participate in the Ultimate Race, so it's an opportunity for each of you to practice Camp Abenaki Valley's tradition of honor and sportsmanship. That means playing the game with integrity and conducting yourselves with dignity, win or lose. Each camper's role is vital. Please keep this in mind when you receive your leg assignment.

"Throughout the coming week, team meetings will be led by your captains, Neil Kennedy and Eddie McCarthy. Where are Neil and Eddie?"

The two captains had been sitting together in the first row directly behind Mr. Gordon. They stood up, both grinning like the Cheshire Cat.

"Yeah! Right on, Eddie Mac! You're our man!" blurted out a Hawk.

A group of Eagles began chanting, "Neil! Neil! Neil! Neil!"

Mr. Gordon allowed the two teams to go back and forth like this for quite some time before attempting to intercede.

"I love your enthusiasm, but we need to proceed with the program—"

"Eddie Mac! Eddie Mac! Eddie Mac! Eddie Mac . . ."

"Neil! Neil! Neil! Neil . . ."

When the chanting had died down, Mr. Gordon turned to the captains and asked, "Have either one of you chosen your baton bearer?"

"No, sir!"

"Would you tell us if you had?"

"No, sir!"

"Okay, boys, you can sit."

Mr. Gordon next went over the schedule for the week. When he was through, he turned to the counselors and asked, "Have I left anything out, gentlemen?"

"No, sir."

"Okay! It's time for the annual Ultimate Race initiation ceremony. Each of you will now be initiated as either an Eagle or Hawk. Captains, please take your places."

Neil and Eddie positioned themselves in front of the fire on either side of Mr. Gordon.

"Now I'd like to see all Eagles form an orderly line in front of Neil and all Hawks do the same in front of Eddie to receive your insignias. When you've gone through your line, take a seat on my right if you're an Eagle and on my left if you're a Hawk."

Sitting in the background on a grassy slope with the other counselors, Wayne stroked his guitar and launched into a rather somber version of "The Battle Hymn of the Republic." Meanwhile, we formed two lines that wound and weaved through the maze formed by the amphitheater's concentric semicircles. I looked over at the Hawks' line and made eye contact with Danny. He smiled and waved. I waved back. Just beyond Danny, I recognized the shadowy shapes of a few of my cabinmates, including Miles, who brought up the rear.

Toward the front of the Hawks' line, the fire cast a grotesquely distorted shadow of Henry Hatfield into the amphitheater. Slouching indifferently next to Henry was a tall boy with long, stringy hair. With thumbs hooked through the belt loops of his cut-off jeans, he spoke to Henry in a cool and detached manner. Elusive. Faceless . . .

*Could this slouching figure be the infamous Spencer Black?*

Henry's shadow leaned in, seemingly whispering to the other in a conspiratorial tone, perhaps suggesting some evil machination for them to pursue after the ceremony. The slouching boy's shadow listened and nodded in agreement. I shuddered and looked upward to the stars for comfort.

Willy, Salad Bowl, and I brought up the rear of the Eagles' line. Soon it was Willy's turn to receive his insignia. I watched with fascination as Neil dipped his index finger into a bowl filled with black ashes and painted a large capital *E* on Willy's forehead.

"Welcome to the Eagle family, brother. Please take a seat."

Neil repeated the same procedure with Salad Bowl, leaving me as the final Eagle to be initiated. I stepped forward nervously and tried to locate Neil's face but saw only darkness. The glow from the fire surrounded him like a giant halo, leaving his face hidden in the flickering shadows. Then I caught a glimpse of an eye, his nose, his mouth. The intense heat of the fire encircled us as he performed the ceremony, painting an *E* on my forehead with ashes that were pleasantly cool to the touch.

"Welcome to the Eagle family, brother. Please take a seat."

There was an open spot on the far end of the first row. Moving quickly under the weight of the entire camp's gaze, I took it. In silence, the two teams sized up each other as the counselors distributed candles. A counselor handed me a lighted candle and instructed me to allow my neighbor to light his candle from mine. Soon the entire amphitheater flickered like a little galaxy.

"On Saturday, you will be engaged in head-to-head competition, doing everything within your power—and the rules—to beat the other team," said Mr. Gordon. "But tonight, your voices will rise together in song as we conclude our opening ceremony."

Right on cue, Neil and Eddie began leading the teams in a two-part round of "Hey Ho, Nobody Home." When the Eagles finished the first line of the song, the Hawks joined in. Together, our voices filled our little galaxy, sprang forth from the precipice, and echoed out into the night and across Parson's Pond.

*In the middle of the pond, a sleeping loon wakes, tilts its head toward the sound, and listens.*

*Hey ho, nobody home*
*Meat nor drink nor money have I none*
*Still I will be merry . . .*

We sang this song and many others until our candles nearly burned themselves out. When the last note had faded into the night air, Mr. Gordon spoke.

"This ends this evening's program. Best of luck to both teams as you prepare for Saturday's competition. Remember always to conduct yourselves with honor and integrity. Make your families proud!"

As we stood to go, a few of the older campers broke into a lively rendition of the camp song. Within seconds, the rest of us joined in. I didn't know the words but caught on quickly.

*Abenaki honor*
*We carry thee*
*Through these woods and home again*
*Ha! Ha! Ha!*
*We will always rise above*
*Victorious for the one we love!*

As we filtered down the path back to Cabin Row, I found myself walking directly behind the towering frame of Mr. Gordon. He carried himself lightly, sauntering along in a manner that suggested he hadn't a care in the world. He didn't seem to be the same man who, just yesterday, had slinked into the administration building without saying hello, or the one who had appeared so ill at ease with the microphone at last night's banquet.

A sudden flash of white light cut through the darkness and lit up the entire forest.

Shortly after my father's death, Stanley, I began seeing things—a glimpse of his face from my bedroom window or a glass of milk spilling moments before it actually happened, and later, much bigger things such as the Twin Towers disappearing in a cloud of black smoke at the bicentennial—but never a vision as vivid and detailed as the one now unfolding before my eyes.

*It's Christmas Day. A young man, his wife, and their little girl are driving along a two-lane country road. They are miles from the next town. A heavy snow is falling. The car hits a patch of ice. It spins out of control and into an oncoming truck . . .*

Mr. Gordon was the only survivor of the crash.

His wife, Caroline, had hair of gold, pure alabaster skin, and sparkling blue eyes that turned bluer when she laughed, which was often. They were married in 1952, less than three months after Mr. Gordon's Olympic experience in Helsinki. The wedding ceremony took place on a glorious autumn day in a tiny New England fishing village. Within a year, Caroline gave birth to a daughter, Anna, who had her mother's features and her father's zest for life.

The accident had robbed Mr. Gordon of all he held dear, yet somehow he found the strength to continue as days turned into weeks, weeks became months, and months disappeared into years. All the while, he never stopped mourning the deaths of his wife and daughter, and he never stopped berating himself for failing to avoid that fateful Christmas Day accident.

*If only I'd been driving more slowly . . . if only I'd been more careful . . . if only I'd reacted more quickly . . . Anna was only six. Six! She never had a chance to go to school, make friends, meet boys, fall in love, get married, have a family of her own . . .*

These and similar thoughts were always with him as he went through the motions of coaching swimming and teaching science and mathematics to his eleventh-grade students at Andover Senior High.

During the summer months, he lived as a hermit, locking himself away in his house and emerging only when necessary to make trips to the market. This pattern continued until his old friend John Lewis asked him to come up to Camp Abenaki Valley for a few weeks in the summertime to serve as swimming instructor and help out with camp administration. After the first summer, Mr. Gordon accepted this commitment on a full-time basis. Ultimately, this arrangement led to Mr. Lewis asking Mr. Gordon to take over as camp director beginning the summer of 1973.

Choosing never to remarry, Mr. Gordon grieved and held on to his guilt for years. Then, in January of 1976, his family physician sent him to an oncologist following a routine physical exam. The oncologist confirmed an advanced case of pancreatic cancer and informed him that he had less than six months to live.

Mr. Gordon told no one of his visit to the oncologist or of his bleak prognosis, resolving to make it through the school year and spend his final summer on earth at Camp Abenaki Valley. The oncologist urged him to consider volunteering for a new clinical trial involving an aggressive course of chemotherapy and radiation treatments, but he refused. When June came, he packed his bags, loaded up the car, and left his home in Andover for Abenaki Valley, Maine.

At camp, Mr. Gordon went about his daily routine, performing his duties as usual. Things proceeded much as they had during his first three years as camp director—until the night before our first campfire together.

*A woman in a long white gown and hair of lustrous gold appears at his bedside. Her fingertips lightly graze his cheek. She whispers into his ear. "Michael . . . Michael, dear, it's me. I'm here, darling. I'm right here." She crawls under the covers and wraps her arms around him. "I've come to tell you that Anna and I are fine. We've always been fine. All these years, we've been right here beside you . . . loving you, always loving you . . . You may not realize this, but you've made such a difference in the lives of your students and your campers. This summer, there's one camper in particular who needs your help. Please be there for him when the time comes."*

*"I will. I promise."*

*"I need to go now, my love." She kisses him tenderly on the lips.*

*"Don't go. Not yet."*

*"You will see us on Christmas Day—both of us."*

*"But—"*

*"In the meantime, you must do two things for me."*

*"Anything."*

*"First, forgive yourself. You must leave the past behind and forgive yourself completely. Can you do that for me?"*

*"Yes."*

*"And second, be happy. Be gloriously happy . . . and share your happiness with everyone around you."*

At dawn, Mr. Gordon awoke to the song of a lark perched outside his window. *Caroline?* He opened his eyes. Lying on his pillow was a heart cut from red construction paper. On the heart, "I love you, Daddy!" was written in the crayoned scrawl of a six-year-old child. With a quivering hand, he picked it up and gazed down at those four sweet words through tears of profound joy. Then he set the heart aside and wept until breakfast.

Mr. Gordon's cancer, which had grown out of a grief he had borne for far too long, would overtake him in his bed at home on Christmas Day 1976. Blissfully happy, he would die alone in his sleep with a contented smile on his lips and the song of a lark in his heart, at last joining his wife, Caroline, and daughter, Anna, in eternity.

# CHAPTER FIVE

*Monday, July 19, 1976*

W*E'RE WAIST-DEEP IN GREEN ALGAE. Our bodies are covered with a thick film of slime. The leeches are sucking us dry. We are prisoners of war building a bridge on the River Kwai. Dooong . . . Dooong . . . Dooong . . . Like robots, we drop our hammers, picks, and shovels into the river and march single file toward the jungle. Each prisoner before me crosses the threshold with a primeval scream and is swallowed up into a dark thicket of jagged twigs and branches. It's almost my turn. I try to resist, but the jungle's pull is too powerful. It opens its mouth into a gaping hole and . . .*

*Dooong*

I jolted upright in bed. *Where . . . where am I?* Rubbing the crusty sleep from my eyes, I scanned the shadowy room but found no answers—only an unfamiliar jumble of beds stacked on beds. I tried to think, but my brain was lost in a thick cluster of cobwebs. Only one thing was clear. I wasn't at home.

Unlike my bed at home, this one was hard and noisy—*very* noisy. When I moved, even a little, the springs responded with a horrible *squeeeak* that sounded like my friend Joey's fingernails on the blackboard in our fourth-grade classroom. *Squeeeak!* Wincing, I held still and listened. *The spider!* Moving only my eyes, I looked up at the ceiling. There was no sign of the little creature, but I knew it must be up there somewhere in the shadows, lurking. Then the rest of it fell into place. I was in a cabin—a cabin painted blue . . . one with a bloodred door. It was the Monday of my first week at Camp Abenaki Valley— thirty-four more days to go.

I peeked over the edge of my bunk and located Salad Bowl's digital clock radio atop his footlocker. 6:28. Time to get ready for breakfast.

After breakfast, I stopped at my cabin to pick up my baseball glove, which, except for the familiar Rawlings red patch on the wrist strap, was as brown as a Hershey's kiss. Taking a moment to admire this, my most prized possession—well broken in from two seasons of use—I allowed the still-fresh leather smell to fill my senses. It was the smell of our basement on a Sunday afternoon when my father used to spend hours cleaning his shoes with saddle soap and then buffing them to an impeccable shine. "Never trust a man who doesn't polish his own shoes," he once told me with a chuckle. The faintest hint of a smile creased my lips. I closed my footlocker and dashed out the door.

The athletic fields consisted of two lacrosse fields and four soccer fields—all but one well groomed. The ungroomed one appeared to serve as a practice field. Upon closer inspection, however, I realized it was actually the outfield of Abenaki Valley's one and only baseball diamond.

The "diamond" was in a hopeless state of disrepair. The infield was mostly crabgrass and dandelions. The pitcher's mound and base paths were made up of a mixture of sandy dirt and pebbles. If there was a home plate, it was buried beneath layers of clay and dust. The chain-link backstop was rusted and filled with gaping holes. I guessed that on a good day, the backstop prevented maybe three out of every four balls from passing through.

Standing at "home plate," I cradled my glove in my arms and waited for the others to arrive. Just when I was beginning to wonder if I had the time right, a group of boys appeared, including Danny, one of his cabinmates, and a couple of others I didn't recognize. A few minutes later, there were eight of us kicking at the dust and gawking at each other. Still no coach. Danny attempted to break the ice by introducing himself, but the response he received amounted to no more than a series of barely audible grunts.

Our coach arrived fifteen minutes late, carrying a large burlap sack filled with bats, balls, and an old catcher's mask and chest protector. After emptying the contents of the bag into the dust bowl, he introduced himself as Phil and explained that we would meet three times a week to prepare for a game against Camp Wildcat in the second week of August. My heart sank. *Eight* boys had signed up for baseball and only *one* game was scheduled.

My second activity that morning was camping. The camping area was situated in a clearing at the end of a circuitous path that led away from the athletic fields and uphill through the woods. Arriving out of breath, I encountered a counselor and six campers chatting casually among themselves. The counselor turned to me and smiled. He had clear crystal-blue eyes and a full but well-trimmed charcoal beard.

"Hi! You must be Ricky."

I nodded.

"Welcome, Ricky. I'm Chad. You're right on time. We'll be getting started in just a sec."

My cabinmate Willy—the one who had warned me about Prell boosters—was among the six campers present. He was having a conversation with a boy whose strawberry-blond locks shone in the few rays of light that managed to filter through the towering pines encircling the clearing. This boy had fair skin and a spate of freckles sprinkled across his cheekbones. He spoke in a very peculiar manner.

"Wawn Ah wus wadda-keyink these mawnink, Ah wawnt awff da key jawmp wid oh-nee one awnd awn da rope! Aw-ha, aw-ha, aw-ha! Eat wus sooo grade!"

"Attaboy, Sam. That really is great."

"Tawnks, Weely." The boy grinned proudly.

After listening for a few more seconds, I realized this boy, Sam, was deaf. I couldn't understand a word he said, but he must have been very good at reading lips because he seemed to understand Willy perfectly. And Willy seemed to understand him.

Chad waved us over to a small campfire pit and welcomed us to Basic Camping Skills and Survival Training, which he described as Abenaki Valley's "Camping 101" course. During the course, we would cover basic camping skills, such as building a fire, pitching a tent, preparing food in the wilderness, orienteering, the proper and safe use of knives and other tools, basic first aid, and respect for the environment. Included within the curriculum were two backpacking trips—a short overnight trip in the last week of July and a longer three-night trip in August.

When he finished the course overview, Chad demonstrated the art of starting a fire by rubbing two sticks together. "This is an advanced skill, but I'd like each of you to give it a try. This should give you an appreciation for how difficult it is to survive in the wilderness. Anyone who can start a fire with these two sticks will get a special reward."

The only boy who succeeded was Sam, who earned, as his special reward, a trip to town with Chad.

*Dooong . . . Dooong . . . Dooong . . .*

We had gone over our allotted time. It was time for lunch. Chad dismissed us "until Wednesday morning."

After a lunch of baked noodle and magic meat casserole, nicknamed "Train Wreck" by the campers, I hurried back to the cabin to use the toilet before my next activity. Feeling an escalating sense of urgency, I bounded up the stairs and swung open the front door. Willy and Keith were taking siestas. Tony and Andrew were playing cards. No one else was there. Tony and Andrew looked up at me and then at each other. I thought I saw Tony wink, but neither one of them said a word. There were three large lumps under the covers of Andrew's bed, but I was in too much of a hurry to give the matter a second thought. Trying to appear casual, I walked directly to the back of the cabin and entered the bathroom. Skipping the first two stalls, I shut myself in the third—I wanted to create as much space as possible between me and the boys in the front of the cabin.

The toilet seat was pleasantly cool. The competing odors of cheap disinfectant and mold surrounded me and swirled into my nostrils. Before me, "Miles Romano is a fag!" was scribbled in black Magic Marker across the inside of the splintered door.

My bowels churned. I prayed that what was about to happen would happen quietly, but then a loud explosion filled the stall, followed immediately by a tremendous splash. Feeling both relieved and embarrassed, I sat very still and listened for a reaction. First I heard giggling. It was muffled and seemed to come from far away. Then footsteps approached and seemed to stop outside my stall. I held my breath until my lungs ached. Finally, I exhaled. *My ears must've been playing tricks on me.* I reached for the toilet paper.

"*Incoming!*"

Three large objects sailed over the top of the door in slow motion—yellow, then blue, then red. Water balloons! Big ones. *Splash!* The yellow one smacked me directly on the forehead and knocked me backward. *Splash!* The blue one hit me square in the face. *Splash!* The red one exploded in my lap. I was soaked. The toilet paper was saturated all the way through to the cardboard roll and completely useless to me. The entire stall was drenched.

The giggles turned into squeals of unbridled laughter.

"Direct hit! Pilot to bombardier, pilot to bombardier—mission complete. Nicely done, bombardier. I'll see you back at home base. Over and out."

"Next time don't try to be a hero, Williamson. Let Romano get what's coming to him."

My heart beating wildly, I let a full minute pass before reaching for my soggy shorts and pulling them up to my waist. My face was hot. My hands were cold. I reached for the door and paused. Tears filled my eyes; it took all my strength to hold them back. With a deep breath, I pushed open the door and stepped out. The first person I saw was Willy. We made eye contact.

"Don't look at me," said Willy. "I had nothin' to do with it." He glanced over at Keith, Tony, and Andrew, who were huddled together and cackling like hyenas.

"Saaah-weeet!" said Keith, slapping Tony on the back. "That was the best one yet. The absolute best. We'll get Romano tonight."

"Look at him," said Andrew. "He's drenched!"

"At least he doesn't stink so much anymore," Keith sneered.

"Yeah," said Tony. "You should thank us, Williamson."

I couldn't take any more. I put my head down and sprinted out of the cabin.

"Where are you going, Ricky?" shouted Willy. "What's the big deal? They were only joshin'."

I never again used the toilets in the cabin—not when sitting was required. At first I tried holding it, but after three days of excruciating stomachaches, I relieved myself in the wooded area behind the cabins, using leaves for toilet paper.

*Tuesday, July 20, 1976*

The following morning, I attended my first riflery class. As it turned out, I was a pretty good shot—"a natural-born marksman," according to Mr. Hardy, a local gun expert whom Mr. Gordon had brought in that summer "to man the range," as he put it.

I liked the sharp scent of gunpowder that greeted me when I entered the shooting range. It gave me a thrill. Mr. Hardy handed me a bolt-action .22-caliber rifle, and my heart skipped a beat. This was really happening! He produced a box of ammunition. The bullets were small yet potent, he assured me. I removed one from the box and held it up to the light. The shell's steely surface shone with a luster that seemed to indicate it had an intelligence of its own. I loaded it into the rifle's chamber. A feeling of sheer power surged through my veins. I took aim at the bull's-eye and slowly pulled the trigger . . .

After riflery, I made my way to arts and crafts, which, according to Salad Bowl, was for fairies. He had shared this information with me the night before when we were getting ready for bed. Miles's bunkmate, Rex, concurred. "Tim's right, Williamson. Arts and crafts is for fairies. You should find another activity. Unless of course . . ."

"Hey, guys," said Ryan. "That's enough. Arts and crafts is not for fairies. You can make some pretty cool stuff in arts and crafts. Give it a chance, Ricky."

Wayne emerged from the bathroom, belched, and turned out the lights.

Ryan's voice slipped through the darkness. "I mean it, Ricky. Arts and crafts is okay."

A burst of giggling filled the room.

"*Quiet!*" hollered Wayne. "Lights out means bedtime, and bedtime means sleep!"

The giggling ceased, but already I had been convinced that arts and crafts was not for cool kids. This was confirmed when only three campers showed up at the art studio: Miles; a rather strange boy named Ernie, who, with his nervous tic disorder, reminded me of a PEZ candy dispenser; and I.

As soon as arts and crafts was over, Miles grabbed his knapsack, slung it over both shoulders, and bolted out of the studio like a rocket. He carried that knapsack wherever he went, but I hadn't ever seen him open it. It was so full it bulged at the seams. I wondered what was inside.

I followed as quickly as I could, but he'd already disappeared down the hallway and out of the lodge by the time I reached the studio door. Pursuing him outside and past a small herd of boys lumbering uphill, I shouted, "Miles! Wait up!" But he didn't seem to hear. Finally, about halfway to Cabin Row, I caught up with him.

"Hey, Miles."

"Oh . . . hey, Ricky." Not slowing his pace, he plowed ahead.

"What do you think of arts and crafts?" I was getting winded from the effort to keep up.

"It's okay, I guess. At least it's a chance to get away from *them*."

"Who?"

"You know, those guys who bully me—guys like Keith Hardaway, who have it in for me."

"Yeah, I know. They're jerks . . . Say, what are you gonna make in arts and crafts?"

He hesitated before answering. "A corncob pipe for my dad. It's a stupid idea."

"No, it's not. I bet he'll like it. Does he smoke pipes?"

He slowed down a little. "Yeah, he's got a whole collection of them at home, but not a corncob one."

"He'll love it then!"

He examined me with his eyebrows knit into a wrinkle of uncertainty, and then suddenly his face burst into a smile. "What are you gonna work on, Ricky?"

"An ant farm. My dad made one for me when I was just a kid, but that was before . . . Well, anyway . . . he knew I liked insects."

Probably sensing I didn't want to talk about my father, he changed the subject. "Hey, do you like comic books?"

"Sure, I guess so."

He stopped walking, removed his knapsack, and opened it, revealing a substantial stash of comic books.

"Wow! There must be, I dunno, fifty in there," I said, starting to wonder whether he really was our cabin's resident thief.

"Forty-seven. And I know what you're thinking—don't worry, none of them are *Batman*."

"I believe you, but why so many?"

"I just like comic books. DC and Marvel are okay, but my personal favorite is *Archie*. Here's one. Wanna borrow it?"

He held up a comic whose cover showed Archie sweating profusely and getting ready to pull the cord on the engine of an old lawnmower while Jughead and Reggie looked on, obviously amused by the spectacle.

I wasn't particularly interested in Archie, Jughead, Reggie, or even Betty and Veronica, but it meant the world that he trusted me enough to show me his prized comic book collection and even offer to lend me one.

"Sure," I said, taking the comic. "Thanks."

"No problem," he replied with a toothy grin, but suddenly his expression darkened. "I'll see you later, Ricky," he said, lowering his head and hurrying off toward our cabin.

I looked over my shoulder and saw the reason for Miles's hasty departure. Tommy Underwood's older brother, Jeffrey, was approaching with three of his buddies in tow. Jeffrey had dishwater-blond hair and, unlike his brother, beady little eyes that seemed to pierce right through me. Tall and lanky, he carried himself with an exaggerated air of authority. His thin lips were bent downward into a sour expression of disapproval.

He got right to the point. "Stay away from that kid, Ricky. He's trouble."

"Miles? B-but, he's my friend."

"Trust me. He's not your friend. He's bad news. Everyone here avoids Miles Romano."

I tried but couldn't imagine what Miles had done to earn this reputation—probably not much. I knew it didn't take a whole lot to earn a bad reputation in this world. I wanted to stand up to Jeffrey. I wanted to tell him that no matter what Miles had done, he was still my friend. Other than Tommy and Willy, Miles was the only camper who had shown me so much as a glimmer of kindness during my first four days at Camp Abenaki Valley, and I was not going to sell him out.

"But—"

"I heard about you sticking up for Miles in your cabin the other day. That was noble but misguided."

"But Henry was going to hurt Miles."

"Henry wouldn't have done a thing to Miles. Henry Hatfield is all talk and no action."

"But you weren't there. If you had seen—"

"Let me give you a friendly piece of advice, Ricky. You need to learn to fall in line, or you're never going to fit in here."

With that, Jeffrey and his buddies marched away, leaving me alone in the middle of the field, dumbfounded.

Jeffrey's words had their intended effect. It was a while before I made another attempt to speak with Miles. In the meantime, I held on to his comic book.

It started to get dark. Once again, dusky shadows stretched across the camp, although it would be another hour before sunset. From his bunk, Keith Hardaway needled away at Miles in a merciless sotto voce. Although his voice was soft, his words pierced the air with the ferocity of a swarm of killer bees.

"Hey, fairy boy. Yeah, that's right—I'm talkin' to you, Romano. Where's my comic book? Whatcha do with my baseball cards? You're a little mommy's boy, aren't you, fairy boy? What would Mommy think of your stealing? Is that a letter from her? Don't feel like talking? That's not very polite. Well, anyway, your mommy's not here now. Is she, fairy boy? You're all alone—how sad, how very sad. Don't worry, fairy boy—I'll take care of you. You're mine tonight."

*Leave him alone!*

Poised on the tip of my tongue, the words were about to leap from my mouth. But then I thought of Jeffrey Underwood's "friendly piece of advice" and swallowed them whole.

Keith got out of his bunk and switched to his normal voice. "Okay, Romano, this time I'm serious. I want my comic book. I want my baseball cards. And I want them now."

Immediately, Tony and Andrew joined Keith in the middle of the room.

Miles sat straight up in bed, clutching his letter from home in trembling hands. "Guys, you know it wasn't me. Why do you keep harassing me?"

"Harassing? That's an awfully big word coming from such a little twerp," said Tony.

"I've had enough," said Keith. "No more words. It's wedgie time."

Miles's eyes grew so large I feared they would pop out of his head. Abandoning the letter, he scooted to the far end of his bed, wrapped his hands around his knees, and squeezed himself into a little ball. But it was pointless. He was only prolonging the inevitable. In a flash, Tony and Andrew were on him.

"No! Leave me alone," pleaded Miles as he tried to fight them off.

"Quit your whining, Romano," said Keith. "With all this fuss, you'd think the world was coming to an end. It's just a wedgie, for God's sake—to teach you a lesson."

"Teach me a lesson? I didn't do anything wrong!"

The boys snatched Miles from his bed and dropped him onto the hardwood floor with a thump. He almost succeeded in crawling back to safety, but Salad Bowl and Rex joined in to help Tony and Andrew retrieve him and hold him down. Even Willy participated—as a cheerleader—clapping his hands and chanting, "Wedgie, wedgie, wedgie . . ."

Soon, all the boys in the cabin, except Miles and me, had taken up the chant. "Wedgie, wedgie, wedgie . . ."

Kicking his feet into the hardwood planks and flailing his arms toward the ceiling, Miles struggled valiantly to free himself. But with four boys holding him down, there was nothing he could do to escape. Once they had him secured, they flipped him onto his stomach and held him flat against the floor. I wanted to do something to help him but instead kept a safe distance.

"You can struggle if you like, Romano, but it's only gonna make it worse for you," said Keith, hovering over Miles's helpless body.

Then suddenly, like a cobra striking its prey, Keith reached into Miles's shorts, grabbed his underwear, and yanked.

Miles yelped.

The other boys cheered.

Straddling Miles's body and holding on to the elastic waistband of the now-exposed tighty-whities, Keith smiled triumphantly—like a cowboy who had just broken his first bronc.

Wayne stomped in and slammed the door behind him. "What are you animals up to?" he roared. "Does this have anything to do with the missing comic book and baseball cards?"

Keith let go of Miles's underwear and stood up to face Wayne. "It does. This little creep stole my *Batman* comic book and my cards, and he still won't admit it."

"Is that so? Okay. This has become a serious matter—an honor violation. We do not tolerate stealing at Abenaki Valley, and we certainly will not tolerate it in this cabin."

Then Wayne did something that surprised us all. He strutted over to Miles, picked him up as easily as a rag doll, and hung him by his underwear on an old nail protruding from the middle of the back wall. His feet dangling uselessly beneath him, Miles closed his eyes tight and crunched up his face in agony. Wayne stepped back and admired his work with his hands on his hips and a disgusting smirk on his face.

Miles Romano wasn't the thief. I knew he wasn't the thief. And I knew this not because he told me so. I just knew. There never was a *Batman* comic book. Or a Carl Yastrzemski baseball card. Or a George Brett. Or a Johnny Bench. Or a Tom Seaver. Yet I did nothing to intercede. Instead I stood there frozen and watched him hang from that nail, swinging from side to side like the pendulum of a grandfather clock. I betrayed Miles to save myself.

"Right on," said Tony. "The nail!"

Miles's body stopped swinging and came to rest, suspended now in a state of eerie motionlessness. It was as if the reality of the moment were too horrible for him to face. Then suddenly, he regained his senses and started to squirm in a desperate attempt to free himself. His feet and legs kicking futilely into the air, he twisted and stretched and reached for the nail, but he was unable to unhook himself.

The boys began a new chant: "The nail must not fail! The nail must not fail! The nail must not fail . . ."

And indeed the nail did not fail.

Miles redoubled his efforts. He twisted and stretched and reached for the nail with such determination that his face turned bright purple. But still the result was the same. Finally, out of sheer frustration, he let out a shriek, like that of a wounded crow. Convulsions rippled through his body. No longer reaching for the nail, he thrashed about as if in the throes of an epileptic fit. His arms and legs swung every which way, blurring into a dizzying swirl of frantic activity. I could hardly bear to watch, yet my eyes remained glued to the human tornado he had become.

"The nail must not fail! The nail must not fail! The nail must not fail . . ."

By this time, it was Miles's tighty-whities that had begun to fail. The back half of the waistband tore away, creating twelve inches of space between Miles and the nail. For a moment, he hung there levitating in midair. Then, finally and mercifully, the underwear gave way altogether. He landed hard on the floor.

Lying there in a heap, he looked up at his tormenters with hatred—*pure* hatred—seething in his eyes.

They laughed. And laughed. They laughed so hard that tears ran down their faces. Wayne laughed hardest of them all.

After a while, the laughter subsided, and everyone went back to their own business. Miles remained where he was, whimpering into the floorboards. A long, thin string of saliva trickled from his mouth and dangled there. I took a step toward him and stopped. Our eyes met. His were filled with such shame and anger as I had never seen. There was no trace of the boy who had smiled and offered me one of his prized comic books only hours before.

Sunset was almost upon us. The interior of the cabin turned a ghoulishly dark shade of split pea green. Someone flicked on the lights. Miles crawled on hands and knees to his footlocker. Finding a fresh pair of underwear, he slinked into the bathroom to clean himself up and change.

The air in the cabin became thick. I couldn't breathe. If I stayed, I'd suffocate. The walls closed in on me.

*Coward. Traitor. False friend. Get out!*

I bolted for the door.

Willy called out to me, "Hey, Ricky! Where you going?"

"Out."

"Out where?"

"Just out."

"Oh, come on, Ricky. Don't be that way. We were just having fun."

I put my hand on the doorknob and stopped. "Miles wasn't."

"Ricky—"

But I was already gone.

*Wednesday, July 21–Friday, July 23, 1976*

After lunch on Wednesday, Neil and Eddie posted the Ultimate Race assignments along with the identities of the two baton bearers. Once again, the boys of Camp Abenaki Valley descended upon the front porch of Lewis Lodge to vie for a peek at the bulletin board. I didn't need to get anywhere near the board to learn that Neil had chosen Johnny Benson as the Eagles' baton bearer and that Eddie had bestowed the honor upon Terry Boggs. Such news traveled fast and loud at Abenaki Valley.

Maintaining a safe distance from the front porch and waiting anxiously for my turn at the board, I overheard two Eagles discussing whether Johnny was the right choice.

"Johnny Benson is one of the best soccer players in camp. He has the most wicked penalty shot I've ever seen. Neil should've assigned him to the soccer leg. Anthony Slater would've been my choice for baton bearer."

"I hear what you're sayin', dude, but I'm not so sure about Anthony's endurance. I saw him smokin' a cig behind Cabin Row last Saturday night. Anyways, Johnny Benson is the camp's best all-around athlete and fastest runner. He was the right choice. Neil knows what he's doin'."

"Doesn't matter who you've got for baton bearer," interjected an eavesdropping Hawk. "We're gonna crush you guys."

"Dream on," retorted the second Eagle.

Finally, I made my way to the bulletin board and located my name. Next to it was a single word:

*Swimming*

My worst fear was confirmed—I was officially one of eight Eagles required to swim a quarter mile through the deep and murky waters of Parson's Pond. A storm brewed in my stomach. My head spun; my vision blurred. No larger now than a postage stamp, the bulletin board faded into a distant fog. Somehow, I found the lodge's front door, wandered into the rec center, and collapsed onto a couch in front of the TV.

*I stare into the screen. At first I see nothing and then . . . a brilliant sun reflects off a mirror of pale-blue water. A few gentle ripples pass through the mirror. A shout reaches my ears. It's a happy sound. Somewhere, not far away, boys are playing . . .*

*Surrounded by the fresh scent of a gulf breeze, I'm standing on a stairway leading into the shallow end of a swimming pool. A Donald Duck inner tube is wrapped securely around my waist. Unable to resist, I step forward and float gracefully into the middle of the pool. Suddenly, I slip through the inner tube and disappear into the mysterious waters below. In a state of sheer panic, I fight my way to the surface only to discover that Donald is floating away . . . tantalizingly out of reach. Gasping for air, I plunge back down into the water . . .*

"Nadia Comaneci, the fourteen-year-old Romanian gymnastics phenom, is seen here on the balance beam during Monday's team competition, scoring her second perfect ten of the Olympics. And here she is again, scoring her third perfect ten, this time on the uneven bars."

The sound of Nadia's name snapped me out of my trance. I looked up at the screen and watched transfixed as she completed her routine on the uneven bars. I was in love.

"After leading Romania to a silver medal in the team competition, Miss Comaneci will be competing in the overall individual competition tonight at the Montreal Forum. Is it possible that this extraordinary young woman has more perfect tens in store for us? Tune in at eight o'clock, Eastern time."

Nadia vanished. An enormous man dressed only in a skimpy red singlet—the Russian weightlifter Vasily Alekseyev—stepped onto a platform and raised 255 kilograms (562 pounds) over his head.

"Holy cow," gasped a boy sitting near me.

My thoughts returned to the Ultimate Race. The depth of the pond's waters concerned me just as much as the distance of the swim. It might have been okay if the water were shallow enough for my feet to touch—I could take a break if I got tired—but I was absolutely terrified of swimming in water over my head. I really believed I would drown.

I had to do something. I had to speak with somebody. But as afraid as I was of the water, I was even more afraid of speaking up for myself. With whom could I possibly share my deepest, darkest fear? Mr. Gordon? No way. A former Olympic swimmer couldn't possibly understand. Neil Kennedy? Maybe. He seemed like a good guy. But would he understand, or would he laugh in my face? Either way, confiding in Neil had to be better than drowning.

Yes. My mind was made up. Somehow I needed to find the courage to speak with Neil, but when would be the right time?

On Thursday, the swim teams reported to the pond for our portion of the course walk-through, which was like a dress rehearsal of the Ultimate Race. Perhaps, just perhaps, I thought, this would be a good time to speak with Neil.

When Johnny Benson and Terry Boggs arrived, they threw themselves onto the shoreline and took a Gatorade break. The

swimmers for each team huddled around their respective captains. Neil marched us to the end of the dock, where he went
over every rule for the swim in excruciating detail. I tried to
listen but couldn't. His voice droned on and on. Finally, he
finished and looked out at the pond as if trying to make up his
mind about something.

After a few moments of quiet contemplation, he said,
"There's no need to do the swim today—save your strength for
Saturday."

I breathed a sigh of relief.

"Everybody can swim, right?"

Everybody laughed, except me.

*Now?* I asked myself. *Should I pull him aside and talk to him
now?*

But it was too late. Neil was already on his way toward
shore, strolling down the dock with my teammates in tow. The
right time had come and gone.

Friday arrived—one day to go before the Ultimate Race. After
lunch, I found Neil next to the Governor's Bell, besieged by
Eagles with last-minute questions, concerns, problems, and
requests. With the hot sun beating down on his bulky frame,
he did his best to keep his cool and deal with each issue on
a first-come-first-served basis. But it was plain he was beginning to lose patience. As the boys vied for his attention, first-
come-first-served went out the window. Shouting all at once, a
half dozen or so surged forward to make their case for switch-
ing events. It seemed everybody wanted to be in the soccer

shootout. Apparently, the shootout was where the Ultimate Race was either won or lost.

"Neil, I'm no good to you on the orienteering course. I'll just get lost. My true skill lies in soccer."

"Back home, I was on the all-city soccer team."

"I'm going to play varsity soccer this fall."

"Have you seen my penalty kick?"

"One at a time!" bellowed Neil. "Please, guys—can we do this one at a time?"

Some boys had arranged trades among themselves. One boy, speaking on behalf of his two buddies, stepped forward and outlined their proposal: "We've got it all figured out—a three-way trade. I'm archery, but I want soccer. Barry's in soccer, but he wants lacrosse. Glen's in lacrosse, but wants archery. So—"

"Stop right there. I see where you're going with this, and the answer is no."

Tommy Underwood's friend, Troy, approached Neil next. "Mr. Hardy won't let me use my personal rifle. Said something 'bout unfair advantage."

"I'll talk to Mr. Hardy."

Another boy asked, "How will we know when the fire is lit?"

"Fire? What fire?"

"In camping. Is a single spark good enough? How will we know?"

"When the race official says so."

I had to talk to Neil even if it killed me. It was now or never. I weaved my way through the tightly packed convocation of Eagles and positioned myself between the Governor's Bell and Neil.

"Neil," I croaked, tapping him on the shoulder, but he didn't notice me.

"The baseball target hasn't been set up," said a boy named Nolan.

*Baseball! I could do baseball!*

"I need to take some practice throws before tomorrow."

"I'll look into it and let you know," Neil assured him.

"Neil. Hey, Neil," I said, tapping his shoulder harder this time.

"What the heck? Oh—hi, Ricky. What's *your* problem? Please tell me you're okay with your event. It's swimming, right?"

How could I explain my fear to him in front of all these boys? It was beginning to dawn on me that this was a bad idea.

"Yeah, but—"

"Thank God!"

"The thing is," I tried to continue, "I played in the little league back home and—"

Another boy jumped in before I had a chance to finish. It was Jihad, the Arab boy who had slugged me in the face in front of the lodge.

"I don't want to do canoeing—it's boring! I want riflery. I'm the best shot in camp!"

I had heard Jihad was good, especially for a kid his age. But everyone knew Troy was the best shot in camp.

"Jihad, we went over this on Wednesday and again on Thursday. My decision is final."

"This is bullshit!"

"Watch your mouth!"

"But—"

"Hold on a second, Jihad." He turned to address the whole group. "Listen up, everybody! *All* my decisions are final. I'm not entertaining any further requests to change events."

"Neil," said a soft-spoken mouse of a boy as he hobbled forward. "I have a note from the doctor. He says I have a sprained ankle. I can do riflery or kayaking or even camping, but *not* the obstacle course."

"Oh, good grief!" Neil rolled his eyes toward the sun. By this time, he was perspiring freely. He wiped his brow, took a deep breath, and let it out. "Okay, I'll see what I can do."

The boy thanked him and pushed his way through the crowd, favoring his right leg as he went. If only I'd been so lucky. Still standing next to the Governor's Bell, I tapped Neil on the shoulder one last time.

He looked down at me and took a moment to peruse my face before speaking. "I'm sorry, Ricky. Things are really hectic right now. Was there anything else?"

"No, I guess not."

"It's settled, then. I need a full team of swimmers. Besides, I have no other place to put you."

# CHAPTER SIX

*Saturday, July 24, 1976*

AFTER A RESTLESS NIGHT OF SLEEP, I woke up moments before sunrise with a pounding between my ears and a hollow feeling in the pit of my stomach. It had been a long, hot night. The bedsheets, moist with sweat, clung tenaciously to my body. The overhead fan provided little relief from the soggy blanket of air that smothered the room. The previous evening at dinner, there had been talk of at least another few days of record-breaking heat.

The first light of day slithered through the front windows and into the shadows that enveloped the rafters above me. I blinked a few times, and the cobwebs began to clear from my aching head. It was Saturday—the day of the Ultimate Race and the impossible quarter-mile swim. Quarter mile? It might as well have been ten miles.

Immediately, my mind went to work concocting ways to get out of participating in the race. I could pretend I was sick, but the doctor would take my temperature and easily expose my attempted deception. I could run away, but how far would I get? After all, home was a six-hour car ride away. I could hide in the woods, but eventually I would be required to account for my whereabouts.

*Face it, Ricky—there's no way out.*

Resigning myself to my fate—at least for the moment—I started to inch out of bed, but the springs attached to the aging metal frame unleashed a sharp bray that stopped me short. Without moving a muscle, I listened for some minutes. No one stirred. I tried again. This time, I moved more quickly and climbed down to my footlocker in seconds flat. There, I slipped on my last clean T-shirt, a pair of shorts, and my sneakers before tiptoeing out of the cabin.

Gently closing the door behind me, I paused at the top of the stairs and allowed the morning air to fill my lungs. Everything was absolutely still. The trees bordering the open field below me stood at attention like a company of well-trained cadets reporting for the day's first inspection. Not a leaf fluttered. Not a blade of grass twitched.

To my right were four cabins, including Danny's, which housed the eight- and nine-year-olds. On my left, a long string of cabins that housed campers up to age sixteen stretched almost to the mess hall. The older boys' quarters, Parson's Abode, commanded a spot of its own, about a hundred yards downhill from Cabin Row. A pale light flickered in the shadows of its front porch.

Like the early-American ghost town in the painting that hung in the back hallway of our home in South Orange, Cabin Row was deserted. Comforted by the solitude of the moment, I relaxed my breath into a steady rhythm and bent down to tie my shoelaces. Only when I had secured them into impeccable double knots did I head off toward the path to Parson's Pond.

The well-worn path wound downward like a spiral staircase through the woods and then opened up at the base of the hill within a hundred feet of the pond's shoreline. Through the hazy mist rising off the water's glassy surface, orange buoys marking the course for the quarter-mile swim appeared. My stomach churned. My heart raced. My jaw clenched itself into a vise grip. A family of loons drifted by, blissfully unaware of the significance of the buoys.

To my left, an old boathouse and equipment shed sat side by side. The red paint on the boathouse's warped planks was peeling like a case of bad sunburn. The doors to the equipment shed were ajar and in desperate need of repair. Stored inside were water skis, ropes, life jackets, paddles, masts, sails, gasoline, and other assorted items. Nearby, wooden racks were filled with canoes and kayaks ready for the day's competition. To my right and about a stone's throw away, our proud fleet of four Sunfish sailboats bobbed gently in the shallow waters along the shoreline.

I walked to the end of the dock and surveyed the course.

The concept for the race was simple. At a quarter past two, sixteen boys—eight Hawks and eight Eagles—would swim out to the floating dock and wait there for the baton bearers. When the first baton bearer arrived, he would run to the end of the main dock, dive into the pond, and swim out to the floating dock. When he touched the dock's side, the official would yell, "Go!" The first eight swimmers would dive in. The remaining eight would wait anxiously for their team's baton bearer. From the floating dock, the competitors would swim toward the center of the pond, past a fifty-yard buoy, and out to a hundred-yard buoy. From there, they would turn right and swim across to the ski jump, around it, and back to the floating dock.

Hopeless. It was hopeless. The course was too long. The water was too deep. I'd never make it to the finish line. The finish line? I'd be lucky to make it to the first buoy. Hell, I'd be lucky to make it out to the floating dock. *Wait! What about a life jacket? Maybe, just maybe . . .* I considered the idea for a second or two and then dismissed it as ridiculous.

The nascent sun burned away the mist. The loon family returned. The water was still except for a few ripples left behind as they swam across my line of vision and proceeded nonchalantly on their way.

*Dooong . . .*

The sound of the day's first bell reverberated through the woods, down the hill, and across the pond. Inclining my head, I thought I could detect its echo coming back to me from the far shore. My tummy growled. I turned my back on the course. I took a step. The dock creaked.

*I'll be waiting here for you . . .*

"Who's there?"

No response.

Without looking back, I sprinted off the dock and up the hill.

I arrived at the mess hall, wheezing and puffing like a steam engine on its last legs. A wave of boys surged past me and disappeared inside. Breakfast had begun. Already the day was slipping through my fingers. The Governor's Bell looked down at me sympathetically but offered no words of encouragement. I faltered forward for a step or two and then scrambled up the stairs and onto the front deck. The double doors towered over me. Lunging forward, I seized one of the handles and pulled with all my might . . .

After breakfast, each team held a last-minute prep session. The Hawks met in the rec center. Neil led the Eagles up to Parson's Peak and stationed himself in front of the campfire pit. Under his watchful gaze, we filled the lower-tier benches. All chattering stopped. He had our full and undivided attention. Stepping forward, he projected his voice into the amphitheater with the natural confidence and poise of an adult.

"All of you heard Mr. Gordon's speech about tradition and honor. You know we're here today to win the Ultimate Race and to do so with absolute integrity. But even more important, we're here to learn to play the game of life with integrity. When the race has been run and the summer is over, we'll return home with something in our hearts that very few people can understand—*Abenaki honor*. It's a tough world out there, but we'll be better prepared than most to persevere and succeed."

"Honor schmoner," the boy sitting directly in front of me whispered to his buddy. "Let's get on with it."

"Today marks the twentieth running of the Ultimate Race. Twenty years ago, the Ultimate Race was much shorter. It lasted less than an hour. And the winning team on that day was the Eagles!"

Everyone leaped up and exploded into a thundering chorus of cheers, shouts, and whistles—everyone but me. My stomach aching with worry, I remained seated.

"Over these last twenty years, the race has evolved into something much bigger. It'll be a long day. The race is scheduled to last three and a half hours, but with the hot weather, it might take longer. So be sure to drink plenty of water."

"Water?" cried out a boy from somewhere in the crowd. "We don't need no stinkin' water!"

Neil frowned at this but carried on.

"The race begins here at one o'clock with a prayer by the chaplain, followed immediately by the starting gun. When the gun fires, the baton bearers will sprint to the first event, which is archery this year. Riflery, camping, and orienteering are next. Unless you're in one of these first four events, you should gather back here by quarter to one.

"Once the race begins, it is your responsibility to be at your event site at least thirty minutes prior to the scheduled starting time. Failure to be at your event on time could get the whole team disqualified from the competition and *will* result in you answering to me personally as well as a face-to-face meeting with Mr. Gordon."

I swallowed hard.

"This has never happened in the twenty-year history of the Ultimate Race. But I assure you, severe disciplinary action will be taken if you don't follow this rule."

I couldn't be certain, but Neil seemed to be looking directly at me as he spoke these words.

"Is this clear to everyone here?"

There was a general murmuring as we nodded in the affirmative.

"Good! Everybody stand up. It's time for the Abenaki Valley Creed."

We came to our feet.

"Who are we?" bellowed Neil.

Our voices rose in unison. "Camp Abenaki Valley!"

"What is our watchword?"

"Honor!"

"What kind of honor?"

"Abenaki honor!"

"And what is the first principle of Abenaki honor?"

"Excellence! We strive for excellence in everything we do!"

"The second principle?"

"Integrity! We speak and act with integrity to ensure justice for all!"

"The third principle?"

"Service! We live our lives in humble and obedient service to family, community, country, and God!"

"Who is going to win the Ultimate Race today?" Neil ad-libbed.

"The Eagles!"

"Louder!"

"The Eagles!"

"I can't hear you!"

"*The Eagles*!"

"That's it! Remember, always strive to be the best at every-thing you do. Okay, get out of here. I'll see most of you back here at quarter to one."

In spite of my fears, I couldn't help but be carried away by the excitement of the moment. As we paraded back to camp in a shared state of exhilaration, I felt, for the very first time, a sense of camaraderie with my Eagles teammates and Abenaki Valley brothers. My stomachache disappeared. I felt empow-ered. Yes! I would be at Parson's Pond thirty minutes prior to my scheduled starting time. And yes! Somehow, *somehow* I would survive this day.

After a surprisingly low-key lunch, I returned with my Eagles teammates to Parson's Peak, where, except for those assigned to the first four events, the entire camp had gathered for the start of the race. The chaplain stood with his veiny hands extended toward the sky. A hush fell over the crowd. After looking us over with a fiery gaze, he lowered his hands and bowed his head.

"Dear Heavenly Father, watch over these boys and keep them safe as they take an important step today in their journey toward becoming responsible young men and contributing members of society. Bless them and teach them the value of sportsmanship in competition and in everyday life. May they strive for and achieve excellence in this race and in all they do throughout their lives." He paused. "Everyone, please join me in reciting the Lord's Prayer."

Our voices came together in a jumbled murmur. "Our Father, who art in heaven . . ."

When the prayer was complete and the last syllable of "Amen" had risen beyond the treetops and into the cloudless sky, a pristine silence filled the woods. Even the birds were quiet. I sent my own little prayer to God. *Dear God, please let this moment last . . .*

"Thank you, boys. Do your best! I'll see all of you at the finish line."

Then, with a nod from the chaplain, a race official raised the starting gun and slowly pulled the trigger until . . . *craaack!* The sound was followed immediately by a puff of white smoke and a whiff of gunpowder in the air. The two baton bearers disappeared down the path, beginning their sprint to the first event and leaving us and our collective hoots and hollers behind in a cloud of dust. The twentieth running of the Ultimate Race had begun.

With an hour to go before I was due at the pond, I snuck away from the crowd and escaped to my cabin to contemplate my predicament. No one was there. Each of my cabinmates was either competing in an event or watching one. I sat on my bed with my back straight up against the wall and stared into empty space.

Outside, the afternoon sun beat down on the cabin's rooftop. Inside, it was a sauna. Drops of sweat fell from my brow and into my lap. I barely noticed. It felt good to be alone. I could relax and let down my guard. I could just be me for a little while. There was no need to perform and certainly no need to prove anything to anybody. And there was no need to protect myself against the random and unprovoked attacks that seemed to be so much a part of life at Camp Abenaki Valley. I was safe.

Then I looked over at the nail on the back wall of the cabin and winced.

Miles Romano was a nice boy. Under different circumstances, he might have been my friend. I tried but couldn't imagine what he had done to deserve being hung on that nail. I only knew it was *not* because he was a thief. Maybe they went after him because they sensed his vulnerability—his vulnerability, his *sweet* vulnerability . . . Whatever the reason, it made my heart ache to think of the pain and humiliation he must have felt as he hung there, twisting and turning and reaching, desperately trying to free himself while a cabin full of boys and even the counselor roared with laughter. When his underwear finally tore and he fell to the floor, the laughter had grown even louder. And then he'd given me that look, as if I'd hurt him worst of all.

Turning away from the nail, I went back to staring into the empty space in front of me. Suddenly it dawned on me that I had no control over the outcome of the day's events, including, of course, the impending swim. Absolutely none. As I continued staring, I felt myself surrendering to my fate, whatever that fate might be.

I crawled down from my bed, changed into my bathing suit, and stepped outside. Cabin Row was deserted. I smiled and strolled down to the pond in a Zen-like trance.

I arrived at Parson's Pond a few minutes before two o'clock. Campers and counselors were scattered about, each busying himself with some mission-critical task, presumably in preparation for the arrival of the baton bearers. They were coming and going, moving back and forth, up and down, this way and that, with random yips and yaps filling the air. These yips and yaps were clearly intended for each other, yet, as far as I could tell, no one was listening. Like characters out of a Richard Scarry book, each of them was completely focused on his own task.

One of the boys turned to me, morphed into a fox, and proclaimed with great pride, "I'm a carpenter!" Another boy transformed into a rabbit and exclaimed, "I'm a baker!" A third became a mouse and bellowed for the entire world to hear, "I'm a policeman!" Having identified themselves so aptly, they promptly returned to work.

I chuckled. I took a breath. I let it go. Then slowly, as if in a dream, I glided toward the main dock, passing dogs, cats, raccoons, bears, chickens, cows, elephants, and monkeys along the way. I was absolutely calm. This was unfamiliar territory. I liked it.

None of the animals seemed to notice when I proceeded to the end of the dock and jumped feetfirst into the pond. *Okay. So far, so good. I can do this.* After a few steps through the waist-deep water, I allowed my body to fall forward, and I began swimming. As if soaring through clouds, I moved steadily toward the floating dock to join the others—a group of Eagles on one side and a group of Hawks on the other, an invisible line between them.

I crawled up the ladder and hoisted myself onto the dock, proud of my accomplishment. No one else seemed impressed, however. A few of the Hawks stole glances at me as if to assess the potential threat. Apparently deciding there was none, they went back to their business. I smiled to myself and imagined them turning into frogs, pigs, and goats.

The two teams bantered back and forth. The words were friendly enough, yet I sensed a competitive tension in the air. One of the Hawks stepped forward. It was Henry Hatfield, the boy who had threatened Miles with a Buck knife and then come after me in our cabin.

"Hey, Randy!" shouted Henry, addressing one of my teammates. "I heard your boy Williamson can't swim."

Right before my very eyes, Henry transformed into a pig, complete with a snout, floppy ears, and a curly tail.

I laughed out loud.

"Got a problem, Williamson?" Henry demanded.

"You're a pig." I smiled confidently. "Isn't it obvious?"

His snout contorting into a grotesque snarl, Henry put his head down and charged.

Randy stepped between us. "Eeeeasy. Take it easy, *mi compadre*. He's just a kid. Let's save it for the race, okay? Okay?"

Henry took a moment to contemplate Randy's words and then glanced over at the race official, who was sitting in a nearby rowboat and shooting him a stern glare.

"Yeah. Okay, Randy. You're right. He's just a kid. No problem. We'll save it for the race."

Patting Randy on the shoulder, he retreated into Hawk territory, crossed his arms, and stared me down in an obvious attempt to intimidate.

My body trembled from head to toe, but, as calmly as I could, I stood my ground and returned his icy stare.

A crackling sound came from the direction of the rowboat. "Station Seven to Station Eight. Station Seven to Station Eight. Do you read? Over."

The race official picked up a walkie-talkie. "This is Station Eight. Go ahead, Station Seven. Over."

"The Eagles just finished lacrosse. Benson's on his way. He's awfully fast, Bert. He'll be there in in just a few. The Boggs kid won't be far behind. Over."

"Understood. Thanks, George. Over and out." He set down the walkie-talkie. "Okay, boys. Get ready. This is turning into a very close race. The swim is gonna be critical to the final outcome."

The blood drained from my face, and my hands turned cold. My vision fogged around the edges. I started to slip away but quickly regained composure, whispering to myself, "Whatever will be, will be . . ."

A large crowd had gathered onshore.

"Whatever will be, will be . . ."

*Everyone's watching. There's no place to hide.*

"Whatever will be, will be . . ."

Johnny Benson emerged from the woods, greeted by a thunderous roar. Johnny was a three-time all-state track star from Harrisburg, Pennsylvania. And he ran like one. With perfect form and grace, he dashed to the end of the main dock and, in one fluid motion, dived into the water.

Within seconds, Terry Boggs burst onto the scene. The crowd erupted. All eyes were on Johnny and Terry. Johnny closed in on the floating dock. Terry dived off the main dock. Our lead was shrinking.

Along with the other Eagle swimmers, I poised myself at the edge of the floating dock and listened for the official to give the word. My heart pounded. The veins in my temples throbbed. A shiver rippled through my body.

Johnny touched the dock with one hand and raised the other to show the baton to the official.

"Go!"

We dived in, a chaotic mass of humanity assaulting the pond with hands slashing and feet kicking in an urgent effort to propel ourselves forward. I tried to locate the first buoy, but when I looked up to scan the horizon, I found myself surrounded by a tightly packed cluster of bodies whipping up a mountain of froth. It was impossible to see anything. Catching an elbow in the face, I put my head down and swam as hard and fast as I could.

Carried by a surge of adrenaline, I kept up with my teammates for the first twenty-five yards. The water was my friend. It seemed to be supporting me. Blindly following the pack, I swam. I swam like never before—breathing, reaching, stretching, dipping, pulling, gliding, kicking, and breathing, again and again and again, using more effort with every stroke. The pond was everywhere. It was in my ears, eyes, and nose. It was crawling down the back of my throat. I turned my head to breathe and swallowed a mouthful of water, yet I kept swimming.

A cramp! There was a cramp in my stomach. At first it was just a little one. But the pain sharpened with every stroke. My breathing became labored. I fell behind the pack.

"Go!"

Behind me, the Hawks dived in and created a second mass of humanity. And this one was coming my way with a full head of steam. A familiar feeling of dread rose from my gut and made its way into my esophagus. Drawing on what strength

I had left, I clenched my jaw, kicked, and, in rapid-fire succession, thrust one hand after the other into the water. My
body grew heavy. My pace tapered off. The adrenaline that had
flowed so freely seconds earlier now felt like inert lead pulling
me downward. The pain in my stomach was agonizing. Still I
kept swimming.

My group was way, *way* ahead of me. They had already
passed the fifty-yard buoy and were coming up on the hundred-yard buoy. I was even with the fifty-yard buoy when the
Hawks overtook me. Once again, I found myself trapped in
the middle of utter chaos. Once again, frothy water was everywhere. Hands and feet splashed and sprayed and showered me
into blindness. Lost, disoriented, and on the verge of panic, I
gagged on the primal taste of fear rising into my mouth. It
tasted of being swallowed into the belly of the whale. It tasted
of no one noticing my absence until hours later when, at dinner perhaps, someone would ask, *By the way, whatever happened to that Williamson kid?* It tasted of never again seeing
Mom or Danny.

The last of the Hawks passed me. I was alone now. *All
alone.*

Right there and then, I realized I wasn't going to make it.
An overwhelming feeling of helplessness consumed me. Panic
set in. Struggling to remain afloat, I flailed my arms and desperately reached my hands toward the sky. I tried to yell for
help but was all out of breath.

Just before going under, I scanned the horizon.

*My angel! Where are you? You told me we were going to make
it right . . .*

*Have faith.*

I stopped flailing. *Have faith?*

*Yes, my love. Have faith.*

*Are you my angel? I can hear you, but I can't see you.*

*Just have faith, Ricky . . .*

As the voice trailed away, I remembered the exquisite peace I had felt gazing into the emptiness of my cabin only an hour earlier. What had I to fear from death? It was living that was so hard. My body relaxed. My muscles became soft and supple. My increasingly heavy limbs dangled from my torso as I descended into the murky water. It was easy. I simply let go and allowed gravity to take over.

My head disappeared below the pond's surface. Fear and panic were replaced by a deep sense of calm. I surrendered. I surrendered to my fate. I surrendered to death. I was so tired of longing for a better life. I was so tired of the struggle. I was so tired of grasping after happiness only to be disappointed time and time again. I was just so tired. So I surrendered and embraced death's lovely promise of peace.

A slew of bubbles escaped from my lips and floated like a fleet of tiny hot-air balloons to the surface. Far, far above, a pale outline of the sun hung in the sky. Its beams fell toward earth and filtered down into the water, where they came to life and surrounded me in a warm tunnel of pure luminescence. Within this tunnel, countless particles of white light performed a dance—a dance in my honor. A death dance.

I smiled. It felt so good to let go after holding on for so long. The chronic exhaustion that had plagued me since the day of my father's death left my body. I fell deeper and deeper into the water until suddenly I felt a sharp jolt. Something or someone had grabbed me by the armpits and was hoisting me roughly out of the pond and back into reality.

It was Bert, the race official. He had maneuvered the rowboat to the spot where I had gone under, reached in with both hands, and yanked my seventy-pound body out of the water. His arms shaking from the effort, he lifted me over the gunwale and deposited me in the bow. The boat lurched, but he steadied it with both hands and lowered himself carefully into the stern.

"So, Williamson," he said, glaring at me, "the Hatfield kid was right. You can't swim. Didn't it ever occur to you to tell someone? Do you realize I almost capsized this boat trying to save your ass?"

I couldn't answer. Having swallowed a mouthful of brackish pond water, I was coughing and gasping for air. Nevertheless, it must have been clear to him that I would be okay. Without another word and without so much as offering me a towel, he dipped the oars into the water and turned the boat toward the dock.

As we neared the dock's edge, Mr. Gordon came into view. His arms were folded neatly across his chest. Apparently, he was waiting for me. But why would the camp director want to see me? What crime had I committed? Had I violated the Abenaki Valley Creed? Probably. Was this the face-to-face meeting about which Neil had so sternly warned us? Most likely. What would come of this meeting? I had brought shame and dishonor to my teammates and the good name of Camp

Abenaki Valley. For this, there would be serious consequences, no doubt.

As the rowboat drifted closer, I attempted to comfort myself. *There's nothing to be afraid of. It's just a meeting with the camp director. You've already faced death. What else could possibly happen?* Clenching my jaw, I braced myself for my first encounter with Mr. Gordon.

The rowboat bumped into the dock. No longer coughing, I crawled out and found myself before the legendary Mr. Gordon, my legs shaking like twigs under my body's weight. He towered over me, much taller up close than I had imagined. Standing in his shadow, I gaped up at him.

He had kind eyes and a look of genuine concern on his face. "Are you okay, Ricky?" He knew my name.

Shivering in spite of the intense heat, I looked down at my feet. "I-I-I think so."

Mr. Gordon placed a gentle hand on my shoulder and offered me a towel, which I accepted gratefully. Kneeling, he asked, "Ricky, didn't anyone ask you if you could swim before assigning you to this event?"

Our eyes met, but I was embarrassed by the question and went back to looking at my feet. "No . . . no, sir. No one asked me. I mean, I tr-tr-tried to explain to Neil that I . . . that I—"

"That you're afraid of the water. It's okay, Ricky. I understand. Really, I do. As a matter of fact, I used to be afraid of the water."

Still shivering, I sputtered, "You? A-a-afraid of the water? B-b-but you were an Olympic swimmer. Everybody knows about your silver medal."

"What they don't know is that until I was about your age, I was terrified of the water. You see, when I was very young, only four years old in fact, I almost drowned. After that, I didn't feel safe around the water. Wouldn't go anywhere near it. I just couldn't shake that horrible memory. It followed me around for years. Then, when I was about your age, I met a man who took me under his wing and made me his personal project."

"Really?" I searched his face in a cautious yet hopeful attempt to verify the truth of this story—a story that so inconceivably mirrored my own.

Mr. Gordon's eyes twinkled. "You bet. He helped me get over my fear and then coached me through high school. His name was Coach Collins. If it wasn't for Coach Collins, I wouldn't have won four consecutive state championships in the freestyle, and I most definitely would not have made it to the Olympics." He paused and looked at me earnestly. "Ricky, would you like me to teach you how to swim?"

I gazed deeply into his eyes and for a moment saw my father staring back at me.

*Say yes, Ricky. It's okay.*

The moment ended. My father disappeared.

I shook my head. "No, I don't think so, sir. No, thanks."

"Are you sure? No one else needs to know. It'll just be the two of us. I promise you it'll be completely safe."

I believed him and wanted desperately to accept his offer, but something inside stopped me. I just couldn't make myself say yes. I think it was because deep down, I didn't believe I deserved his kindness.

"No, thanks, Mr. Gordon," I said with as much conviction as I could muster.

Mr. Gordon leaned in close and lowered his voice. "I have a feeling we're going to be good friends, Ricky. So why don't you call me Mike?"

I smiled at the idea.

With a wink, he patted me on the shoulder and stood up. "If you change your mind, Ricky, or if you just feel like talking—about anything, anything at all—come pay me a visit. My door is always open." He turned and made his way along the dock toward shore, whistling a light tune.

Remembering what he had been through with the loss of his wife and daughter and what he was going through now with the cancer, I watched with admiration as he sauntered toward the path that led up the hill and back to camp. His feet never touched the ground. He moved through space gracefully and effortlessly, as if he had all the time in the world. He seemed to be truly at peace with himself. And *free*. I continued watching until he reached the path and disappeared into the woods.

"Made a new friend, Williamson?"

I swung around with a jolt. It was Henry. He and a few other Hawks had just climbed out of the water and onto the dock.

"Everybody knows that old man has a few screws loose. You know he's crazy, don't you, Williamson?" Dripping wet and glaring at me, Henry crossed his arms and waited for an answer. Receiving none, he snorted and changed the subject. "I was right. You can't swim."

My face and neck flushed; my ears prickled.

"What a worthless piece of shit. You're nothing but a fucking disgrace."

I bowed my head in acquiescence.

Letting out a sigh of exasperation, he strutted by me and threw an elbow into my side. I cried out and stumbled, almost falling off the dock. The other boys snickered and followed him to shore.

I was bent over and still trying to recover my senses when Randy—the boy who had come to my defense earlier— mounted the ladder and climbed onto the dock. Glowering at me, he passed by without a word. With saltwater tears stinging my eyes, I cast a tentative glance along the shoreline. The canoeing event had begun. The two baton bearers were drinking Gatorade while the canoers paddled frantically in a dead heat. It was going to be a very close race.

It was a very close race—the closest race in camp history. In the end, Terry completed the run through the Tunnel of Doom and crossed the finish line seconds before Johnny. After catching his breath and receiving congratulations from the large cast of Hawks gathered there, Terry remarked that running the last two miles along the out and back had been like running through a greenhouse. With the thick foliage overhead and no breeze to provide relief, the Tunnel of Doom had been almost intolerable. Johnny agreed and shook Terry's hand, congratulating him on a great race.

There was no report from either boy of Burning Sky coming out of the forest to seek revenge for his murder.

At dinner, the Hawks celebrated their victory with singing, chanting, and good- and not-so-good-natured needling. About halfway through the meal, they broke into a spontaneous version of "Na Na Hey Hey Kiss Him Goodbye." Their voices flew upward. The mess hall's rafters shook. A number of boys got up on tables and, swaying from side to side, waved farewell to us Eagles as they sang the song's mind-numbing chorus over and over and over again. Meanwhile, we accepted our medicine with our heads hung low.

The only Eagle who seemed to take the loss well was Neil. He kept his chin up and maintained a dignified posture throughout the evening. The rest of us slouched mournfully at our tables as the Hawks continued to celebrate. I felt like I had let my team down. Even though my performance had no impact on the final result, I felt terrible.

During dessert, Neil came up from behind me and whispered in my ear, "I'm sorry, Ricky. I didn't know you couldn't swim. I really thought you could. I know you tried to tell me, but I was too distracted to listen. I'm so sorry." He returned to his table.

I took a bite of my Dutch apple pie. The apples, sugar, and cinnamon swirled together into a syrupy bouquet that performed a little dance for my taste buds. The tip of my tongue passed over my lips. A smile arose.

It was movie night once again at Camp Abenaki Valley. Movie night—an opportunity to forget all about the Ultimate Race, Eagles versus Hawks, baton bearers, the murky waters of Parson's

Pond, Mr. Gordon, Neil Kennedy, Henry Hatfield, and all the rest. This week's movie was *The Guns of Navarone*, starring Gregory Peck, David Niven, and Anthony Quinn. For two and a half blessed hours, I was transported to the island of Navarone, where I disappeared into the World War II story of a team of Allied soldiers whose mission was to destroy two very large cannons installed in a German fortress perched high on the island's cliffs overlooking the Aegean Sea. Thank God for movies.

That night, I had a revelation.

Soon after lights-out, Keith Hardaway, who was still riding high from his Hawks' victory, had a special message for the three Eagles in our cabin—one he delivered in a melodramatic whisper. "Good night, Eagles. Better luck next year, suckers. By the way, Williamson, I heard about your performance in the quarter-mile—I mean fifty-yard—swim. Couldn't make it to the second buoy, huh? Don't feel too bad. Everybody knows the swimming leg doesn't matter. Anyway, the Hawks were a team of destiny this year."

I really couldn't tell for sure if Keith was being sincere. I suspected this was his twisted way of trying to be nice. Sincere or not, it didn't matter, because that was when it hit me like a shot between the eyes. Keith Hardaway didn't care whether I could swim. His only concern was that his team won.

At dinner, the Hawks had been too busy celebrating and the Eagles had been too busy feeling glum to notice what I was going through. The only person in the room who cared about my humiliation was me. No one else cared that I had failed to finish the race. Each boy was concerned only with his own personal story, not mine.

My deepest, darkest secret—not just that I could barely swim but that I was deeply flawed and incapable of performing any worthwhile activity—was out there for the entire world to see. Yet no one cared. Imagine that! My deepest, darkest secret, when exposed to the light of day, turned out to be *nothing*—a mere phantom vaporizing helplessly into the sun's rays as they appeared from over the horizon to illuminate the earth.

I yawned. "Thank you, Keith." Then, closing my eyes, I turned onto my side and snuggled into the mattress of my squeaky bed—my wonderfully squeaky bed! Within seconds, I began to descend into a deep and dreamless state of unconsciousness. But just before I got there, wavering—like a spinning top—on the verge of wakefulness and sleep, I felt a hand gently stroking my hair.

*I love you, Ricky . . . very much. You're doing just fine . . .*

# CHAPTER SEVEN

*Wednesday, July 28, 1976*

Dear Mom,

Sorry for not writing sooner. Camp got off to a rocky start. You know how hard it is for me to make friends. To make matters worse, my counselor, Wayne, is kind of a grouch. Anyway, there are eight boys in my cabin, plus Wayne and Ryan (remember him?). On the first night, the movie *Bridge on the River Kwai* was playing at the rec center, but I got sick and didn't see the ending.

The next day I felt much better. That night, we had a campfire under the stars. Did you know they have lightning bugs here, just like back home? And crickets too! At the campfire, we had an opening ceremony for something called the Ultimate Race. For the Ultimate Race, the entire camp was divided into two teams, the Eagles and the Hawks. I was an Eagle. They put a big *E* on my forehead (don't worry, it washed off). Danny was a Hawk. He got an *H*. The Hawks won. There was a closing ceremony at our second campfire the following Sunday night (campfires are always on Sunday nights). During the closing ceremony, they honored the victors. Danny was very happy.

This week, I scored my personal best in both archery and riflery. In archery, I'm a bowman. In riflery, I'm a marksman first class, just a few points short of sharpshooter. Mr. Hardy (my riflery instructor) says I'm a natural-born gunman. Only eight boys signed up for baseball. I'm not sure if we will even get to play a game. In arts and crafts, I'm building an ant farm, like the one Dad made a few years ago.

Today I was in a sailing regatta. I was part of a two-man crew with an older boy named Frank. I was kind of scared (really scared, actually), but Frank said he knew what he was doing. We almost capsized but still took second place (don't worry, I was wearing a life jacket!).

Danny is doing fine. As always, he is making lots of friends. He got up on water skis on his very first try. He was very proud of himself.

Tomorrow I'm going on an overnight backpacking trip with the boys from my camping activity. The camping activity counselor's name is Chad. He's nice. We leave for Baldface Mountain in the morning after breakfast. We will be back in camp on Friday afternoon. This Saturday night is the annual dance. Girls from Camp Crystal will be there. I've never been to a boy-girl dance before. I'm a little nervous.

The food here is good, especially dessert, and I love the bug juice! Can you make us shepherd's pie when we get home? Please send a care package with comic books, baseball cards, candy, and cigarettes (just kidding about the cigarettes, but PLEASE send everything else!!!).

Your loving son,
Ricky

*Thursday, July 29–Friday, July 30, 1976*

"Bug spray?"

"Check."

"Flashlight?" Willy looked up from the crumpled piece of paper in his hand. "Flashlight?"

"Check." I rolled my eyes. It was Thursday morning, and we were supposed to meet Chad and the others in the parking lot. But Willy insisted we go through our checklists again to make sure we weren't forgetting anything. I knew I wasn't; I'd checked it all twice the night before.

"Canteen?"

"Check." I tugged my Mets cap down over my forehead. It was time to go.

"Sleeping bag?"

"It's right there." I pointed to the rolled-up sleeping bag fastened securely to the aluminum frame of my backpack.

"Great! Are you ready to go?"

"About time." I hoisted my backpack onto my shoulders. It wasn't heavy. After all, I had packed only for an overnight trip.

At the welcome area, Chad and Sam were loading their gear into a burnt-orange Volkswagen Bus with skinny tires and curtains hanging in the side windows. Gossamer-thin, the curtains were decorated with a floral print of faded pink and yellow daisies. Next to arrive were Bruce and Raymond, who, at twelve, were the oldest members of our expedition. Raymond was well into puberty. His shoulders were broad, and his voice was deep. There was even a little peach fuzz growing on his upper lip. Bruce was almost a head shorter than Raymond and slim as a reed. He wore glasses and spoke in a self-conscious whisper.

After loading our gear, there was nothing left to do but wait for the comedy team of Chuck and Patrick, a couple of eleven-year-olds, who, by then, had earned the title of "Unreliable Ones." Checking and rechecking his watch, Chad announced he was going to look for them. But then they appeared.

Chuck had a chubby, round face and body to match. He was built like a Weeble—he wobbled but didn't fall down. His light-blond hair was cut so short I could see his scalp perspiring in the morning sun. He had the inexhaustible energy of an Airedale terrier pup. Patrick was slender and wore an ever-present smirk, which seemed to imply that either your fly was down or you were about to be made the butt of some shameless practical joke. He had long brown hair with bangs that fell carelessly over his eyebrows. Chuck looked as though he had been up all night and was still going strong. Patrick looked as though he had just rolled out of bed.

"Hi, Chad," said Chuck. "Sorry we're late, man, but the line at breakfast—wow! Was it ever long!"

"Nice try, Chuck, but breakfast was over an hour ago."

"Oh. Yeah. Well, we're here now. Did I mention we're sorry?"

"Yes, you did."

"Oh. Well, we are. Right, Patrick?"

"Righty-o, daddy-o," said Patrick, borrowing the phrase from an old Beat flick he'd seen that Sunday on TV in the rec center.

The phrase had caught fire. It seemed everyone in camp had been running around all week saying, "Righty-o, daddy-o." By the time we returned from our trip, however, it would be something else. It was always something else at Camp Abenaki Valley.

"Apology accepted," Chad said. He wasn't the type to stay mad at anyone for very long. "Now listen to me, guys. Remember what we talked about earlier this week? We're a team. We have to *know* we can depend on each other in the wilderness. Dig?"

"Dig," said Chuck, his lower lip protruding a little too far to pass for sincerity.

"Got it, Patrick?"

"Got it, *kemosabe.*"

"Keep your *kemosabes* to yourself. Let's go—load up your gear. It's almost nine o'clock now. And it's a good two-hour drive to the trailhead."

Chuck and Patrick loaded their gear, and we were on our way. It wasn't long before Chuck began telling jokes. He was in rare form.

"Hey, Patrick, have you ever read *Under the Bleachers* by Seymour Butts?"

"No, I haven't—hey! That's a good one, Chuckles."

"Do you know who wrote *Yellow River*?"

"I dunno. I give."

"I. P. Daily. Do you know who wrote *Brown Spots on the Wall*?"

"Don't tell me. I know this one . . . Okay, I give."

"Who Flung Poo."

"Wicked funny, Chuckles. Keep 'em comin'!"

"How about *Fifty Yard Dash to the Outhouse*, written by Will E. Make-it and illustrated by Betty Won't?"

Between bursts of laughter, Patrick said, "These are great. How come you haven't told them before?"

"I've been saving them for this trip."

"Chuck, do you have any idea how old those jokes are?" asked Chad from behind the wheel of the van.

"Sure. They're classics."

"Yeah, they're classics, all right," said Raymond. "They're classically stupid."

"Aw, you just don't appreciate good humor," said Patrick.

I was in the back row of the van with Willy and Sam. Willy and I couldn't help ourselves. We were laughing hysterically.

Sam, of course, couldn't hear Chuck's jokes and wasn't in position to read his lips. "Wad's so fawnee?" he asked.

"I'll tell ya later, Sam," Willy managed to say before succumbing to another round of the giggles.

We cruised north across the Maine countryside, only slowing down to negotiate the main streets of a dozen or so small towns, each with a filling station, a Ben Franklin, a pub, and a diner with a neon sign over the door that read: *Eat.*

After two hours, we crossed the Maine-New Hampshire border. A sign welcomed us to Coös County. A few minutes later, Chad pulled the van into an unpaved parking lot. We unloaded our gear, crossed the road, and found the Baldface Circle trailhead a short distance away. In addition to their own gear, Chad and Raymond carried the tents, our food, a cookware set, an ax, a first-aid kit, and some other assorted items. The rest of us were responsible only for our personal belongings.

From where we stood, we were a good hour's hike from the base of South Baldface, the first of two peaks along the Baldface Circle trail—the second being North Baldface. Both mountains were in the eastern part of the White Mountains, which, in turn, were part of the Appalachians. The plan for the day was to hike to a swimming hole known as Emerald Pool, where we would break for lunch before continuing our trek to the summit of South Baldface. At the summit, we would take as much time as we needed to enjoy the view, which Chad assured us was spectacular. Then we would descend into the pine forest between the two Baldfaces and set up camp for the night.

When we arrived at the aptly named Emerald Pool, Chad told us we had just enough time for a quick dip before lunch. The pool was in a clearing at the base of a small waterfall with a twenty-foot drop. To one side of the waterfall was an eight-foot-high rocky ledge—perfect for use as a launching pad. Letting out a series of war cries that echoed throughout the valley, the others paused only long enough to tear off their T-shirts and hiking boots before racing for the ledge and hurling themselves into the sky, one after the other in rapid-fire succession.

"Cannonball!"

*ker-PLASH!*

"Jackknife!"

*ker-PLASH!*

"Can opener!"

*ker-PLASH!*

The can opener produced a fifteen-foot splash that arced elegantly into the air and caught the sun just right, giving birth to a mini rainbow.

"*Eeeyah*! Oh my gosh, is it ever *cooold*!"

"Yeah, but it feels so great!"

Each of the six boys took his turn, climbed out of the pool, and ran straight back to the ledge. On his second try, Sam allowed himself a moment to prepare for a backward flip and then executed it with the precision of an Olympic diving champion. In spite of his disability, Sam was one heck of an athlete. With a twinge of envy, I realized he had the same natural skill and grace as Danny.

It was a blazing-hot day. I would have done *anything*—well, almost anything—to join the others. Instead I sat at the water's edge just downstream from the waterfall and dangled my feet in the icy cold water.

"Don't you want to swim?" asked Chad, approaching me from behind.

"No, I'm fine," I said, staring down into the water, where a small school of minnows played hide-and-seek among the rocks.

"Okay, I'll join you."

"But I'm just sitting here with my feet in the water. Won't you get bored?"

"Bored? Out here in nature, sitting in the shade by this beautiful stream? No way. I love being outdoors. It's my life." He removed his hiking boots and sat down.

I looked over at Chad and smiled. He smiled back at me. Together we lounged on the bank of that stream and watched the others jumping into the pool. They jumped and jumped and then jumped some more. I was convinced they would have continued jumping until nightfall if Chad hadn't announced it was time for lunch.

After a meal of beef jerky, peanut butter on hardtack, and gorp, which we gobbled up by the fistful (it really is true that being outdoors makes you hungry), Chad reminded us all to fill our canteens, and we were on our way.

At first, the going was easy as the well-marked trail wound its way casually through the forest. There was an occasional uphill climb, but for the most part, the trail was smooth and flat. Every once in a while, we would encounter a creek, which we crossed by hopping from one rock to the next without so much as getting our feet wet. "Careful," Chad cautioned us. "Some of these rocks are slippery." No one fell.

After a while, the terrain became steep. My backpack felt heavy. I needed a break. We weren't yet above the tree line, but there was a clearing ahead with blueberry bushes growing from a ledge on the side of the mountain. Sam had taken this as an opportunity to stop for a midafternoon snack. Chad, Raymond, Bruce, and Willy continued on, apparently unaware that he was no longer with them. Without looking back, they disappeared around a bend in the trail.

When I caught up with Sam, I removed my backpack from my aching shoulders and joined him. The late-July sun glared down at us. It seemed to fill the entire sky. I lifted my baseball cap from my head, ran my fingers through my sweat-drenched hair, and replaced it before getting down to business. I picked the largest blueberry I could find and placed it in my mouth. I chewed it, savored the flavor, and swallowed. I picked another blueberry and popped it in my mouth . . . and another . . . and another. Soon I was eating them hand over fist. These wild blueberries were exquisite—not at all like the store-bought ones back home. They were plump, juicy, and sweet with just a hint of tartness in the background. *Perfection!*

Sam flashed me a smile that revealed a set of violet-blue choppers. Neither of us spoke. We just kept picking and eating.

Bringing up the rear as they so often did, Chuck and Patrick caught up with us, giggling mischievously. They were up to something. Sam was engrossed in picking blueberries and didn't notice them until Chuck tapped him on the shoulder. When Sam turned around, both Chuck and Patrick got in his face and, without making a sound, moved their lips in a random and wildly exaggerated fashion, forming not words, but a deaf person's equivalent of utter gibberish. Again and again and again, they stretched and contorted those hideous lips across Coca-Cola-stained teeth, opened their mouths into gaping holes, and transformed their faces into a pair of grotesque Halloween masks. Chuck became the fiendish murderer from *The Texas Chainsaw Massacre*, and Patrick became a zombie from *Night of the Living Dead*.

"Stob id!" cried Sam.

"Stob id! Stob id! Stob id!" Chuck and Patrick sang out. They stomped their feet. They clapped their hands. They threw their heads back and laughed a cruel and vicious laugh. It was sickening yet strangely . . . what? Intoxicating?

It's been more than forty years since that day, Stanley, and still I cannot fathom what came over me in that moment—that surrealistic nightmare of a moment, perched there on that blueberry-carpeted mountainside. Inexplicably unable to control my motor functions, I found myself lifting my hand to tap Sam on his shoulder as I prepared to repeat Chuck and Patrick's vile deed. A monstrous cloud materialized overhead and blocked out the sun. A cold wind blew down from the mountain's summit. All sounds in the forest came to an abrupt stop. Time slowed. It slowed to a crawl. My hand continued upward until it reached its apex, and then I watched helplessly as it began its descent. When my index finger finally touched his shoulder, he began to move his body in an agonizingly slow 180-degree turn. When this turn was complete, he focused his gaze upon my lips and waited for me to speak. I could see in his face that he trusted me. *Wholeheartedly.* It didn't occur to him that I was capable of stooping to Chuck and Patrick's level.

I was sorry—oh, how sorry I was!—as soon as I opened my mouth. But I felt powerless to stop. My face stretched into a caricature of itself as my lips performed the same silent, non-sensical dance Chuck's and Patrick's lips had performed only seconds earlier, except that my dance was in slow motion and seemed to last for an eternity. Sam's calm expression of abso-lute trust morphed into one of shock and horror. He trusted me, and I betrayed him in the worst possible way.

The cloud vanished. Birdsong burst from the forest. Time was restored to its normal state. I glanced over to see if Chuck and Patrick were watching, but they were gone. Then I looked back at Sam. Although all outward signs of shock and horror had faded, the corners of his mouth were drawn downward into a frown of disappointment.

I knew I had done wrong and that I should apologize. Instead I buried my remorse, grabbed my backpack, and hur-ried to catch up with Chuck and Patrick to validate my initi-ation into the cool kids' club. Running up the trail, I left Sam behind, standing by the blueberry bushes with a single uneaten blueberry in his hand and violet stains on his teeth. Needing to distance myself from what I had just done, I increased my speed and disappeared around the bend in the trail.

Chuck and Patrick had seemed so sure of themselves when they teased Sam, yet I knew in my heart they were wrong. On the other hand, there was a part of me that admired their cruelty. It was decisive, unflinching . . . *powerful*. I wanted to be like that—powerful, just like they were. Unfortunately, it hadn't worked. I felt just as weak and powerless as I did before joining the cool kids' club.

Something my father once told me was just now beginning to make sense. He said that every thought of separation, no matter how small, eventually leads to an act of violence. That meant there was a thought of separation rattling around in my head that caused me to treat Sam the way I did. But what was that thought? I pondered this question with all the intellectual might my ten-year-old brain could muster as I continued up the increasingly steep trail in hot pursuit of Chuck and Patrick.

It was undeniable that I thought of myself as a *me* and Sam as an *other*—in other words, as separate from me. There was no *we* in the equation. Thinking of Sam as an *other* rather than a *we* made it easy for me to disregard his feelings and make fun of his disability, as long as it served my selfish needs. Could it be that simple? What would the world be like if there were no such thoughts of separation?

*If we could see and know that only love is real, there would be no thoughts of separation. If there were no thoughts of separation, young boys would not tease each other, and older boys would not learn to fight. If boys never learned to fight, men would not go to war defending abstract concepts such as right and honor. The world would only know peace.*

*Daddy?*

"Hey, Williamson."

It was Chuck and Patrick. I had just caught up with them.

"Where's your friend, the *deeeaaaf* boy?" Patrick asked.

Chuck giggled.

"He's not my friend," I said.

"Okay," said Patrick, shrugging his shoulders indifferently. "Whatever."

Chuck, Patrick, and I caught up with the others, who were taking a water break at the side of the trail. We dropped our packs and pulled out our canteens. When Sam joined us, he was smiling as if nothing had happened. I felt like crying and turned away to avoid making eye contact.

We resumed the hike and, before long, arrived at the 3,547-foot summit of South Baldface. Chad was right. The view was spectacular. From the bare mountaintop, we could see for miles in all directions. Everywhere we looked, the cloudless sky served as a solid indigo backdrop for the sun-parched but abundant forests, rolling hills, and protruding mountains that surrounded us and expanded outward like rows of dominoes extending into the horizon. To the west, the tallest peak within view stood watch over the other peaks, commanding their respect and humble obedience.

"That's Mount Washington, Ricky," said Chad. "It's the tallest mountain in the entire northeastern region of the United

States and notorious for its extreme weather conditions. Back in 1934, they measured a wind speed of 231 miles per hour at its summit. It's a magnificent view from here, isn't it?"

"It sure is."

Outlined by a faint haze, the charcoal-gray mountain ascended majestically into the brilliant sky toward heaven. I was awestruck.

"Decent view," said Patrick.

"Far out," said Chuck, and he was off, with Patrick in close pursuit.

They ran around the summit like little mice seeking shelter from the bright sunlight, but there was none to be found. Their high-pitched squeaks evaporated into the thin mountain air. I listened for an echo but heard nothing.

While Chuck and Patrick flitted about, the rest of us stood at the precipice of the rocky summit, soaking in every square inch of the expansive panorama.

"The winds are shifting," said Chad. "A front will be moving in tonight, tomorrow morning at the latest. It's going to cool things off and bring some rain with it for sure."

Bruce followed Chad's gaze out to the northwest horizon and then peeked up at the clear blue sky. "You can tell that from the wind?" He sounded skeptical.

"We really need the rain—it's been a wickedly dry summer. Feel that breeze? It's coming out of the northwest, which is very unusual for this time of year. Don't be surprised if it's storming when we wake up in the morning."

Chad's ominous tone concerned me. I stuffed my hands into the front pockets of my shorts and shifted nervously in my hiking boots. The northwest breeze blew steadily in my face. I knew Chad was right. I could *feel* it, and I could *smell* it. That deceptively gentle breeze carried an undercurrent that stank of something dark and cold and ruthless. Suddenly, I couldn't breathe. With a violent gasp, I began to panic. Fiery beads of sweat erupted from my clammy skin. Then, as quickly as it came, the episode passed. My lungs swelled with a welcome blast of air and slowly deflated as I let out a sigh of relief. I looked over at Chad. His gaze was still focused on the northwest horizon. Neither he nor any of the others had noticed my near-panic attack.

Yes, a storm was coming, and it would wreak more havoc than Chad could possibly imagine. Nothing anyone said or did would change that fact. Any efforts to stop the storm would be met by unrelenting force. Of this, I was certain. I removed my hands from my pockets, crossed my arms, and stood rooted on the precipice in my very best defensive posture as the northwest wind continued blowing in my face. It felt harmless enough but carried a very clear message: *Beware!*

Chad placed a hand on my shoulder. "Don't worry, Ricky. We'll be fine. Just to be on the safe side, we'll change our itinerary. But we'll be fine. I promise."

I appreciated his attempt to comfort me, but I was inconsolable. The best I could manage was a pencil-thin smile through tightly pursed lips.

After a while, Chuck and Patrick grew tired of running around and sat down with the rest of us by a tower of neatly stacked rocks—a monument of some kind erected by past visitors to the summit.

"Okay, guys," said Chad, "there's been a small change in plans. Originally, we were going to camp in the forest between the two peaks, then tackle the northern peak in the morning." He paused and looked over at North Baldface, which stared us down with a scornful glare.

*C'mon. I dare ya. I double-dare ya! What are ya . . . chicken? I'm not gonna hurtcha. Hell, I'm just a mountain. I don't bite. What's a little rain, anyways? C'mon, show some courage. You'll be fine. I promise. Trust me . . . cowards!*

"But with the changing weather pattern, we're going to backtrack and camp below the tree line on the eastern side of this peak. If it rains in the morning, and I think it will, we don't want to be caught climbing up and down these ridges. They get very slippery in the rain. Sound like a plan?"

"No way!" Chuck said. "It does not sound like a plan. I say we continue. We've come this far. Let's keep going."

"Sorry, Chuck. This is an executive decision. There's a front moving in, and it's just too risky."

On that note, with North Baldface scoffing at us, we gathered up our gear, retreated from the summit, and retraced our steps down the trail.

It was late afternoon, and the sun had begun its lazy descent toward the western horizon. Long, crooked shadows crisscrossed the rocky path as we approached the tree line. My stomach growled. I was hungry and looking forward to stopping for the day. We entered the shaded forest and hiked until we reached a stream. Instead of crossing it, Chad took a sharp right and led us away from the mountain for about a quarter mile to a small clearing near a bend in the stream. It was the perfect spot for an overnight campsite—just far enough off the beaten path and plenty of freshwater and firewood nearby.

When the tents were pitched, Bruce and Raymond unpacked their gear and went fishing while the rest of us collected firewood. The fishermen returned an hour later with two good-sized brook trout, both caught by Bruce. By then, the fire was roaring, thanks to Chad's expertise and Sam's skill.

After an appetizing meal of trout à la Bruce and freeze-dried soybean stew (just about anything tastes good in the outdoors after a long day of hiking—even soybeans), we gathered around the fire, roasted marshmallows, and told ghost stories.

When Chad started to tell the story of Burning Sky, I took the opportunity to grab my flashlight and slip away for a bathroom break. I had already heard all about the infamous Mohawk warrior and how he frequented the woods along the dirt road leading into camp, seeking revenge for his murder. I didn't need to hear it again.

By this time, the sun had set over Mount Washington. Enshrouded within the great mountain's shadow, the forest was pitch black except for the narrow stream of yellow light glimmering pitifully from my flashlight. *But the batteries are brand new . . . I changed them myself!* The wind picked up. The trees swayed. The leaves shivered. There was a biting chill in the air. For the first time all summer, I felt cold. *Really* cold.

*Snap!*

*Burning Sky?* I spun around with my heart in my throat and pointed my flashlight into the darkness.

Willy stepped forward into the yellow light. "Scare you?"

"Yeah, a little," I said, lowering my flashlight. "Well, more than a little, actually." After a half dozen ghost stories, I was more spooked than I realized. Breathing normally now, I felt grateful for Willy's company.

After taking care of business, rather than returning to the campsite, we wandered downstream to a clearing where we found a flat rock just large enough for two to lie on side by side. Reclining on its surface, worn smooth by the elements, we gazed upward into a sky covered with a thick blanket of stars. I fancied we were back at Parson's Peak. A feeling of peace washed over me. Except for the wind, it was quiet— there were no crickets chirping and no critters stirring. At least five minutes passed without either one of us speaking.

"I heard you made fun of my brother this afternoon," said Willy.

"Your *brother?*"

His brother? Sam was Willy's brother? How could I have missed it? A thin but brilliant sliver of light shone down upon us from the crescent moon rising above the treetops. I inspected Willy's face. Now I saw it. It had been there the entire time in the shape of the eyes, nose, and chin. Willy had red hair and Sam's was blond—strawberry blond, actually—but they both had the same fair complexion with the same spate of pale freckles sprinkled generously across the cheekbones. There was a family resemblance—a very distinct one.

"Yeah. Sam's my big brother. I can't believe you would do that, Ricky. He can't help that he's deaf. Don't you think he would do *anything* to hear? What do you think it's like for him living in a world where he's so different from everybody else?

He doesn't let it show, but it really bothers him when people tease him. It's bad enough coming from dorks like Chuck and Patrick, but you should know better. You didn't like it when Keith Hardaway and his buddies threw water balloons at you in the toilet, did you? Well, this is much worse. I thought you were a decent guy, but you're just like the rest of them. You're a loser. I hope you can live with yourself."

He stood up and turned to go.

"But, Willy, I didn't know he was your brother."

"Should it matter? Brother or not, he's a good person and doesn't deserve to be treated the way you treated him. He's got feelings, you know. He's a human being with feelings, and you had no right to do what you did. I was actually starting to feel sorry for you because you're having such a hard time fitting in. But not anymore. You deserve what you have coming to you."

"But, Willy—"

"Good night, Ricky."

"But, Willy, I'm sorry. I'm really sorry. I was sorry as soon as it happened."

"Don't tell me. Tell him." He hopped off the rock and disappeared into the forest.

*Oh my God. What have I become?*

The wind was blowing much harder and much colder now. It penetrated my skin and sank deep into my bones. I stood up on the rock, folded my arms across my chest, and shivered. It was so cold I could see my breath escaping in wisps of steam that hovered in front of my face before floating across the stream and dissipating into the mountain air.

*I'm all alone now.*

I slept in a tent with Chad, Chuck, and Patrick. Actually, *slept* was the wrong word. I was awake most of the night, crammed between a snoring Chad on my right and a muttering Chuck on my left (yes, he even talked in his sleep). My sleeping bag was positioned directly on top of a large tree root that had been overlooked when we pitched the tent, and there was no way to avoid the root without bumping into either Chad or Chuck. To make matters worse, I was suffering from an overwhelming case of claustrophobia. There was almost no room to move around inside my sleeping bag. I tried to get comfortable but succeeded only in getting my limbs hopelessly bound up in its nonbreathable synthetic material. *I'm stuck!* The bag was eating me alive like a Venus flytrap. Eventually, the feeling passed, but I lay there all night, drifting in and out of sleep while Willy's tongue-lashing played itself over and over again in my head.

*What do you think it's like for him?*

*I don't know.*

*. . . you should know better . . .*

*But . . .*

*. . . you're just like the rest of them.*

*I'm not!*

*He's a human being with feelings . . .*

*I know.*

*You deserve what you have coming to you.*

*I do? What's coming to me? Willy! What's coming to me?*

I jolted awake and sat straight up. It was still dark, but I knew by the distant squawking of a murder of crows that morning was about to arrive. "What's coming to me?" I whispered into the darkness. Trembling, I lay back down but was too agitated to sleep.

*What's coming to me?*

The rhythm of Chad's breathing changed. He began to stir. I closed my eyes and pretended to be asleep. He yawned, unzipped his sleeping bag, yawned again, rummaged around for his clothes, got dressed, and exited the tent.

I waited for a few minutes and then followed him outside, where I was greeted rudely by an unseasonably cold gust of wind in my face. The previous night's thick blanket of stars had been replaced by an even thicker blanket of dark-gray clouds. It looked as though it could rain at any moment. Per Chad's prediction, the weather had done a complete one-eighty since we'd reached the summit of South Baldface the previous afternoon.

At breakfast, we huddled around a fire Sam had built and ate hot oatmeal with brown sugar, cinnamon, and raisins out of tin cups. Wearing multiple layers—including a T-shirt, sweatshirt, and windbreaker—I hunched forward over my cup and thought of how my mother often said that oatmeal sticks to your ribs. I closed my eyes and prayed that this oatmeal would hurry up, stick to my ribs, and insulate me from this cold and gloomy morning.

Sam sat across the circle from me. The cold didn't seem to bother him. He wasn't shivering or hunching over his cup like the rest of us. Instead he sat straight up and invited the cold in. He wasn't even wearing a coat. He wore only a pair of blue jeans and a bright-red T-shirt with two words emblazoned across the front: *Loving Heart.*

*Loving heart?* Okay, so maybe he wouldn't spit in my face when I tried to apologize. But when would be the right time to approach him? I was nervous, but I knew apologizing was the right thing to do and that I should do it sooner rather than later.

We made it through breakfast without any rain. But just as we began to tear down the tents and break camp, a fine mist filled the air. Soon the mist became a drizzle, and then the drizzle turned into a light rain that prompted us to don our foul-weather gear. Even Sam put on a raincoat. His was olive green. Mine was bright yellow and made of thick rubber with awkward metal buckles down the front. The rubber had a funny, smothering odor, which I did my best to ignore. In the store, I had complained to my mother about the hood, thinking it made me look like a doofus. But on this particular morning, I was grateful for it.

We finished breaking camp and commenced the long hike back to the trailhead. I brought up the rear behind Chuck and Patrick to give myself time to build up my courage. Fifteen minutes into the hike, and without feeling any more courageous, I broke into a sprint. When I caught up with Sam, my heart was beating rapidly. I touched him lightly on the shoulder. He looked at me. I spoke as slowly and clearly as possible so he could read my lips through the rain.

"I am so sorry about yesterday by the blueberry bushes, Sam. I don't know what made me do such a stupid thing.

There's no excuse for my behavior. I'm really sorry." I braced for his response.

"No problem, Ricky," he said graciously. "I forgive you." He still spoke with an impediment, yet I understood him perfectly.

Forgiving me seemed to come as naturally to Sam as breathing. It was as if he'd been practicing forgiveness for a lifetime—and in all likelihood, he had. I felt a little better but was still besieged by pangs of guilt. I had hoped they would go away, but they hadn't, at least not yet.

I touched him again on the shoulder. "At breakfast, I noticed your T-shirt. What does *Loving Heart* stand for?"

"That's my school," he said proudly. "I go to Loving Heart Preparatory School in Morristown, New Jersey. It's a private school for kindergartners through twelfth graders."

It seemed like an odd name for a school, and I had all kinds of crazy ideas in my head about what kind of school it was. *Is it a cult? A school for hippies? Is Sam a flower child?* I was careful, though, not to share any of them with him.

"Do you like it?"

"Yes, I like it very much. I would not go to any other."

The rain turned into a steady shower. By the time we reached Emerald Pool, the shower had become a deluge. It was coming down so hard I could barely see Chad—who, as far as I could tell, was no more than twenty feet in front of Sam and me. With our eyes fixed on the muddy trail and our feet swimming in waterlogged hiking boots, we passed Emerald Pool and continued our solemn march toward the trailhead.

As we trudged on, my feet turned numb, and my head burned with fever. The rest of my body was covered with goose bumps. Between sneezes, my teeth chattered maniacally, like those of some demented clown. I felt awful.

"Are you okay, Ricky?" asked Sam.

I tried to sound brave. "I will be as soon as I get out of this rain and into the van."

With the rain coming down as hard as it was, I doubted he understood me. Nevertheless, he gave me a pat of encouragement on the arm. "Hang in there, buddy. We'll be there soon."

We passed a sign that read: "You are now leaving White Mountain National Forest. We hope you enjoyed your visit. Come again soon!" After a few more laborious strides through the thick mud, we finally arrived at the trailhead by Route 113. We crossed the road, loaded the van with our rain-drenched gear, and drove off.

It was a long ride back to Camp Abenaki Valley. Except for the steady sound of rain pelting the van and my intermittent sneezing, it was a silent one as well. Even Chuck and Patrick were quiet. There wasn't a word uttered or single joke told for the entire two-hour drive.

# CHAPTER EIGHT

*D*OOONG . . . *D*OOONG . . . *D*OOONG . . .
I woke with the sound of the Governor's Bell reverberating inside my head. I no longer felt feverish but was too tired and achy to move just yet. Instead I lay in bed listening to the pitter-patter of raindrops on the rooftop of the cabin painted blue. It had been raining nonstop ever since we broke camp at the base of South Baldface. The storm had followed us all the way back to Camp Abenaki Valley and now hovered overhead with no sign of moving on anytime soon. I let out a groan, rolled over, and buried my face in my pillow.

What day was it? I probed the thick web of grogginess that had settled into my brain for an answer. *Let's see . . . I slept most of Friday, sooooo . . . it must be Saturday!*

It *was* Saturday, and something special was planned for that night. But what? Something fun? Then I remembered—it was the night of the annual dance. Realizing the dance would preempt movie night, I let out another groan—this one with some real force behind it. With no movie to look forward to, my third Saturday at Camp Abenaki Valley was about to begin.

The rain continued to pitter-patter as I contemplated breakfast. Wayne, Ryan, and the others had already left. The cabin was mine. Stretching my arms overhead, I let out a primeval yawn that shook the rafters. *Better.* I was still weak but on the mend. It must have been one of those twenty-four-hour bugs. I'd had them before.

I climbed down from my bunk and visited the bathroom. Then I changed into my foul-weather gear and went out into the rain. Turning toward the mess hall, I made my way along Cabin Row and noticed a number of canvas pup tents set up on the field. Each tent had a large *Reserved* sign posted on its front flap. *Reserved? Reserved for what?*

"Hey, Ricky," said Ryan, approaching me from the direction of the mess hall. His navy slicker glistened in the rain. A droplet or two rolled off the front of his hood.

"Hey, Ryan. What's with all these tents?"

He stopped and regarded one of them with a sly grin on his face. "It's the same every year. For some guys, it's a joke. Other guys actually believe they're gonna get lucky tonight."

"Huh? Oh! I get it."

After a light breakfast, I spent the rest of the morning at the riflery range, where my scores continued to soar. I felt energized. Empowered.

*Dooong . . .*

It was lunchtime. Instead of following the horde into the mess hall, however, I ambled down to the lodge. Inside, I shook off the rain and approached the door leading into the rec center. A sign read: *Closed.* I gave the door a nudge and peeked inside. It was deserted except for a couple of technicians setting up a sound system. The pool tables, Ping-Pong tables, foosball tables, and pinball machines had been put into storage, leaving behind a wide-open space and revealing an expansive network of parquet that would serve as the dance floor. Feeling a twinge of anxiety, I left the rec center and shuffled down the hallway toward the art studio.

At the studio door, Miles appeared. He glanced up from the floor. His eyes were lifeless, like glass. He was somewhere else—another world perhaps. Without a word, he plodded down the hallway and departed through the lodge's front door. With a sigh, I entered the studio and spent the remainder of the afternoon finishing my ant farm.

As evening approached, the rains stopped, the winds picked up, and the temperatures plummeted. On the front deck of the mess hall, the thermometer hovered between thirty-nine and forty degrees. Inside, where dinner was being served, the radiators clanged to life. No one at my table could remember the temperature ever falling so low while camp was in session. The cold air was indeed bone-chilling, especially after a long summer of record-breaking heat.

Back at the cabin, we spent the hour between dinner and the start of the dance first bathing and then primping and preening. It wasn't long before the hot water ran out. I was the last one to shower. The water was so cold I could only endure it for the few seconds it took to get my hair wet. After drying myself, I competed with the other boys for position in front of one of three bathroom mirrors. Framed by the mirrors, we combed our hair, brushed our teeth, and gargled with industrial-strength Listerine—all the while assuming the demeanor of fierce warriors preparing for battle. Finally, we dressed in our very best, which meant jeans and a flannel shirt for most of the boys. I wore a pair of stiff khaki dress pants and a blue-and-white-striped oxford my mother had purchased for me with the camp dance in mind. I admired myself in the mirror, thinking how grown-up I looked in my new shirt.

Word reached our cabin that the buses from Camp Crystal had arrived. Hurriedly, we put on jackets and made our way to the lodge. The dance was to begin promptly at eight o'clock.

Our hair was still wet when Willy and I entered the rec center with Sam, whom we had picked up along the way. It had been cold outside, but a wave of heat met us at the door. The rec center–turned–dance hall brimmed with the nervous energy of boys and girls striking not-so-subtle poses for each other while doing their best not to appear overwhelmed by the pomp and circumstance of the event. The boys stood a little taller, puffed their chests out a little farther, and, as a group, spoke even louder than usual. Meanwhile, the girls practiced the fine art of glancing furtively over their shoulders to see if any boys had noticed their freshly feathered hair or glossy lips smeared with Bonne Bell Lip Smackers. Wide eyed, we removed our jackets and left them lying in a growing heap by the door.

The disc jockey cued the first song of the night, "Saturday Night" by the Bay City Rollers. Stationed behind a table at the back of the room, he was surrounded by miles of wire, piles of various and sundry electronic components, two turntables, and at least a dozen plastic milk crates filled with record albums. Strategically placed speakers blasted the music into the rec center, through the walls, and into the cold night beyond.

Over the middle of the dance floor, a disco ball hung from the rafters and checkered the shadowy room with rotating bursts of light. The stage was set for an evening of dancing, prepubescent flirtation, and young romance. But not one camper had found his or her way to the dance floor. The boys remained obstinately camped out at one side of the room, the girls on the other.

I stayed close to Willy and Sam, well within the boundaries that defined the boys' side, and took in the scene. Something was not quite right. All boys were required to be present, but my instincts told me someone was missing. Taking a quick survey, I spied Danny (check) and his bevy of friends (they all got mental checkmarks) by the refreshment table, drinking punch hand over fist. Snickering, Willy pointed out Jihad (check) and his three brothers (check, check, check), all of whom were dressed to the nines in black sport coats and dress slacks. With the possible exception of Neil Kennedy (check), who was cleaned and pressed to his usual tee, the rest of us looked shabby in comparison to the Arab brothers from New York.

All senior and junior counselors were required to be present as well—presumably to ensure we behaved ourselves. I easily located Wayne (check) and Ryan (check) in the crowd.

Chad (check) had just crossed the invisible line separating the boys from the girls and was chatting with a very tall and attractive female counselor from Camp Crystal. I assumed this towering beauty, a Cher look-alike with a dynamite smile and chestnut mane of hair flowing all the way down to her waistline, was his girlfriend. This assumption was soon confirmed when he put an arm around her shoulders and kissed her on the cheek.

Chuck (check) and Patrick (check) flitted about the room in their usual way but kept a safe distance from the dance floor. I spotted Henry Hatfield (check) and his two overgrown sidekicks, Theodore Smith (check) and Thaddeus Smith (check), lurking in a dark corner with a shadowy shape I recognized as Spencer Black (check) from the night of my first campfire.

"I wonder what those thugs are up to," mused Willy.

Jeffrey Underwood (check) stopped briefly to congratulate me on no longer hanging around with Miles Romano.

*Miles?*

"Wise decision, Ricky," he said before moving on.

*Miles?*

"Not much for conversation, is he?" observed Willy.

Miles was missing. Where was he? I hadn't noticed it at the time, but he hadn't been in the cabin when we were getting ready for the dance, nor was he now in the rec center. I rescanned the room carefully and didn't see him anywhere.

"Willy, do you see Miles? I don't think he's here."

"I haven't seen him at all today. I wonder where he's hiding this time. Don't worry. He's done this before. Sometimes he just disappears for a while."

Mr. Gordon and Miss Howard, who were chaperones for the evening, made the first move to the dance floor. All eyes turned toward them as they began to dance to "The Hustle." At first, their presence on the dance floor was met by a smattering of nervous laughter. But soon, everyone in the rec center was cheering and clapping their hands to the music. In spite of his lanky physique and awkward appearance, Mr. Gordon's athleticism showed through as he performed his own personal version of the Hustle. Together, Mr. Gordon and Miss Howard made quite a pair.

About halfway through the song, my gaze drifted past Mr. Gordon and Miss Howard to the far side of the room, where I spotted a girl—much shorter and more petite than her companions—whose eyes, even from that distance, I recognized instantly.

*My angel! I thought I'd never see you again, but now you've come back to me . . .*

A sudden commotion arose and rippled through the rec center like a wave in the ocean. My angel disappeared. *Was she ever there at all?* A small cluster of girls, apparently emboldened by Mr. Gordon's and Miss Howard's foray onto the dance floor, had ventured from their side of the room and started dancing. Without a moment's hesitation, Sam sprinted out to join them.

"Does he know those girls?" I asked Willy.

"No, I don't think so," he said. "He just likes to dance. He's been chomping at the bit ever since we got here."

If only I possessed Sam's irrepressible spirit, his fearlessness, his . . . his chutzpah! Surrounded by a growing circle of girls, his body moved with ease as he allowed the music to work its magic through him. He danced without a speck of shame, as uninhibited and free as the stars on campfire night. I felt a twinge of envy, just like the one I'd felt watching his natural athletic ability shine through as he jumped from the rocky ledge into Emerald Pool while I sat on the bank of the stream, dangling my feet in the cold water.

Soon the entire dance floor was filled with campers, including Danny and all his buddies. Basking in the glittering light of the silvery disco ball, they moved together in perfect harmony. There were no Eagles or Hawks. No winners or losers. No taunting. No teasing. No bullying.

Sam tilted his head back and lifted his eyes toward heaven as if to thank God for the gift of this precious moment.

*I want what he has. What's his secret?*

*Gratitude, Ricky. Gratitude.*

Without taking his eyes off his brother, Willy said, "Sam told me you apologized. Thanks, Ricky. It meant a lot to him, and it means a lot to me."

"Thank *you*, Willy—I mean, for setting me straight, you know?"

"I was hard on you that night, but you need to understand. Sam's not only my big brother; he's also my best friend."

"He is?"

"Yes, he is."

"By the way, how can he dance so well? I mean, if he can't hear the music, how can he, you know, move to it?"

"He might not be able to hear the music the same way you and I can, but he can feel the vibrations. He loves music, and he loves to dance. He's been a dancer all his life."

"And quite a ladies' man too."

"Yeah, Sam's a real Casanova."

"Come on!" a voice shrieked.

At Sam's urging, one of the girls grabbed Willy by the hand and dragged him onto the dance floor. Shrugging, he tilted his head and shot me a glance as if to say, "If you can't beat them, join them," and then he left me standing there with my feet only inches from the parquet. *I could join them too, but . . .* What was I afraid of? Dancing? Looking like a fool? Toni Tennille belted out the megahit "Love Will Keep Us Together," which was followed by Maxine Nightingale's "Right Back Where We Started From."

I buried my hands in the front pockets of my khakis. Trying to appear casual, I bobbed my head to the music a few times. *Don't do that! You look stupid.*

Then it happened.

My angel reappeared. She was in the middle of the room with the disco ball spinning directly over her head. And she wasn't alone. She was dancing with a boy! When the song ended, another boy approached her to ask for a dance. And then another. And another. With each new song, another boy appeared. They were lining up to dance with *my* angel. And the line was growing! Somehow word must have gotten around that she was too sweet and too polite to say no to anybody. All the boys who had been too afraid to venture onto the dance floor had found their courage—all the boys, that is, except me.

Doe eyed, she peeked up at her dance partner as her lips curved upward and blossomed into the delicate petals of an enchanting smile—one capable of melting even Lucifer's cold and stony heart. *No! That smile is for me!* I would have cut off my right arm if I thought it would help me get past my fear and onto the dance floor, where I would be reunited with my angel. Instead, I stood at the edge of the parquet, simmering with jealousy and playing the part of the consummate wallflower.

*Mistaking her smile for an invitation, her dance partner leans in for a kiss . . . That does it! I've had enough! I hurl myself out onto the parquet and shove him aside. He falls to the floor with a thud. The music stops.*

*I delve into my angel's eyes . . . they're exactly the same—each a swirling river of chocolate . . . "My dear, precious angel. It's me—Ricky Williamson. We're together again. You remember when we first met, don't you?" No response—only a blank stare and a confused smile. "Of course you remember. It was at the pool. You know, the one by the gulf . . ." She continues staring. Her smile fades. My voice becomes shrill. "How can you not remember? I was drowning. You saved my life!" An expression of absolute terror spreads across my angel's face. She opens her mouth wide and screams . . .*

*Four, maybe five, boys pounce and wrestle me to the floor. I thrash and claw and gouge and kick. But they're too strong. They drag me across the room and deposit me in front of Mr. Gordon.*

*"What in God's name has gotten into you, Ricky?"*

*"But, Mr. Gordon, that girl is my angel."*

*"You know her?"*

*Neil Kennedy interjects. "Mr. Gordon, I just spoke with the young lady in question, and she's very upset. She has no idea who Ricky is. She just wants to go home now."*

*"Ricky, aren't you ashamed of yourself?"*

*"But, Mr. Gordon—"*

*"Not another word, Ricky. I'm afraid your behavior requires
we take drastic measures. We're going to take you to the pond now."*

*"The pond? What's at the pond? I don't want to go to the pond."*

*"Don't make this any harder than it already is." He reaches for
me with his bony claws.*

*"No!"*

*He wraps them tightly around my neck and . . . and . . .*

Bursting into the chorus of "Turn the Beat Around,"
Vicki Sue Robinson snapped me back into reality. *Reality?* Still
standing at the parquet's edge with my hands buried deep in
my pockets, I looked on as my angel danced the night away.
Twirling around the room with carefree abandon, she threw
her head back and let out an "Ah!" followed by a laugh that
rose over the music—a clear expression of the joy of being
fully alive. Watching her dance, I felt my heart overflow with
both delight and sorrow.

"That little girl is quite a fox, isn't she?"

Startled, I snapped my head around. It was the infamous
Spencer Black, hovering over my shoulder. Willy had advised
me to avoid Spencer at all costs, yet there he was—so close
I could smell the faint but unmistakable odor of cigarette
smoke on his clothes. My heart pounded. My defenses went
up. Within seconds, all systems were operating on high alert.

Spencer Black was tall and very lean. His bare forearms
revealed long, sinewy muscles and ropy veins that popped
dramatically through his pale skin. Bony thumbs dangled
casually from the belt loops fronting his tattered blue jeans.

He slouched—his shoulders and neck rolling forward and his upper back rounding into the curve of a tortoise's shell. A few more years of such slouching, and his posture would rival that of Quasimodo. His drab hair was long, stringy, and greasy. A few random flakes of dandruff lay scattered on the shoulders of his black Led Zeppelin concert T-shirt from the band's 1975 US tour. Clearly, *he* hadn't bothered to primp and preen himself for the big dance.

The checkered light of the disco ball highlighted a marred landscape of blemishes, blotches, craters, and scars that covered much of his face. His long neck featured a prominent Adam's apple that bobbed up and down when he spoke. The corners of his thin mouth pointed upward as if to suggest a warm smile, but his dark eyes were cold and inhuman, more like the pitiless eyes of a great white shark stalking its prey than those of a sixteen-year-old boy at a camp dance. Obeying an instinct of self-preservation, I took a step to my right to create some space between us.

My initial impression was that Willy had been correct. Spencer Black was to be avoided at all costs. When he spoke, however, he spoke in a soothing tone that belied both his reputation and appearance. Leaning toward me to close the gap I had just created, he repeated himself over the music.

"That little girl is quite a fox, isn't she?"

"Huh? What? Oh . . . ah . . . yeah, she is . . . I guess. I mean, yeah, she's a fox."

"Too young for me, of course. But still a fox. Otherwise, this dance is a real drag. Don't you think?"

He was asking *my* opinion. "Yeah, I guess so."

"My name is Spencer Black," he said, extending an open hand in my direction.

I was caught off guard by the formality but recovered in time to pull my hand out of my pocket and shake his. He had good manners and was charming. I wasn't expecting that. My defenses began to melt.

"I'm Ricky Williamson."

"Yes, I know. It's nice to meet you. Listen, Ricky, I hope you don't mind, but I'd like to get right to the heart of the matter. I understand there was some bad blood between you and my boy, Henry Hatfield, and I want you to know that I think he was acting way out of line."

Was I hearing him correctly?

"When I heard you stood up to Henry not once but twice—in your cabin and then again on the floating dock—I was extremely impressed. You've got real guts, man."

"I do?"

"Did you really slug him in your cabin?"

"Well, yeah."

"Wicked cool! He deserved it, man."

"Yeah, he sure did."

"Did you really call him a pig at the Ultimate Race?"

"A pig? I mean, yes . . . yes, I did."

"Radical, man! You're too good to be true. You're really a man who knows how to handle himself. I wish I'd been there to see the look on his face."

"He wasn't happy."

"I'll bet." Spencer stepped closer and touched my arm as if he were about to share a secret with me. "By the way, buddy, no one cares that you didn't finish the swim. It's just a stupid race anyway."

I gazed up at him and blinked in wonder.

"May I ask you a personal question, Ricky?"

"I guess so."

"You don't have many friends here at Abenaki Valley, do you?"

That stung. There was Willy and Sam, but . . .

"No, not really."

"I'll be your friend."

An older boy wanted to be my friend! Spencer was not at all the way I thought he would be. He was actually a nice guy. He really liked me, and I liked him. For the first time since arriving at Abenaki Valley, I felt special. Maybe, just maybe, I could belong to his group—as long as I didn't say or do anything too stupid.

"Okay."

"Great! What do you say we blow this pop stand?"

"Huh?"

"Would you like to come outside with me and my buddies? Just for a little while?"

"Will Henry be there?"

"Yes, he will."

"Gee, I don't know . . ."

"I get it, Ricky. I really do. I can understand why you're reluctant, especially after the way Henry treated you. But don't worry—I've put him in his place. Henry does what I say."

"Always?"

"Always. Besides, he feels real bad and wants to make amends."

I looked over at my angel. She was slow-dancing with Keith Hardaway to the Eagles' "The Best of My Love." My heart sank.

"Okay, I'll come."

"Great! Let's go." Slipping one of his sinewy arms around my shoulders, he added, "I'm on your side, buddy. Trust me. Henry is not gonna be a problem."

Unknown to me at the time, Sam had been watching my entire conversation with Spencer from the dance floor. When he saw us heading toward the door, he excused himself from his partner, ran after us, and grabbed me by the arm. "Where are you going, Ricky?"

"Just outside with Spencer for a little while."

Pulling me aside, he whispered urgently, "Don't go! Spencer is a bad guy—a *real* bad guy."

I studied Sam's face. His forehead was contorted into a mountain range of concern. Jeffrey Underwood had said essentially the same thing about Miles, but Miles wasn't a bad guy—far from it! I glanced over at Spencer, who smiled innocently as he slouched by the door with his thumbs once again dangling from his belt loops.

"Come on, Ricky," said Spencer. "We'll only be gone for a short while."

Turning back to Sam, I said, "I'll be okay."

"Are you sure?"

I nodded and turned to go.

"Ricky! Be careful!"

Sam was really worried about me. I hesitated and then pushed all doubts out of my mind. "I will. See you later."

Spencer and I grabbed our jackets and went out into the cold and damp night. Pausing on the open-air porch, I looked up at the starless sky. A chill ran up and down my spine.

"Come on, Ricky."

I zippered up my summer-weight jacket and followed Spencer around the perimeter of the lodge until we reached the very back of the building.

Examining the murky edge of the woods, he muttered something like, "Shoulda brought a goddamned flashlight . . ."

The driving beat of music percolated through the lodge's walls and infused the night with sound. Turning away from Spencer, I reached for the side of the building. The entire structure vibrated under my fingertips. *It's KC and the Sunshine Band.*

The song came to an abrupt end and was followed by a softer, fainter sound that beckoned me closer. Leaning in, I placed an ear on the roughly hewn surface of the building's white-pine exterior. The wood was cold. I pulled away immediately. I tried again. The melody was sad but strangely hopeful. The lyrics . . . I couldn't quite make out the lyrics . . . Something like . . . *I'm a butterfly . . . I'm . . . I'm . . .*

*Free?*

"Ah, here it is."

Spencer had found an opening in the woods—Tommy Underwood's secret path. We followed the path for about fifty feet before three mysterious points of light appeared in the distance, hovering in midair and radiating an orangey glow through the thick brush. *Lightning bugs?*

"There they are," Spencer said.

We left the path and hacked through the brush for some minutes. Drawing closer to the points of light, I realized they weren't lightning bugs at all but rather the smoldering ends of cigarettes. Attached to those cigarettes were the hands of three figures assembled in a small, remote clearing. I doubted even Tommy had ever ventured this far. It was dark, but I could just make out the faces of Henry and the two giants, Theodore and Thaddeus. Henry raised his cigarette to his lips, took a drag, and released a billowing cloud of smoke into the gloom that encircled them. The smell was acrid. I began to think this wasn't such a good idea after all. I should have listened to Sam. It wasn't too late to go back . . .

"Hey, hey, hey—look who's here!" exclaimed one of the giants.

"That one's Theodore," said Spencer. "You can tell by the big, ugly growth on the end of his chin."

I squinted. Sure enough. There was a wart or a mole or some kind of birthmark on Theodore's chin. It was the size of a penny.

"Hi, Ricky." Henry flicked the ash off his cigarette. "Welcome to our little hideout in the woods. Here, have a seat." He motioned to a fallen log.

I sat down. Henry sat next to me. I smelled both cigarettes and alcohol on his breath.

Without beating around the bush, he said, "Listen, Ricky—I'm really sorry about the bad blood between us. I was way out of line when we met in your cabin and again on the floating dock."

He sounded sincere.

"No hard feelings?" He offered me his hand.

Not knowing what else to do, I shook it. Henry had completely transformed himself. He was no longer a snarling pig but rather a docile kitten. Spencer really did have control over him.

"Have a beer, Ricky," said Theodore, joining Henry and me on the log.

Sandwiched between Henry and Theodore and unsure what to do, I looked up to Spencer for help.

"It's okay, Ricky. Go ahead. You're one of the guys now."

"Um . . . I don't know, Spencer. We're not supposed to be drinking."

"Don't worry about it, Ricky," he said in a comforting voice. "It's just one beer."

"It's the one beer to have when you're having more than one," said Theodore before bursting into a side-splitting cackle.

Henry followed suit and doubled over before reaching across my lap and slapping Theodore on the thigh.

Spencer shot them a look that would freeze hell over ten thousand times. The laughing came to an abrupt halt. Cowering under Spencer's watchful eyes, Theodore pulled a bottle opener out of his jacket pocket, pried the cap off a Schaefer, and handed it to me. The woods became very quiet.

I had never tasted beer and didn't want to start with that Schaefer. But I had no choice. They were watching me like a bug under a microscope. It was my duty to perform. I slowly raised the bottle to my mouth and took a tiny sip. It was bitter! I would have done anything for a bottle of 7Up instead. I took another sip. It was still bitter, but if I took very small sips, I thought I could survive the ordeal.

After about fifteen minutes of small talk, I began to relax. In spite of a few acerbic comments about how I was nursing my Schaefer, Spencer and his gang seemed to accept me as one of their own. For most of the conversation, I just listened while making sure to laugh and nod my head at the appropriate times. Topics covered included women (Raquel Welch was the group's unanimous favorite) and music (favorite bands ranged from Led Zeppelin to Black Sabbath to KISS). According to Spencer, Zeppelin was the best of all time. What was my favorite rock 'n' roll band?

"I . . . I don't know. The Beatles?" The Beatles weren't really my favorite band, but the question had caught me off guard.

"The Beatles!" exclaimed Thaddeus. "They suck. Besides, they broke up years ago."

"Put a lid on it, Thaddeus," said Spencer. "The Beatles were a cool band."

The group was unanimous in their condemnation of Mr. Gordon. Unimpressed by his Olympic medal, they thought he was doofus as well as a pencil-necked geek with a stick up his ass. It was probably no more than his thick glasses and reclusive nature upon which their opinion was based. Nevertheless, they were adamant.

*If they only knew what I know*, I mused.

They held an even lower opinion of Neil.

"The golden boy? Mr. Fancy-Pants? Is he ever full of himself!" Spencer exclaimed. "What a phony. That fat fuck is nothing more than a smug asshole and a suck-up. Did you know his father is a highfalutin politician from New Hampshire? A politician! Everybody knows politicians are just a bunch of scumbags."

"What do you guys think of Camp Abenaki Valley?" I asked.

Spencer answered on behalf of his gang. "All that talk about Abenaki honor is horseshit. No one actually believes in that stupid creed, except maybe Neil Kennedy. The only creed that matters is the Spencer Black creed."

"What creed is that?"

"I'm glad you asked, Ricky, my friend. It's very simple: 'Look out for number one, and don't ever let anyone fuck with you!'"

"Right on!" Theodore raised his bottle into the air, spilling half of it on himself in the process.

Thaddeus cackled. "You said it, man!"

Focusing all his attention on his beer, Henry had become strangely quiet.

After a few more minutes of Spencer ranting and raving over Abenaki Valley hypocrisy and other such matters, the conversation reached a lull.

"Have a smoke." Theodore inched closer and extended an open pack of Marlboros toward me.

I stiffened. "No, thank you. I don't smoke."

"Oh, come on, Williamson. Don't be such a pussy. It's just a fuckin' cigarette."

"Hey!" bellowed Spencer. "That's enough. Lay off my buddy Ricky. If he doesn't want a cigarette, then he doesn't have to have a cigarette. And that's the end of the story."

"Okay, Spencer," Theodore said defensively. "Jesus."

"Why don't we just get this whole goddamned thing over with?" mumbled Thaddeus from the edge of the clearing.

"What was that, Thaddeus?"

"Why don't we . . . nothing."

"Is there something you want to share with the group?"

Thaddeus opened his mouth as if to speak and then stopped himself.

An awkward silence ensued. Henry was to my right. His head was bowed, and his eyes were glued to the ground. Theodore was to my left. He too had his eyes focused downward as the silence stretched from one agonizing moment to the next.

Desperate to fill that insufferable silence with some sound—*any* sound—I found myself saying, "Thanks for sticking up for me, Spencer, but I think I will try a cigarette."

"Right on!" said Theodore.

"Are you sure, Ricky?" asked Spencer, sounding genuinely concerned.

"Yeah, I'm sure. I'd like to try just one puff, if that's okay."

"Sure it's okay." Spencer motioned to Theodore. "Go ahead, give the man a smoke."

I took a cigarette from Theodore's pack and placed it carefully between my lips. The unlit tobacco smelled sweet, like hot cider sprinkled with cinnamon. The aroma reminded me of autumn in South Orange. *Halloween and jack-o'-lanterns . . . Thanksgiving and stuffed turkeys roasting in the oven . . . and pumpkin pie for dessert!* My mouth began to water.

"Okay, Ricky. When Theodore lights that cig, you'll need to suck in a little. Can you do that?"

I nodded, and Theodore held a lighter to the end of the cigarette.

"A little more than that, Ricky," said Spencer. "You need to suck a little more. That's right. You got it."

I inhaled. A thousand red-hot pins and needles assaulted the back of my throat. The pain was excruciating! Gasping for air, I gagged and coughed until finally I could breathe normally again. Wiping tears from my face, I looked up at Spencer.

"I thought I was gonna die."

"Good effort, Ricky," he said. "You can try again some other time. Right now, we're gonna head down to the pond."

*The pond?*

My failed attempt at smoking had left me in a cold sweat. "I'm cold, Spencer. I'd like to go back to the dance now."

He left no room for discussion. "Nonsense. We're all going down to the pond."

*The pond.*

Shivering on the sandy shoreline of Parson's Pond and feeling an onslaught of trepidation gurgling in my stomach, I looked out over the watery expanse and into the eastern sky, covered thick with a heavy curtain of clouds. A speck of pale light appeared. The clouds parted. A crescent moon waxed overhead and scattered its silvery beams throughout the valley. The light reflected from the pond's glassy surface and comforted me, replacing my trepidation with feelings of hope and gratitude. I smiled.

"Thank you, Spencer. Thank you for—"

"*Take that!*"

Before I knew what was happening, I was facedown in about six inches of water, eating silt from the bottom of the pond. In a flash, I raised my head and came to my hands and knees, emerging from the water with a thick strand of fetid algae pasted across my eyes and mouth like a blindfold and gag. Horrified, I tore the algae from my face and flung it as hard as I could toward the middle of the pond. Then I looked back over my shoulder at my assailant. It was Henry.

"That was for the lucky sucker punch in your cabin!" Thick puffs of hot smoke burst from his snout as he spoke.

Just as I was recovering from the shock of that first blow, he delivered another—a ferocious kick that landed directly on my tailbone and sent me flying face-first into the water. I reemerged just in time to hear: "—for calling me a pig! No one disrespects me in front of my buds!"

My tailbone on fire, I started crawling through the silt toward the main dock. There was a dim thought in my head that somehow I would be safe if only I could reach it before Henry struck a third time. Then I remembered what Spencer had said back at the lodge, and it stopped me dead in my tracks. *Henry does what I say. Always? Always.* Could it be true? Was Spencer responsible for this? No. He said he would be my friend. I believed him.

"Spencer!" I cried out. "Help me. Henry's gone crazy. Make him stop!"

My pleas were met by a full and lively round of devilish cackling.

"Are you for real, Williamson? You're an even bigger moron than I thought," snorted Henry, sounding fully confident of Spencer's support.

Thumbs dangling loosely from belt loops, Spencer stood on the shore and said nothing. But then the faintest sliver of a grin appeared on his face.

That was when it hit me. And it hit me hard. This was Spencer's doing! I had fallen easy prey to his flattery and charms. How could I have been so stupid? Why, oh why, oh why had I refused so pigheadedly to listen to Sam? He was right. Spencer was a bad guy—a *real* bad guy.

The clouds returned, once again obscuring the crescent moon from view. I was alone. I was alone crouching on my hands and knees in six inches of bone-chilling water. I was stupid, and now I was all alone. Still, there was a part of me that refused to believe Spencer was responsible for Henry's actions. With nothing left to lose, I decided to make one last desperate appeal.

"Spencer, the water is really cold. I want to go back to the dance now."

An ominous silence filled the air.

"Wh-wh-wh-why . . . why don't you say anything?"

Henry answered for Spencer. "You don't get it, do you, Williamson? You're not going back to the dance."

Finally, Spencer broke his silence in a voice an octave lower and a hundred times more sinister than the one he had used to lure me to this spot. "For you, the dance is over."

*The dance is over?*

Spencer's betrayal was confirmed.

"B-b-b-but, Spencer . . . I'm r-r-r-really, really cold," I managed to utter through teeth that were chattering beyond all control.

"For Chrissakes, Williamson. Enough with the goddamned whining. You whined about drinking a beer. You whined about smoking a lousy cigarette. And now you're whining about the cold. What a wuss! You dug your own grave, so just shut up and lie in it. This experience will teach you not to mess with us. You're gonna learn if you mess with one of us, you mess with all of us."

Under my breath, I muttered, "You said you would be my friend."

Spencer shot a glance at Henry. "What did he say?"

Henry kicked me hard in the ribs. "Speak up, Williamson!"

Gritting my teeth against the pain, I repeated, "You said you would be my friend."

"Louder," said Spencer.

My voice exploded with the force of a cork from a violently shaken bottle of champagne. "You said you would be my friend! You said you would be my friend!"

"Quiet!"

"You said you would be my friend! You said you would be my—"

"I said, *quiet!*"

"—friend! You said you would—"

Charging into the water and pushing Henry aside, an infuriated Spencer grabbed me by the hair and dunked my head into the frigid pond. I swallowed a lungful of water and thrashed about in a desperate attempt to reach the surface, but he held me under with his powerful arms. After an eternity, he loosened his hold. I came up, coughing, then sputtering, then retching, until finally I spit up a cocktail of pond scum and Schaefer beer. Recovering my breath, I renewed my pilgrimage toward the dock, which in my confused mind still represented a safe haven. My pathetic attempt to escape, however, just made Spencer angrier.

He grabbed me by the hair again. "Just where do you think you're going? I'll teach you to sit still and take your medicine. Theodore! Thaddeus! Find me a stick—a big one. Make sure it's long and slender but strong."

The two giants hastened to the edge of the tree line in search of a stick that would match Spencer's specifications. Theodore was the first to return. He held up a stick roughly two feet in length. "How's this?"

"No. Bigger and longer!"

Thaddeus returned, brandishing a three-foot-long branch that had the girth and consistency of a riding crop. "How 'bout this one?"

"Hickory. Perfect." Spencer took the branch from Thaddeus. "Now, tear off his shirt."

"Tear off his shirt?"

*Tear off my shirt?*

"You heard me. Tear off his shirt."

I tried to scramble away, but Thaddeus was too quick. He wrapped his arms around my torso, grabbed the front of my brand-new oxford—the nicest shirt I'd ever owned—and pulled with both hands. The cotton-and-polyester-blended material held fast. He pulled again. This time, there was an audible rip at the seams. But still the material held. Finally, on the third pull, the shirt's buttons went flying into the night as he savagely tore the oxford away from my body, leaving abrasions across my chest and under my arms.

*How will I ever explain this to Mom? Mom? Mom, is that you? Mom! I'm sorry. I'm so sorry . . .*

I fell forward and landed on my hands just before my face reached the water. *My shirt! Where is my shirt?* I had to find my shirt, but just when I turned my head to look for it, I caught a glimpse of a frightful image out of the corner of my eye—Spencer's shadowy silhouette looming above me and raising the hickory branch overhead.

*Whi-kisssh!*

The sturdy branch came crashing down on my naked back and ignited a raging inferno. With a shriek, I squeezed my eyes shut and dug my fingers into the silty bottom of the pond. The fire quickly burned itself out and turned ice-cold, like a straight-edged razor slicing through flesh.

"Now lie still and take your medicine, you worthless little shit."

There was no need for Spencer to worry about me trying to get away. The pain was so intense, I could hardly move. Instead I just lay there whimpering and waiting for the next blow. I didn't have long to wait.

*Whi-kisssh!*

"Take that! Couldn't even finish a quarter-mile swim. What a pussy!"

"You said n-n-no one c-c-cared about that. You said—"

*Whi-kisssh!*

"Daddy! Daddy, help me! Help me, please!"

Other than the rhythmic thumping of a distant disco beat, there was no answer.

"We need to shut him up," said Spencer. "You!" He pointed at Theodore. "Take off one of your socks and stuff it in his mouth."

I was too weak to fight. Theodore went about his business, and soon I was gagging on a grimy tube sock. I tried to spit it out, but he had shoved it in deep.

*Whi-kisssh! Whi-kisssh! Whi-kisssh!*
*Whi-kisssh! Whi-kisssh! Whi-kisssh!*

The lashings ceased. Warm streams of blood flowed freely over the lacerated contours of my back and trickled into the pond. With my head hanging barely an inch over the water, I whimpered into the tube sock. A voice scratched the surface of my befogged brain. It sounded concerned. *No, not concerned . . . worried. No, not worried . . . shocked. Shocked? Shell-shocked? Yes, that's it—shell-shocked like a soldier in one of those World War II movies after the big battle . . .* I thought maybe the owner of the voice was Henry, but I couldn't be certain.

"Jesus Christ, Spencer," said the voice. "You're gonna kill him."

"He better live. We're not through with him yet. You're up."

"Huh?"

"It's your turn, Henry. This is your chance to settle the score."

"No . . . no, that's okay, Spencer. I . . . I think the Williamson kid has suffered enough. Let's just call it even. In fact, what do you say we call it a night?"

"Nonsense. The night is young. Besides, I got him ready just for you."

"What do you mean?"

"I mean, he's ready for you, Henry. He's an awfully nice-looking piece of ass, don't you think? Go ahead, Hen— fuck him. He won't put up a fight now. This is your big chance.

You've been talking all summer long about how badly you wanna get laid. Did you mean it, or was that just talk?"

"But he's a boy!"

"For Chrissakes, Henry! Don't be such a virgin. Beggars can't be choosers. You've got to work your way up to girls." Spencer lowered his voice to a whisper. "There he is, Henry. He's barely conscious. This is your big opportunity. Don't blow it. Go ahead, Hen. Fuck him. Fuck him now. Fuck him while you can."

"Yeah, Henry—fuck him," said Theodore.

"Go for it, Henry," said Thaddeus.

"Fuck him, Hatfield!" Spencer screamed.

"I can't, Spencer."

"Okay, Henry. You give me no choice. Either you take off your pants right now, or I have the Smith brothers remove them for you."

"Please, Spencer. Don't do this."

"Gentlemen . . ."

Theodore and Thaddeus closed in on Henry, who stood frozen in the water not far from me.

"Okay, okay, okay. *Okay!* Back off, guys."

But the two giants kept coming, lumbering through the shin-deep water until they towered over him, ready to strike at Spencer's command. Henry shook convulsively. Theodore grabbed him by the arm.

"Don't touch me!" screeched Henry. "I'll do it. I'll do it! Spencer, call them off. I'll do it. I swear I'll do it!"

"Okay, guys. You can stand down. But stay close—just in case Mr. Hatfield changes his mind."

Henry slowly unbuckled his belt, removed his pants, and threw them onto dry land.

"Undies too," Spencer said.

Tears streamed down Henry's cheeks. "Don't make me do this, Spencer. Can we *please* just stop? I have nothing against this kid."

"You have nothing against this kid? Are you joking? He sucker-punched you, then he called you *pig* in front of at least a dozen guys. He insulted your manhood. He humiliated you. And you're gonna let him get away with it? What kind of man are you?"

By now, Henry was crying like a baby.

"Okay, okay. Stop your freakin' blubbering. You can put your pants back on."

Sniffling loudly and wiping his nose, Henry plodded through the water to the shoreline and retrieved his pants. When he attempted to put them on, however, he encountered a problem. One of the pant legs had become tangled. When he shoved his foot in, it got stuck. Teetering precariously on the other foot, he tried to maintain his balance but fell headfirst onto the hard sand before scrambling to his feet to complete the task.

The once-proud Henry Hatfield was now unrecognizable to me. He was neither a pig nor a kitten but simply a fourteen-year-old boy. He was no longer crying openly, but his cheeks were soaked with tears, and half his face was covered with sand. Apparently, he was unaware of the sand, for he made no attempt to remove it. I felt sorry for him.

As soon as Henry zipped up his fly, Spencer handed him an empty beer bottle. "Here. Take this bottle and fuck him with it."

Henry gaped at Spencer, horrified.

"You heard me. Fuck him with this bottle."

Henry opened his mouth, but no words came out.

"Go for it, Henry," said Theodore.

"Yeah, Hen. Do it. Just like Spencer said," chimed in Thaddeus.

Henry took the bottle from Spencer and reentered the pond as if in a trance.

"Attaboy, Henry. Show him what you've got," said Spencer.

I was aware of what was about to happen but too weak now to attempt an escape. Spencer instructed Theodore and Thaddeus to remove my trousers and underwear, which they did in haste and with little resistance from me. Lying naked on my stomach, which was turning numb in the frigid pond, I used every last bit of my remaining strength to raise my head and look back over my shoulder at Henry.

"Please don't . . ."

Averting his eyes, Henry knelt down, placed the beer bottle between the cheeks of my buttocks, and gave it a halfhearted push.

"Spencer, this isn't right. He's defenseless."

"Do it. *Do it now!*"

Theodore and Thaddeus began a chant that escalated steadily into a crescendo. "Do it. Do it. Do it. Do it . . ."

Henry pushed the bottle a little harder. My seventy-pound body tensed and turned as rigid as stone in a desperate attempt to prevent advance of the foreign object. Bracing myself with my hands dug into the silt, I raised my head well above the waterline and arched my back into an impossibly steep angle.

My muscles quivered and shook. Henry twisted the bottle a few times like a screwdriver, but with no success.

"Spencer, it's no use. He's too tight. The bottle isn't going to fit."

"Push hard!"

"I am pushing hard."

"If you can't do this, Hatfield, I'm gonna give this job to the Smith brothers, and when they're through with Williamson, *you* will be next."

Henry bent down close to me and whispered in my ear, "I'm sorry, Ricky. I have no choice. If you try to relax, maybe it won't hurt so much."

Without any further warning, a bolt of lightning entered my body and shot through my insides, leaving in its wake a path of seared flesh. A flash of white light appeared. Unable to see and paralyzed by the pain, I fell face-first into the pond. The white light faded into a cold and desolate darkness. A stark terror rose up from within my bowels. I snapped my head out of the water and screamed into Theodore's grimy sock, producing a muffled sound that carried no farther than the dock, which was only about ten feet away.

The entire neck of the bottle was inside me, but Henry was just getting started. Obeying Spencer's orders, he pulled the bottle out and thrust it back in. Again and again and again, the bottle's neck tore through my flesh. With the intense pain and pressure came dizzying waves of nausea. My head spun. I choked on the sock. I clenched my teeth together. I thrashed from side to side in a futile attempt to escape the thrusts, but the wounds on my back screamed out in protest. I stopped thrashing. At this point, it was all I could do to prevent my face from dipping into the water.

Theodore and Thaddeus's chant increased in volume and tempo. "*Do it! Do it! Do it! Do it!*"

Spencer's scarred face materialized inches from mine. "How does this feel, Williamson?" he demanded, breathing his rancid breath into my face. "Not so good? That's too bad. You're gonna think twice before messing with one of us again, aren't you? *Aren't you?*"

I nodded my head weakly.

"Faster, Henry! Faster! Harder! Faster! Harder! Fuck this Williamson kid like the little girl that he is."

Henry complied, thrusting the bottle even more savagely into and out of my helpless body. Finally, out of pure exhaustion, I surrendered. No longer was every muscle in my body in a state of contraction. Rather I lay there limp like a rag doll bleeding into the pond, no longer caring whether I lived or died. My head hung loosely from my shoulders. The tip of my nose scratched the pond's surface.

"*Do it! Do it! Do it! Do it!*"

Depleted, Henry collapsed. The bottle fell into the pond. It was over.

"Good work, Henry," said Spencer. "You've done your duty, and you've done it well. Your honor has been restored. You should be proud, *mi compadre*."

I lifted my head and caught sight of Henry. Looking anything but proud, he picked himself up and made his way listlessly to shore.

"What?" Spencer called after him. "Too tired to celebrate? Oh, well. We'll have a beer later. Now that you've loosened him up, I'll take it from here."

Taking a long drag off a cigarette, Spencer threw the butt into the pond. It fizzled out. He unzipped his fly. He circled me. He circled me for what seemed like eons. Then, without warning, he stopped, pulled down his pants, and drilled himself into me from behind.

I gasped.

This time, there was no chanting. Other than Spencer's rhythmic grunts echoing across the pond, there was not a sound to be heard. Even the crickets had stopped chirping.

I summoned one last burst of energy in an attempt to squirm free, but it was no use. Spencer was in complete control. As before, I succumbed to the attack. There was not an ounce of fight left in me.

*It's my own fault. I deserve this. I deserve to die. They hung Miles on the nail, and I did nothing to help . . . when he needed me most, I thought only of myself . . . I'm sorry, Miles . . . I'm so sorry . . .*

Tears streamed down my cheeks. I looked out past the dock. Nothing. Murky—like peering through the rain-streaked pane of my bedroom window. But then an object appeared. A plank—a warped and splintered plank. Another plank. And another . . . The time-weathered doors of the dilapidated equipment shed came into focus. *If only I could free myself and make it through those doors, I might be transported into another world . . .* I closed my eyes and tried to imagine becoming weightless.

*Leaving my body behind, I float into the air, glide over the dock, and drift toward the shed . . . my fingertips graze the doors, which make not a sound but fly open as easily as silk curtains in the breeze . . . I pass over the threshold and find myself in the warm comfort of my bedroom . . . I'm home . . . my head sinks into my pillow . . . a colonial American lighthouse—my night-light—casts a beacon of soft light across my face . . .*

*My eyelids grow heavy . . . the light dims . . . "You're safe now, Ricky." It's Daddy. He says nothing more but gazes down at me with pure love shining in his eyes . . . I'm in his arms . . . he's hold-ing me so close I begin to melt into his chest . . . we're becoming one . . . yes, I'm safe now . . . nothing can hurt me . . .*

*Weightless again, I float up into the Maine sky . . .*

*I'm hovering over Parson's Pond . . . below me, a little boy is lying flat on his stomach in six inches of murky water . . . a sinewy-armed, long-haired monster straddles the boy's hips. There's another boy . . . he's sitting at the water's edge with head in hands . . . he appears to be crying. Two giants stand nearby—motionless and gaping at the little boy and monster engaged in a horrifying dance . . .*

*The scene fades . . . I'm falling . . .*

Spencer's body erupted into a series of convulsions, and it was finally over.

A voice drifted into my ear canal and crackled like a broken transmission arriving at its destination after a long journey through light-years of space. "Theodore . . . Thaddeus . . . would you . . ."

". . . uh, no, I . . ."

". . . me neither . . ."

". . . what if he talks?"

"Yeah, if . . . we'd be . . ."

"Listen up, Williamson. If you . . . we'll kill you . . . and your brother too . . . Understand?"

I raised my head toward the voice and nodded.

The patter of footsteps faded into the woods and dwindled away. *They're gone* . . . I crawled to the edge of the pond, dropped my head onto the hard sand with a *thunk*, and passed out.

*Dooong . . . Dooong . . . Dooong . . .*

The lonesome sound of the Governor's Bell rang out across the countryside. When the bell's first tones reached me, they tumbled into my ears and gently tapped the tiny drums there into vibration. On the twelfth and last *dooong*, I woke with a start. Curled up in the fetal position and shivering, I was still at the pond's edge. But now, my body was covered by an adult-sized hunting jacket like the one my father used to wear. Without getting up, I craned my neck to search for my clothes and discovered them lying neatly folded on the dock. Wincing, I staggered to my feet, waddled over, and got dressed in the crescent moon's jaundiced glow. A cold breeze blew in from the far side of the pond. I donned the hunting jacket, which hung down to my ankles, and began a clumsy, arduous trek up the hill and back to my cabin.

Bracing myself against the pain that shot through my body with each step, I climbed the stairs to the cabin's front door and pulled it open.

"You're late, Williamson," Wayne stated flatly.

From the doorway, I peered into the room. Miles sat up in bed and gazed at me. His dark eyes were fraught with pity. *He knows!* I stepped inside. He turned away to hide the tears that had begun to flow.

"Where were you?" asked Ryan.

"Walking. I got lost."

"Holy cow, Ricky! It's past midnight. We were about to send out a search party."

I said nothing and went straight to bed.

# CHAPTER NINE

*Sunday, August 1, 1976*

I WOKE BUT DIDN'T DARE MOVE. If I moved, my whole body would scream out in pain. *Easy does it, Ricky . . . one breath at a time . . .* Cautiously, I took a slow and deliberate breath. It was morning. I had slept through the first bell of the day. The other boys moved busily about the cabin, getting ready for breakfast. I waited for them to leave before inching out of bed . . . *take it nice and slow . . .* and climbing down the side of the bunk. From there, I stumbled into the bathroom. Every square inch of my body was on fire. When I was finished in the bathroom, I returned to bed.

Breathing hard from the exertion of scaling my bunk, I curled up in the fetal position and rested on the cardboard-thin mattress. Every muscle in my body cried out in protest. I closed my eyes, focused on my breath, and felt the expansion and contraction of my chest as it gradually steadied itself.

I thought back to the day of the Ultimate Race, when Mr. Gordon told me to pay him a visit if I wanted to talk. *My door is always open . . .* But there was no way I could ever tell him, or anybody else, what had happened at the pond. After all, it was my own damn fault. I was stupid and paid the price for my stupidity. In Spencer's words, *You dug your own grave, so just shut up and lie in it.* Besides, Spencer had threatened to kill me and Danny if I breathed a word to anybody. My life no longer meant much to me, but I had no right to put my brother's life at risk. Mom would never forgive me if he were killed on my account.

Finding me still in bed when he returned from breakfast, Willy asked, "Are you okay, Ricky?"

"I'm not feeling too good this morning."

"Maybe you should go to the infirmary."

"No. I'll be fine."

"I could go with you—"

"I said I'll be fine!" The words came out much more forcefully than I had intended. Feeling remorseful, I began to apologize, but Willy cut me off.

"Suit yourself," he said and left the cabin in a huff.

The door slammed. The front steps creaked with each footfall. Then it was quiet. I waited. And waited. When I was absolutely certain he was gone and not coming back, I stripped the bloodstained sheets from my bed and buried them in the woods behind Cabin Row.

I made only a token appearance at lunch, entering the mess hall just long enough to grab a glass of bug juice and a slice of bread. Sneaking out the back, I made my way around the perimeter of the building and started down Cabin Row. About halfway to the cabin painted blue, Sam and Willy overtook me.

"Hey, Ricky," said Willy, out of breath from running. "Wanna come down to the rec center with us? We're gonna watch the closing ceremony for the Olympics."

I kept walking. "No, thanks."

Putting a hand on my shoulder, Sam asked, "What happened to you last night, Ricky?"

I could tell he was really concerned, but still I rebuffed him. "Nothing."

"Come on, Ricky," said Willy. "Something must have happened. You didn't get back to the cabin until after midnight."

"What did Spencer do to you?" asked Sam.

"Nothing." I quickened my pace in an attempt to lose them, but they kept up easily. "Leave me alone!"

"Why are you walking so funny?"

"I fell."

"You fell?"

"I was climbing up the far side of Parson's Peak, and I fell," I lied. "It's no big deal. I just bruised my tailbone."

"There's been talk of an investigation," said Willy.

I stopped. *An investigation? No!*

"Mr. Gordon has already questioned Spencer. But word is, Spencer didn't admit to anything."

"Good, because nothing happened."

"Ricky, no one believes that."

"Well, it's the truth. Now just leave me alone!" I resumed my awkward waddle back to the cabin, leaving behind my worried friends.

Willy shouted after me, "Mr. Gordon is gonna have a talk with you!"

*We gather for Sunday campfire. A blanket of wistful stars gazes down at us. Our voices float upward into the mysterious ether and fade into nothingness . . .*

*Monday, August 2–Wednesday, August 4, 1976*

Mr. Gordon summoned me to his office first thing Monday morning.

When I arrived, I stepped haltingly into the reception area. Miss Howard was stationed behind an old-fashioned manual typewriter perched on a desk piled high with papers, folders, notebooks, and thick, ink-stained ledgers. Peering through her horn-rims, she greeted me with a thin smile that failed to hide an expression of deep sorrow carved into the creases of her face. It had been just over two weeks since our arrival, but she seemed different now—like a little old lady hunched over a cart at the grocery store.

Mr. Gordon entered the room. On this, our second face-to-face encounter, the twinkle in his eyes was noticeably absent. Without wasting any time, he directed me to his inner sanctum, shut the door, and asked me to take a seat as he settled behind an imposing mahogany desk.

The interview commenced.

Taking a deep breath and clearing his throat, Mr. Gordon expressed "grave concerns" regarding the night of the dance. Informing me he had already spoken with Spencer, he then asked me to describe my version of the events of Saturday night. I assured him I had no version of the events, that nothing had happened.

"Ricky, a dozen witnesses saw you leave the rec center with Spencer Black."

"Yes, sir."

His eyes narrowed. "Well?"

"Well . . . we went out for some fresh air."

He leaned forward across his desk. "That's fine, Ricky, but you didn't return to your cabin until after midnight."

I looked down at the floor. "Yes, sir. I know. I'm sorry. I went for a walk and got lost."

"Were you alone?"

"Yes, sir, I was."

"Ricky, I want to help you, but there's nothing I can do unless you tell me the truth—the whole truth."

"I am telling you the truth, Mr. Gordon."

The interview went on like this for another thirty minutes. Mr. Gordon continued interrogating me, and I continued assuring him nothing had happened. He was unconvinced. Without my cooperation, however, he had no choice but to drop the investigation.

The heat returned to Abenaki Valley that morning and covered the entire camp under a heavy blanket of oppression.

Virtually everyone and everything sagged under its weight. Campers dragged themselves from one activity to the next. Trees, shrubs, and plants wilted under the sun's harsh rays. The yellow grass turned brown and died. Even the sound of the Governor's Bell languished as it announced the beginning of lunch. In response, the boys of Camp Abenaki Valley gathered what strength they could muster and stormed the air-conditioned mess hall for an hour-long reprieve. Then, revitalized, they set out in various directions to attend their afternoon activities.

All but oblivious to the weather, I hobbled around camp in a daze, hardly speaking or making eye contact with anyone. The other campers seemed not to notice me. It was as if I had become invisible, which suited me fine. My only wish was to be left alone.

Moving methodically from one activity to another, I listened to the counselors' instructions and did exactly as I was told. At the archery and riflery ranges, I practiced my technique while adhering strictly to the letter of all safety procedures. In riflery, I achieved a personal best score and advanced to the rank of sharpshooter. In baseball, we continued practicing, even though there was talk of canceling our game against Camp Wildcat due to lack of interest on both sides. In camping, we began planning our second backpacking trip—this one to Mount Katahdin, Maine's highest peak. Chad kept challenging us to start a fire without a match. On Wednesday morning, I finally succeeded, starting a fire in record time. By simply going through the motions, I had become a model camper.

On Wednesday afternoon, Danny and I received care packages from home. Feeling neither excitement nor anticipation, I carried mine back to the cabin and opened it to discover a treasure trove of such goodies as Bubble Yum, Pop Rocks, and Twizzlers, as well as comic books, Wacky Packages, and baseball cards. Tossing the candy and comic books aside, I sat with my legs hanging over the edge of my bed and thumbed mindlessly through the cards until I sensed I was being watched. I glanced up. Sure enough, there he was. Miles was sitting cross-legged on his bed, watching me, watching me with those dark eyes and that eternally mournful expression on his face . . . watching me, watching me as he had grown so accustomed to doing since the night of the dance . . . watching me, watching me, and waiting so maddeningly for me to say or do something—I knew not what—or perhaps wanting desperately to reach out to me but not knowing how.

I returned my blank stare to the baseball cards and resumed thumbing, thumbing, thumbing . . .

*Thursday, August 5, 1976*

Dear Mom,

Thanks for the care package. Everything is fine.
I love you.

Ricky

*Friday, August 6, 1976*

It was late in the afternoon. A light breeze had begun to blow, one that offered welcome relief from another long day under the hot sun. All activities had just wrapped up for the week. On the way back to my cabin from the archery range, I decided to stop at the lodge and check the mail. Expecting nothing and receiving nothing, I shrugged, exited the post office, and lumbered toward the front of the building, my footsteps echoing ponderously in the empty hallway.

"Psych!"

Someone in the rec center had just scored a goal in foosball.

"You're goin' down!"

"Dream on."

Reaching the end of the hallway, I put all my weight behind the front door and pushed. It opened with a lazy rasp. I stepped out onto the porch and was greeted by a warm gust of wind seasoned with just a hint of balsam. A counselor sat on the front steps, drinking a Coke and reading the sports section of the Portland paper's afternoon edition. A couple of campers had recovered enough from the heat of the day to play Frisbee on the desperately parched field in front of the lodge.

For no particular reason, and not being in any kind of a hurry, I elected to take a detour. Instead of the usual and more direct route straight up the field's steady incline to Cabin Row, I took the low road along the tree line and found myself approaching the revered two-story cabin reserved exclusively for senior campers, the only cabin in camp that merited a name: Parson's Abode. I stopped to take in the sight of this preeminent structure.

Like the lodge, Parson's Abode was made of white pine and had a front porch, only this porch was much smaller than the lodge's and was screened in on all three sides. For the moment, shadows covered the porch, making it impossible to see inside. The second-story windows looked down upon me like the eyes of a spoiled child of the aristocracy observing an insect. I imagined this child might have nothing better to do than pluck off this poor insect's wings and then, one by one, each of its legs.

I started to move on, but then, emerging from the darkness of the porch, Neil appeared at the front door and invited me to come inside. I hesitated, but he waved me in. "It's okay, Ricky. There's nothing to be afraid of."

I followed him through the porch and into the cabin's interior where I was struck by the sheer spaciousness of the first floor, which opened up into a much wider and deeper configuration than that of the cabin painted blue. At the apex of the room's vaulted ceiling, a massive fan whirled at dizzying speed. A few streaks of late-afternoon sun cut through the shadowy porch, cascaded into the cabin through oversized front windows, and accentuated the hardwood-paneled walls, which were stained a warm shade of yellow. The sleeping area occupied the back half of the room. There were no bunk beds in Parson's Abode; rather, each resident slept in his very own full-sized bed. In the far-right corner, a door labeled *Gents* marked the entryway into the first-floor bathroom. The front half of the room was set up as a living area with a faux-leather sofa, coffee table, chairs, and a television set with rabbit ears. To my right there was a kitchenette complete with a mini-refrigerator, toaster oven, sink, and a breakfast table built for no more than two. To my left, a spiral staircase disappeared upward into the loft.

Following my gaze, Neil said, "That's where the other six guys sleep. Altogether, there are twelve of us here. You might have heard—there are no counselors in Parson's Abode. Senior campers are considered mature enough to look after themselves. But that's not always true, Ricky."

"Are you sure it's okay for me to be here?" I asked, feeling rather uncomfortable standing on such hallowed ground.

"Of course it is. I invited you in, didn't I?"

"Yeah, but . . ."

"Would you rather leave?"

"No . . . it's just that I, uh . . ."

"Well, then, have a seat, sport," he said, pointing to the sofa.

*Sport?* I sat down. It was just Neil and I. No one else. Fidgeting nervously, I tried to make myself comfortable.

"What do you think of Parson's Abode?"

"Nice."

"Yeah, we're living in the lap of luxury here, that's for sure. I just got a care package from home. Would you like some licorice?" He extended a bag of black licorice toward me.

"Me too . . . I mean . . . sure. Thanks," I said, taking a long rope of licorice from the bag.

Neil lowered his hefty frame into an overstuffed wingback chair, leaned forward, and asked, "Is everything okay, Ricky?"

"Yeah. Everything's fine, I guess."

"How are your activities going?"

"Pretty good. I just got sharpshooter in riflery."

"Really? That's a great achievement, especially for a first-year camper. Good job, Ricky."

"Th—"

Just as I started to thank Neil for the compliment, I was overcome by a sudden bout of dizziness and almost lost my balance. Grabbing the sofa's arm, I steadied myself, but then my vision became fuzzy. Neil's features were distorted and indistinguishable. The outline of his face blurred into a cold and distant sun. Parson's Abode dissolved into a swirling multitude of pale-blue bubbles. Everything turned black.

*I'm at the range. The smell of gunpowder tickles the tiny hairs in my nostrils. My .22 feels good in my hands . . . together we're invincible. I load my weapon with a single round of ammo, flick off the safety, and aim at the target . . . it morphs into the shape of a human face—Spencer Black's. He smiles coldly, daring me to pull the trigger. He vanishes in a flash. Another face materializes . . . it's too blurry to make out at first, but then it becomes clear. It's a face I know very well—my own. I'm wearing a black-and-white-striped prisoner's uniform. It's my execution day. I take aim and squeeze the trigger . . .*

"Ricky? Hey, Ricky! Are you okay?"

I returned to Parson's Abode. Neil was still leaning forward in his chair, now with an expression of alarm plastered across his face.

"It seemed like you were a million miles away. Can I get you a glass of water or something?"

"No, thanks."

"Are you sure?"

"I'm sure. Thanks anyway."

"Is there *anything* I can get for you?"

"No. Really, I'm okay. I was just daydreaming." *Daydreaming?* "I do that sometimes."

"Oh. You didn't hear a word I said, did you?"

"No, I guess not," I said, beginning to feel embarrassed.

"Don't worry about it. I was just making conversation. I was asking you what your dad does."

I stared at him, uncomprehending.

"You know . . . for a living. What does your dad do for a living?"

"Nothing."

"Nothing?"

"Yeah, nothing. I mean . . . I'm sorry, Neil. My father died."

"Died? When?"

"Two and a half years ago." I was too numb to feel any pain, and the words came out easily.

"Gosh, I'm sorry, man. I had no idea."

"It's okay."

After a long silence, Neil said, "I want to apologize again for what happened at the Ultimate Race—you know, the swim. It was my fault. I should have listened when you tried to tell me, but . . . oh, heck, but nothing. I have no excuse. I should have listened, period. I was your captain. As captain, it was my duty to listen." His voice softened as he continued. "Even more than that, I should have listened because that's what people do for each other—they listen. They listen and they watch out for each other. I should have been there for you when you needed me, and I wasn't. I'm sorry."

Spencer burst into the room and stopped short. "What's *he* doing here?" he demanded, pointing an accusing finger at me.

The finger quivered and then turned rigid.

I felt nothing.

"I invited him in," Neil said in his confident politician's voice.

"He's a junior camper. You can't just invite him in. He doesn't belong here."

"Neither do you, Spencer."

At a loss for words and unable to respond, Spencer slithered upstairs.

"Spencer isn't supposed to be in Parson's Abode," Neil said. "This cabin's always been for seventeen-year-olds only. The sixteen-year-olds didn't want him, so, unfortunately, we've been stuck with him all summer."

I stood up and turned to go.

"You don't have to leave."

"I should go get ready for dinner." I started for the door and then stopped. "Thanks for the licorice, Neil."

*Saturday, August 7, 1976*

On movie night, the rec center was packed with campers eagerly awaiting the beginning of Alfred Hitchcock's *Dial M for Murder*. Armed with a bag of popcorn and looking forward to escaping my barely tolerable day-to-day existence, I settled into a back-row seat. But there was a delay. For some unknown reason, the film refused to thread properly. Three times, the movie commenced and stopped abruptly, sparking a thunderous chorus of boos and hisses from the audience. On the fourth attempt, the problem with the film resolved itself, but then the projector's bulb burned out in a sudden and dramatic flash of light. It was as if there were some mysterious force at work—a force whose mission was to prevent us from watching that movie. It took another fifteen minutes to locate a new bulb and replace the old one. Finally, the movie began.

Very much in the Hitchcock tradition, *Dial M for Murder* was a hair-raising story of blackmail, deception, and murder. After discovering that his beautiful wife had been unfaithful, a dashingly handsome professional tennis player devised an elaborate plan to have her killed. In the scene of the attempted murder, the tennis player's wife, played by Grace Kelly, came out of the bedroom, dressed only in her nightgown, to answer the telephone. She picked up the receiver and answered with a sleepy hello. There was no response.

"Hello?" she repeated.

As the suspense mounted, I heard a strangely familiar voice at the other end of the line. It belonged to Spencer Black.

*That Williamson kid is gonna talk. We need to do something before he does.*

"Hello?"

I closed my eyes and found myself in the middle of my own movie, crouching stealthily behind a tree in the woods. It was nighttime and very, very dark.

"I don't know, Spencer. If he was gonna talk, he would've said something to somebody by now."

*Hello?*

Cautiously sticking my head out from behind the tree, I peered through the thick brush and into a clearing where Spencer, Henry, Theodore, and Thaddeus were holding a meeting in their secret hiding place behind the lodge. Cigarette smoke formed a cloud above them. Stuck into the ground at their feet, a flashlight pointed upward and illuminated their faces with the subdued brilliance of a small campfire.

"I tell you—he's gonna talk. I saw him yesterday in Parson's Abode getting chummy with Neil Kennedy."

*Hello?*

"We need to shut him up . . . permanently."

"Permanently?" asked Henry. "What are you talking about, Spencer?"

"What do you think I'm talking about, dimwit? We need to kill that little shit, and we need to do it soon."

*Hello?*

"And here's how we're gonna do it: Tomorrow night, when everybody's asleep, we'll sneak into his cabin, pull him out of bed, carry him outside, and hit him over the head with a baseball bat—nice and clean. Then we'll haul his body out to Parson's Peak and throw it over the cliff."

"And just how do you propose getting him out of the cabin without his raising bloody hell and waking up the entire camp?"

"Simple—the element of surprise. We'll stuff a sock in his mouth and cover it with duct tape for good measure. Before he knows what's happening, the Smith brothers will carry him outside. If we do this right, it'll look like he threw himself over the cliff. Williamson's been acting strange all week. He's been walking around like a zombie. Everybody's noticed. Everybody knows he's unstable and capable of anything, even suicide."

*Hello?*

"This is a stupid plan. Someone is bound to wake up while we're dragging him out of the cabin. And even if it succeeds, we'll be the first ones they suspect. I think we should come clean. I'm going to see Mr. Gordon right now."

Henry started to go, but Spencer grabbed him by the arm.

"You're not going anywhere. If you breathe a word to anybody, we'll tell them it was all your idea. Besides, Henry, you were the man at the helm."

Theodore nodded. "That's right, Henry. You were."

"But, Theodore, you know Spencer made me do it! Thaddeus? Help me out here."

"I'm with my brother and Spencer on this one, Hen. Sorry, dude."

"One more thing." Spencer smiled coldly. "I've still got that bottle, and it has your fingerprints all over it."

*Hello?*

Opening my eyes, I was instantly transported back to the rec center. Grace Kelly was putting the phone down when a man with a thin moustache wearing gray gloves and an overcoat stepped forward from the shadows. He slipped a scarf around her lovely neck and proceeded to strangle her. The phone fell from her hand. Her husband, who was on the other end of the line, listened as she fought for her life. During the struggle, she reached for a pair of scissors and stabbed the man in the back, killing him.

I sat straight up in bed in a cold sweat. The cabin was pitch dark. The other boys were sound asleep. *It was just a dream, just a dream, just a dream . . .*

*Sunday, August 8, 1976*

After dinner, I snuck away to my very own private bathroom facility in the woods. This "bathroom facility," located a few hundred feet behind Cabin Row, was nothing more than a fallen tree trunk and a shallow crater I had dug into the earth a few days after the water-balloon incident. It had been storming most of the afternoon. The ground was still moist. The trunk's bark glistened.

For the first time since the day of the dance, I lowered myself into squatting position. A sharp jolt rose up from deep inside my body. I had been feeling severe discomfort and pain throughout the week, but nothing like this. It was like a serrated knife tearing through the flesh between my legs. Tears filled my eyes and spilled onto my cheeks. *It hurts sooooo much. Please, God, make it stop.* In spite of my desperate appeal to God, the pain skyrocketed. Little yellow stars swirled all around me, slowly at first and then more and more rapidly. Finally, I blacked out.

When I came to, I was lying in the dirt a few feet from the tree trunk. It was still light out, so I knew not much time had passed. With my shorts wrapped snuggly around my ankles,

I somehow managed to stagger to my feet and peer over the trunk, where I discovered a filthy, bloody mess strewn across the crater. *Oh my God! Is that from me? Now what? Should I go to the camp doctor? No. No way. He would only ask questions— questions I can't answer.* Resolving to keep my medical condition a secret, I dropped to my knees and scooped one handful of loose soil after another into the hole. Soon, the evidence was concealed.

After cleaning myself with rain-drenched leaves, I reached for my shorts, which were still binding my ankles, and then I stopped. A curiously shaped object was nestled at the base of a tree not far from where I had been squatting. I pulled up my shorts and waddled over. It was a stone, no larger than a buckeye. I picked it up and cradled it in the palm of my hand. Bronze with a reddish hue, the stone was shaped exactly like a heart—not so much an anatomically correct human heart, but rather the kind of heart one might see on a Valentine's Day card.

I looked west. A golden sun hung low in the August sky. Its rays filtered through the trees and created a patchwork network of shadows that stretched from the heart of the forest to the tips of my sneaker-clad toes. A single tear burned a path across my face and fell into the compost of musty leaves and rich soil below.

My thoughts turned to my father. He had been gone for over two years, but I could still *hear* his deep and resonant voice soothing my ears with words of encouragement as I made my first attempt on a bike without training wheels, *see* his amber eyes twinkle and dimples deepen as his face broke into a warm smile of fatherly pride, and *smell* the rich, leathery aroma of his skin as he comforted me with a hug following my first fall.

The sun dipped below the treetops, and a stiff breeze barreled through the forest. A chill coursed through my bones. I looked down at the heart-shaped stone for comfort. "It's perfect," I decided out loud. Swaying in the wind, the trees bowed and nodded their agreement. "More than perfect." I placed it carefully into my pocket and made my way back to the cabin.

I arrived to find the others busy with Sunday evening chores—cleaning the bathroom, sweeping the floor, returning random personal items to their footlockers, changing their bedsheets, and stuffing their laundry bags for pickup in the morning. Everything had to be absolutely flawless for inspection; we wouldn't be permitted to attend campfire until it was. The screen door slammed a little too loudly behind me. Wayne glowered disdainfully but didn't bother to articulate his displeasure. A few of the boys, including Miles, glanced up and then quickly returned to their chores. Not a word was spoken. I hurried over to my bunk to tidy up my personal area.

Kneeling in front of my footlocker to put away my shoes, I reached for the latch and opened it.

*FAGGOT*

The word was scrawled hideously across the inside of the lid in big red letters. I slammed it shut and became very still. *They knew.* They knew all about what had happened at the pond. I was stunned but didn't cry. I wouldn't give them the satisfaction. My face turned red hot, and my heart thundered in my chest like an orchestral timpani, but still I didn't cry.

One of the boys, probably Keith, snickered. "He's crying."

A few others giggled.

"I'm not," I said in as brave a voice as I could muster.

I understood what the word *faggot* meant. But even as early as age five, I had known I preferred girls. Preferred them? *Loved them!* Inevitably, all blood would rush from my head and my knobby little knees would turn to jelly at first sight of a pretty face. More than once, I had to reach for a nearby object—a table, a chair, or even a wall—to steady myself.

I got up off the floor and shimmied up the back end of the bunk I shared with Salad Bowl. As I started to make my bed, the memory of my first love, a five-year-old named Amy, flashed into my mind. Amy had blonde curls, sparkling electric-blue eyes, and a mischievous smile. She was filled with such exuberance and unbridled passion for life that a career on stage was all but inevitable. And then there was Christine, full of life like Amy, but so different from her in every other way. Christine had long, straight chestnut hair that flowed well past her shoulders and eyes the color of warm mahogany. There was nothing mischievous about Christine. Kind and generous to all—perhaps to a fault—she was adored by everyone at school, even our third-grade teacher, Mrs. Copeland. I never spoke to anyone of my feelings for either Amy or Christine but rather kept them hidden in a secret place that belonged only to me.

My heart fluttered. I allowed a momentary smile to light up my face—but then caught myself. I had no right to be happy. Feeling good was an indulgence I didn't deserve. There was something horribly wrong with me, and that would never ever change. I was defective. I couldn't articulate the nature of my defect, but I knew it was there. I could feel it. *If only . . . if only Daddy were here, he would make everything okay. If only he hadn't . . . hadn't . . .*

Pulling my bedsheets tight and tucking them into make-shift hospital corners, I decided nothing mattered anymore, not after what had happened at the pond. Keith Hardaway could write or say whatever he wanted about me. I didn't care.

Then, for a brief moment, I felt a presence. A loving hand on my shoulder. The scent of leather . . . and Old Spice.

*Ricky . . .*

"Daddy?"

I took a furtive look, but he wasn't there. The other boys had returned to their chores, and Wayne was sitting on his bed, tuning his guitar. *I'm being stupid. It's just my imagination . . .* I returned my attention to my hospital corners and finished making the bed. Inspection was in ten minutes, and I didn't want to miss campfire. It was one of only two activities I really looked forward to each week—the other being movie night, of course.

The bedsprings let out a sigh of relief as I began my descent. Floorboards creaked under the weight of my foot and the feet of others moving purposefully about the room. Wayne lightly strummed his guitar. A rogue wind rustled hauntingly through the leaves of the red maples clustered behind Cabin Row. A cheer arose from a few cabins away, announcing the first successful inspection of the week.

Everything stopped. The world became perfectly still. The only sound was the sound of my beating heart. *Lub-DUB, lub-DUB, lub-DUB . . .*

*Ricky . . .*

*Daddy? Is that you?*

*Yes, Ricky.*

*Daddy, please help me. I can't . . . I can't do this anymore. It's too hard. I need you.*

*Everything is going to be okay . . .*

*How, Daddy? How will it be okay?*

*Listen to me, Ricky, and listen carefully. Very soon you will find yourself at the end of a dirt road, only inches from a threshold . . . a threshold into another world—a glorious world, one of infinite possibility. You'll be standing there contemplating your next move when a gust of wind whispers, "Have faith." When you hear those magic words, it'll be time for you to cross the threshold and begin your journey . . .*

*Home? My journey home? All I want to do is go home, Daddy.*

*First you will need to face your greatest fear . . .*

*My greatest fear? I don't think I can.*

*Yes, you can, Ricky. Trust yourself and have faith.*

*But, Daddy . . .*

*Have faith.*

*But, Daddy . . . Daddy? Daddy?*

Outside, the maple leaves rustled in the wind. Inside, the floorboards resumed their creaking under the feet of boys busy putting the final touches on the cabin for weekly inspection. A soulful chord rose from the strings of Wayne's guitar and lingered for a moment or two before diffusing into the rafters.

My other foot tapped the floor, completing my descent from the bunk.

*Daddy?* The voice had sounded like my father's, but . . .

*Have faith, Ricky.*

Arriving at Parson's Peak minutes before the beginning of campfire, I found a spot toward the top of the amphitheater and settled in beneath a star-glazed sky. No one sat within ten feet of me in either direction. I had room to breathe. A few wisps of campfire smoke floated upward and formed a wreath above my head before fading into the darkness. From my vantage point, I could see all the lower tiers, which were inundated with a roaring sea of campers. The noise reverberated throughout the amphitheater and pierced my eardrums like an arrow from the bow of Burning Sky. Digging into my pocket, I clasped the heart-shaped stone and rolled it around in my fingers.

Mr. Gordon rose from his seat, and the campers settled down. As he rattled off a series of announcements, I gazed mindlessly into a small and isolated cluster of boys sitting near the fire on the opposite side of the amphitheater. After a few moments, their faces came into focus. It was Spencer, Henry, Theodore, and Thaddeus, huddled together at the far end of the second row, perhaps plotting their next conspiracy.

Spencer looked up at me, his cold eyes catching the fire's light, and he winked. Even from that distance, there could be no mistake—the bastard had winked at me. My blood ran cold, but I didn't flinch. My face remained expressionless. As I stared back at him, my fear gradually evaporated into the still night air until I felt nothing, nothing at all.

Conceding defeat in our meaningless game of chicken, I broke eye contact, looked away, and rested my gaze into the fire. At its core, the flames writhed and twisted like a raging pit of snakes. Yet I remained unmoved . . .

A sound drifted into my ear. It was the evening's first few notes of music.

A senior counselor named Dennis stood alone in front of the fire, playing a guitar and crooning a bittersweet melody into the night. Dennis was the only African American in camp. Unlike most of the other counselors, who sported long hair and scruffy beards, he was well groomed and clean shaven. His wiry curls were cut so short that his scalp gleamed in the campfire's light. He carried himself with a dignified, professorial air, wearing small-framed spectacles with lenses that formed perfect geometric circles. He had a square jaw and large forearms yet held his guitar in a gentle and loving embrace. His demeanor was quiet but confident. His voice comforted me yet left me feeling sad and lonely.

He sang Don McLean's "Vincent," homage to the life of tragically misunderstood artist Vincent van Gogh, a song inspired at least in part by his painting *The Starry Night*.

The snake pit mellowed into a steady crackle. Its amber glow reflected off the faces of scores of boys falling one by one into a collective hypnotic trance. *I wonder if we're listening to the same music . . . if it's touching their hearts in the same way it's touching mine.* I yearned to connect with them, to be a part of their community. But that wasn't possible. I didn't belong. I could never belong. I was separated from their world by a hopelessly high stone wall that cast a dark shadow of shame across my face. There was no escaping the shadow's reach. It followed me wherever I went.

*I don't belong here. I need to leave . . . tonight . . .*

After a brief pause, the sound of another guitar swept through the amphitheater. I looked down. It was my cabin's junior counselor, Ryan. *Ryan?* He'd been nice in the beginning but had become all but invisible over the past couple of weeks. Sitting now in the first row and staring intensely into the fire, he performed an achingly soulful version of Bob Dylan's "You Ain't Goin' Nowhere."

*This song's for you, Ricky.*

*But I can't stand it here any longer . . . if . . . if only I could fly . . . fly far, far away . . .*

Wayne and the camp's water-skiing instructor, a California transplant named Logan, stepped forward for a performance of dueling guitars. Logan was a tall and exceptionally lean young man with shoulder-length blond hair that seemed to flow from his scalp like a waterfall. Pausing to sweep the hair out of his eyes, Logan glanced at Wayne before striking the first chord of America's "Sandman."

*The Sandman is coming for you, Ricky . . .*

*Who's there?*

*He's coming . . .*

*The Sandman? Who is the Sandman?*

An easterly wind blew across the exposed side of Parson's Peak, swirled into the amphitheater, and left me shivering against its cold chill. Feeling naked and more than a little vulnerable, I folded my twiggy arms across my chest in a protective posture. But the chill passed through my skin and seeped into my bones, turning them into brittle icicles. Meanwhile, Wayne and Logan, the latter with his long blond hair flying free in the swirling wind, strummed their guitars with ever-increasing ferocity. The song soared to a dramatic crescendo and came to an abrupt stop.

In the ensuing silence, Wayne and Logan receded into the shadows. Once again, Dennis stepped in front of the fire. He took a moment to retune his guitar and then played, his fingers moving over the strings with the kind of fluid grace one would expect only from one of God's most favored creatures. In response, the strings came to life and fluttered into the most exquisite and hauntingly beautiful sound I had ever heard. It was Paul Simon's "The Sound of Silence." Ever so gradually, my bones began to thaw.

*Is it possible? Is it possible such music can exist in a world where we treat each other the way we do . . .*

*Just listen, Ricky.*

*Miles . . . so misunderstood . . . and the way they bully him . . . it's just so unfair! Spencer . . . Spencer Black . . . those cold, lifeless eyes . . . that terrible breath . . . the pond . . .*

*Just listen . . .*

*Daddy? Is that you again? Are you there?*

*Yes, Ricky, I'm here.*

*Where?*

*Look inward . . . keep looking inward . . . you will find the answers to all your questions in the silence . . .*

*In the silence?*

*. . . your wisdom is within you . . . in the silence . . .*

*But . . .*

*. . . all true wisdom lies in the silence . . .*

I tried listening but was overwhelmed by a flood of emotion that filled my chest before rising upward and becoming lodged in my throat like a feculent piece of raw brisket. Choking on it, I could barely breathe. Tears stung my eyes, but I refused to cry—to do so would be unthinkable. Summoning all my strength, I pushed the emotion down into the pit of my stomach and held it there as tightly as I could—as if my life depended on it. Then I remembered my father's words and listened to the silence.

When campfire broke for the night, the boys of Camp Abenaki Valley filed quietly out of the amphitheater. Only when the last of them had vacated the premises did I stand up and descend toward the fire, which had already begun to burn itself out. The chill that had taken up residence in my bones was almost gone. I passed the fire and left Parson's Peak behind. Making my way in the dark along the narrow and winding path back to Cabin Row, I became acutely aware of the faint smell of campfire smoke in my hair and in the fibers of my clothes. Up ahead, a murmur grew into the sound of boys singing in a subdued yet melodious tone.

> *Abenaki honor*
> *We carry thee*
> *Through these woods and home again . . .*

*Remember, Ricky—all true wisdom lies in the silence . . .*

# CHAPTER TEN

*Sunday, August 8–Monday, August 9, 1976*

"LIGHTS OUT!" HOLLERED WAYNE.

I climbed into my bunk and pulled the sheets and blanket up to my chin. Clutching my heart-shaped stone in both hands, I felt strangely comforted. Drowsiness set in. Somehow, the stone found its way to my lips; I kissed it softly. It smelled and tasted like the earth. I wondered how old it was. Like all things, I reasoned, it must have been born . . . *millions . . . maybe even billions of years ago . . . but would it, could it ever die* . . . Pressing my lips to the stone again, I drifted off to sleep.

It was a fitful sleep fraught with ghostly images moving in and out of form. With Wayne and Logan's version of "Sandman" playing in the background, faces appeared and disappeared in a gradually accelerating montage projected onto the silver screen of my subconscious mind. Willy, Sam, Danny, Mom, Mr. Gordon, and Neil Kennedy came and went.

*The Sandman is coming for you, Ricky.*

Miles watching me, watching me . . .

*He's coming.*

. . . Jihad, his eyes ablaze and fists poised to deliver a knock-out blow . . .

*You want another one?*

. . . Henry Hatfield as an anthropomorphic pig transforming into a translucent lamb and prancing through a pasture blooming with wildflowers—a brilliant spray of reds and oranges radiating into a glistening sea of yellow, blue, indigo, and violet . . .

. . . my father . . .

*The Sandman is coming.*

. . . a dark and faceless figure shrouded in a hood . . .

*He's here!*

Again my father appeared and was replaced by the hooded apparition . . . and again . . . and again . . . and again as I bounced back and forth between the polar extremes of hope and despair.

The music stopped, and all images retreated through a cobweb-draped door fitted with medieval wrought-iron strap hinges. The hinges were held in place by bolts the size and shape of human eyeballs. One of them winked. The door swung shut with a heavy thud. There was no sound and no light, only silence and darkness. Then, slowly, very slowly, the hooded figure rematerialized before me. But this time, it bore a face—the face of Spencer Black.

I opened my eyes, and Spencer vanished. The wind blew. A coyote howled. The branch of a maple knocked at the cabin's rear window. I sat up.

"I've got to get out of here," I whispered, the words passing over my lips and trickling unheard into the darkness. *Now. Right now.*

First finding my precious stone, I slipped out from under the covers and inched toward the end of the bed. Once there, I managed somehow to hoist myself over the footboard and begin my descent without causing the metal frame to squeak. Determined not to disturb the rhythmic sound of breathing that filled the room, I reached ever so gingerly for the floor with the tips of my toes and gradually transferred my full weight onto its surface. The board under my feet creaked. I froze. Wayne let out a snort. Salad Bowl yawned, shifted his body, and returned to never-never land. Only when I was absolutely certain everybody in the cabin was once more sleeping peacefully did I take a cautious step in the direction of my footlocker, and another, and then another, until I was looking straight down at the enormous casket that housed all my worldly belongings.

The easy part was behind me. Next I needed to retrieve a set of clothes, negotiate a minefield of creaky floorboards, and sneak out the door without waking anybody.

My heart beating furiously, I bent down slowly until I was kneeling on the floor. My head pounded. My stomach gurgled. My knees ached. I placed my sweaty fingertips on the footlocker's latch and paused. Extreme caution was required at this juncture. My footlocker was situated against the wall and wedged between two bunk beds—the one belonging to Salad Bowl and me on one side, and the one occupied by Tony and Andrew on the other. Tony slept on the top bunk, so he was less a concern than the others. But I was no more than a whisper away from Andrew on my left and Salad Bowl on my right. The slightest miscue would most certainly wake either or both of them.

Holding my breath, I clicked open the latch. Salad Bowl stirred but didn't wake. Dead to the world, Andrew didn't so much as twitch. *So far, so good.* I raised the lid. Ignoring the big red letters painted on its inside cover, I grabbed my sneakers, a pair of jeans, and a blue-and-white Camp Abenaki Valley T-shirt. Gently closing the lid, I turned away and tiptoed to the front door. *Almost home free . . .*

I reached for the doorknob. Something behind me rustled. I stopped breathing and listened. It was the sound of sheets and blankets being pushed aside by a waking camper! I spun around and peered into the dark room. At first I saw nothing, and then a shadowy silhouette slowly rose from the bottom bunk of the bed nearest the bathroom. Continuing its ghostly ascent, the silhouette emerged from the darkness like the Great Pumpkin from Linus's pumpkin patch—only this Great Pumpkin was not Snoopy but Miles Romano.

Sitting straight up in bed, Miles said not a word and moved not a muscle. He looked right at me, those eyes of his boring into my skull with a blank, otherworldly stare. It was as if the Miles I knew weren't there at all. I felt totally exposed, like standing naked before a perfect stranger.

For a full minute—I knew it was a minute because I counted the seconds in my head—I stood motionless by the door. His stare didn't waver. Then it occurred to me that he might be asleep, that he might not be able to see me at all. But how could that be possible? His eyes were wide open! Suddenly they melted into a warm, buttery gaze. Recognizing me now, he smiled and gave the thumbs-up sign before lowering himself back into his bunk. Thinking I would never see him again, I waved goodbye, but it was too late. His eyes were closed, and he was fast asleep.

With my clothes tucked safely under an arm and my shoes and the stone in hand, I rotated toward the door and carefully placed my free hand on the knob. Slowly, very slowly, I turned it until the latch clicked and released. Trying to breathe normally, I opened the door just wide enough to slip through, leaned my shoulder onto the outer screen, and gently pushed. It opened with a screech, but there was no turning back now. I stepped out into the cool night air and, exercising the utmost degree of care, closed both doors behind me.

*Free at last!*

Under a clear sky lit by a moon just one day shy of becoming full, I sat down on the front steps and quickly dressed. Feeling more exhilarated than scared, I began walking briskly along Cabin Row toward the mess hall. Thus, under the guidance of that brightly shining gibbous moon, my life's journey was set inexorably into motion. Nothing would ever be the same.

A long, slow, high-pitched screech, like fingernails on a chalkboard, stopped me dead in my tracks. A cluster of pins and needles sprouted on the back of my neck. Cringing, I held still until the screeching ended abruptly with the slam of a screen door, which very nearly caused me to jump out of my skin. A loudly whispered "Damn!" echoed from below and faded into the night.

From my vantage point at the far end of Cabin Row, I spied a tall, lanky figure slouching forward and striding swiftly away from the front porch of Parson's Abode. It was Spencer Black. Even from a distance equivalent to the length of a football field, I recognized his long gait and distinctive posture. Although the moon was more than bright enough to light his way, he carried a flashlight and pointed it at his feet while making a beeline up the hill and toward my cabin. Instinctively, I stepped back and attempted to hide myself in the shadows cast by the red maples behind me.

Spencer met three shadowy figures at my cabin's front steps. One of the figures held something that resembled a baseball bat. After a few minutes of what appeared to be a heated discussion, Spencer and the two largest figures climbed the steps and disappeared inside. One figure, who I deduced was Henry Hatfield, remained outside and glanced around nervously. I stepped forward to get a better look. He turned in my direction and spotted me. I froze, waiting for him to alert his accomplices. But instead, he did a curious thing. Without making a sound, he waved his arms in a frenzied shooing motion, as if urging me to continue my journey away from Cabin Row.

Just when it dawned on me that Henry might actually be trying to help, Spencer and the two Smith brothers emerged from the cabin and caught him in the act. Hesitating for only a split second, they ran down the steps and right over him. Henry fell to the ground. Spencer and the two colossal Smiths sprinted in my direction.

"Run, Ricky!" Henry shouted, his voice echoing up and down Cabin Row.

By this time, I was in no further need of urging. I turned to run but was stopped short by a sharp pain between my legs, just like one I had experienced a few hours earlier behind Cabin Row. I tried to run through it but fell to the ground. The little yellow stars returned, swirling cyclonically in front of my eyes. I couldn't afford to lose consciousness, not this time. I glanced over my shoulder. Through a starry kaleidoscope, I could see them coming for me and gaining ground fast.

I struggled to my feet and tried once again to run, to be the runner I had been in school, where they nicknamed me the "Roadrunner." Yet the best I could manage was to limp through the sensation of a samurai sword slicing through the middle of my body.

Again I fell.

Getting back up and gritting my teeth, I created forward momentum by grabbing one leg with both hands and forcing it to swing forward through the pain. Then I grabbed the other leg and forced it forward. I repeated this procedure over and over until I was hobbling forward at a decent clip, no longer needing my hands to create momentum.

When I reached the mess hall, I veered left. A blast of adrenaline propelled me forward. I gained speed. Continuing to accelerate, I passed the mess hall and left it behind. I was actually running now! I could still feel the pain but no longer cared. All that mattered was outrunning the three boys on my tail and somehow finding a way to survive the night.

I glanced back—they were gaining on me. Shifting into overdrive, I ran faster than I ever had in school and made it to the welcome area and visitors' parking lot in seconds flat. Still they came, a pack of ravenous hyenas, the ground rumbling beneath their feet. Without slowing, I continued on until I reached the totem poles, beyond which lay the dirt road leading out of camp.

*The Tunnel of Doom.*

I stopped short. The moonlight would be unable to penetrate the thick canopy of tangled branches and overgrown foliage that covered the mile-long dirt road. If I went on, I would be blind—and at the mercy of Burning Sky and any other evil spirits that haunted these woods.

Spencer, Theodore, and Thaddeus crossed the visitors' lot. The ground thundered now. They would be on me in seconds.

I flung myself headlong into the tunnel's mouth.

Running like an escaped convict, I passed the first sharp bend in the road. The moonlight faded into oblivion. The tunnel swallowed me whole. I was all alone and without any means of navigation, yet I didn't slow down. Running past the point of exhaustion, I disappeared deeper and deeper into the whale's belly.

A rut in the road leapt up and caught me by the ankle. My face hit the dirt. I got up, looked back, and saw nothing—only an endless black hole. The only sound was the sound of my own breathing. Perhaps they were too scared, or too smart, to follow.

A menacing voice filled the tunnel. "We'll get you when you come back, you—you lousy son of a bitch . . . if Burning Sky doesn't get to you first, that is . . ."

"I'm not coming back!" I yelled defiantly.

There was no reply.

I reached into my pocket and clutched the heart-shaped stone, drawing from it both strength and courage. Then I peered ahead and stepped forward with both hands stretching out into the darkness. Completely blind, I inched along until I bumped into a tree by the side of the road and stumbled into the woods. Righting my course and feeling my way from one tree to the next, I continued on. Eventually, my eyes adjusted to the dark, allowing me to discern a vague line of demarcation between the edge of the woods and the dirt road. Using this line as a guide, I navigated the road one step at a time.

Backed by a chorus of crickets filling the woods with a steady rhythm of chirping, an owl launched into a solo performance, apparently curious as to my identity. "Whooo . . . ooo . . . ooo-oooo? Whooo . . . ooo . . . ooo-ooooo?"

Feeling like an intruder in the owl's domain, I replied tentatively, "I'm Ricky."

"Whooo?"

The owl was interrupted by a rustling at my feet. A large four-legged creature with eyes ablaze emerged from the woods, darted across my path, and scurried to the other side of the road, where it disappeared into the thick underbrush.

My heart beating wildly, I blurted out after the creature, "What are you? A coyote? A wolf?"

*A werewolf?*

My snail-paced trek continued.

*Ba-da-dum, ba-da-dum, ba-da-dum, ba-da-dum . . .*

I became very still and strained my ears to hear this new sound—an eerie cadence that seemed to come from deep in the woods and gallop through the middle of my head.

*Ba-da-dum, ba-da-dum, ba-da-dum, ba-da-dum . . .*

It faded away.

*Was that . . . could that be . . . the horse of Burning Sky?*

As if in response, a sinister voice echoed up and down the tunnel. *These are my woods . . . woods . . . woods . . .*

*Burning Sky? Ridiculous. Burning Sky is nothing but a myth.*

Pushing all thoughts of Burning Sky out of my head, I pressed on. Up ahead, a tiny dot of light appeared. An ear-splitting wail ballooned into a maniacal falsetto and descended into a long series of raspy sobs. *Someone's crying!* As I drew closer, I could see the light was coming from a lamp perched on a nightstand conspicuously situated in the middle of the road. Discolored and covered with dust and scorch marks, the lamp's shade diffused a circle of pale-yellow luminescence around the stand and surrounding area. Within the circle, a woman sat on the edge of a bed with her head buried in her hands. *It's Mom!* A lump swelled in my throat.

"What . . . what is it, Mom?" I asked, my voice quivering with dread.

She looked up at me with red, puffy eyes. *Ricky, come sit down*, she said gravely, reaching her arms out to me.

"Mom, you're scaring me. What is it? Where's Dad?"

Grasping me by the shoulders, she looked me straight in the eyes and said, *Your father died last night . . .*

Before I could respond, my mother and all the furniture vanished, leaving me alone again in the desolate blackness.

I pressed on with my hands reaching out into the void. My eyes hadn't yet readjusted to the dark when suddenly the entire tunnel was lit up by the luminous image of a boy with skin the color of a shiny penny flying out of the woods in a heart-stopping flourish. It was Jihad. He glared at me with his fists cocked. *You want another one?*

Another image flew out of the woods. It was Henry Hatfield, coming at me with his Buck knife drawn. *You're really asking for it, aren't you, Puke?*

"You're not real," I declared with as much conviction as I could muster. Keeping my eyes focused straight ahead in a Herculean effort to avoid seeing these ghostly images, I continued down the dirt road. As if responding to my will, Jihad and Henry receded into the forest, leaving me alone in the dark once again.

Just as I was breathing out a sigh of relief, the horse returned.

*Ba-da-dum, ba-da-dum, ba-da-dum, ba-da-dum . . .*

My blood turned cold. This time it wasn't nearly as distant as before. And this time, the ground trembled under the soles of my feet.

*Ba-da-dum, ba-da-dum, ba-da-dum, ba-da-dum . . .*

Approaching from all directions, the sound grew louder and louder. But just when it was about to reach its crescendo, it broke off and faded away, leaving only silence in its wake. The Tunnel of Doom was devoid of all sound. Even the owl and crickets had decided to retire for the night.

I walked in this blessed silence until the tunnel started to tinkle like a chorus of bells in a horror movie. It was a group of boys giggling mischievously. From the prepubescent pitch of their voices, I guessed they were about my age. I couldn't see them, but I knew I was surrounded. They had been stalking me, and now they had me. I stopped in my tracks.

*Incoming!*

Three objects came at me from above in rapid-fire succession. Water balloons—yellow, blue, and red—passed right through me and disappeared into the ground at my feet. The giggling exploded into a frenzy of laughter.

*Direct hit! Pilot to bombardier, pilot to bombardier—mission complete!*

The laughter subsided and faded into the woods. It returned, though, louder and meaner. Light flooded the tunnel and revealed a room full of boys with their backs to me. They were clustered together in a chaotic semicircle, pointing and laughing at something. I pushed my way through the crowd and saw the object of their torment: Miles. He was nailed to the back wall by his underwear, his feet dangling uselessly beneath him, his face tangled into a knot of anguish.

*Ricky! Don't just stand there with your hands in your pockets. Do something. Help me. Please!*

*Don't listen to him*, a voice interjected. *If you want to fit in here, you won't do a thing.*

It was Jeffrey Underwood, standing next to me with his arms crossed. He wasn't laughing. To Jeffrey, this was a very serious matter.

I took a step backward.

*Coward.*

I opened my mouth to attempt an explanation, but Miles dematerialized, leaving behind nothing but an old rusty nail on the wall. Crooked and pointing downward at the floor, the nail seemed hardly capable of supporting the weight of a ten-year-old boy, even one as scrawny as Miles. I stepped forward to investigate, but Jeffrey and the entire scene disintegrated in a sudden flash of light.

Again the Tunnel of Doom's insatiable darkness swallowed me whole. It was quiet—quiet as an abandoned graveyard on a cold, moonless night in the dead of winter. I forged ahead.

Somewhere out there in the world, a clock was keeping track of time, but not in that infernal and seemingly endless tunnel. It might have been a matter of seconds since my encounter with Miles. Or minutes. Or even hours. I had no way of knowing, as I had lost all ability to sense the passage of time. Adding to my distress, there were no visible landmarks by which to judge my progress. *Progress?* Was I even making progress? It was possible, I concluded, even likely, that I had become turned around somewhere along the way and was heading back toward camp. Disoriented, tired, and discouraged, I was ready to give up all hope that I would ever reach the tunnel's end.

Something behind me skittered. A loose piece of gravel?

I stopped.

"Hello? Is someone there?"

No response.

*It must have been just . . . just my imagination . . . but it seemed so real! Didn't it?*

I increased my pace.

*The Sandman is coming for you, Ricky.*

In my haste, I tripped over the uneven terrain and fell forward through space—*I'm so damn clumsy*—until . . . *splash* . . . I landed facedown in a shallow pool of water. *Water? Where did the water come from?* I peeled my face out of the silt and was confronted by the gaping eye sockets of a rotting skull.

*Ricky, my boy, I'm afraid you have no one to blame but yourself . . .*

*Mr. Gordon?*

The water evaporated and left me on dry land, lying flat on my stomach and unable to move. I was paralyzed from head to toe. I tried to get to my hands and knees, but my muscles refused to obey my commands.

*You dug your own grave, so just shut up and lie in it!*

*Whi-kisssh!*

The hickory branch crashed down across my back. My flesh ignited.

*Couldn't even finish a quarter-mile swim . . .*

Everything went black.

The foul odor of cigarettes and beer smacked me in the face. I opened my eyes. Spencer's nose was inches from mine. I gagged and choked on the stench of his terrible breath.

*Fuck this Williamson kid . . .*

"You're not real!"

*Do it! Do it! Do it!*

"None of this is real!"

*Good work, Henry. You've done your duty, and you've done it well . . . I'll take it from here . . .*

"*No!*"

All images dissolved into the darkness. Silence returned to the tunnel. I picked myself up off the ground and brushed the dirt from my T-shirt. Then, feeling my way along the edge of the road, I resumed my trek. There was no end in sight.

Something behind me disturbed the silence.

*That sound again! I knew I hadn't imagined it.*

I stopped. It stopped. I moved. It moved. It sounded like footsteps—a single pair of footsteps.

Mr. Gordon's rotting skull reappeared. From behind a desk, it peered at me through Coke-bottle lenses. *I have grave concerns, Ricky . . .*

The footsteps got louder and closer. I walked faster.

*Ricky, I want to help you, but there's nothing I can do unless you tell me the truth . . .*

The footsteps were almost on top of me. Hampered at first by the pain between my legs, I worked my way up to an awkward trot and accelerated into a full sprint. The footsteps drew closer. Then suddenly they were drowned out by the thunder of a horse at full gallop.

*Ba-da-dum, ba-da-dum, ba-da-dum, ba-da-dum . . .*

On horseback and carrying a giant bow with arrow drawn, Burning Sky charged right at me. His jet-black beast had fiery crimson eyes. Hot smoke billowed from its flaring nostrils. Its teeth were stained yellow. Riding without a saddle, the chiseled warrior was naked from the waist up. Lit from within, his translucent skin glowed with a bronze tint. His hair was cut in classic Mohawk style, forming a sable racing stripe that stood straight up from the top of his otherwise bald head. Three eagle feathers dangled loosely to one side of his face, which was hidden behind a thick screen of bloodred war paint and set in a hard scowl. Glaring down at me, he let out an earsplitting war cry and bellowed over the sound of his beast's hooves pounding the earth.

*These are my woods . . . I will have my revenge!*

I closed my eyes and braced for impact, but nothing happened. I opened them and saw no sign of Burning Sky or his horse. *They must have passed right through me.* What I did see, however, was a soft speck of light—a radiant ball of cotton shining from a point about a hundred yards ahead.

*I've made it! I've made it through the Tunnel of Doom!*

Turning around to see if Burning Sky had left behind any trace of his visit, I was confronted by a dark figure towering over me with a baseball bat raised over its head. It was Spencer Black! He had been following me the entire time. And now, he was upon me, preparing to strike what would surely be a fatal blow.

"Gotcha!" he growled.

Without pausing to think, I delivered a swift kick that caught him right between the legs. The bat flew into the air. He went down in a lump, rolling on the ground and clutching his gonads with both hands. I dashed for the end of the tunnel and left him behind, writhing in agony and howling into the night like a mortally wounded cur.

I reached the tunnel's end. The sky opened above me. The moon greeted me with a brilliant smile. I stopped, raised my arms overhead, and sang out a euphoric "Thank you!" before bending forward and resting my hands on my knees. Taking a moment there to catch my breath, I looked down at my feet, which were planted firmly in the grainy dust of the dirt road. No more than an inch or two away was the smoothly paved, shiny black surface of the state highway gleaming in the moonlight. One more step, and I would be standing on Maine State Route 4.

I had arrived at the threshold. On one side lay Camp Abenaki Valley and all my demons. On the other side lay the world of infinite possibility the voice in my cabin had promised would be awaiting me. If that voice was to be believed, the other side represented a fresh start—the new beginning I had been longing for.

But I was not yet willing to cross the threshold. Something held me back. Something heavy. I was both relieved and exhilarated to have made it this far yet plagued with worry and doubt regarding the future—an uncertain future at best. I was excited at the prospect of taking my life into my own hands yet terrified of the possibility of failure. And what if the voice in my cabin didn't belong to my father but to the devil assuming a pleasing shape? What then?

Standing at the edge of this tantalizing threshold, I pictured myself on a high dive. It was the grand opening of the South Orange community swimming pool. I was eight years old. My father had been gone for eight months. With my feet at the very end of the board and my toes hanging perilously over the edge, I gazed down upon a golden ring of sunlight reflecting off the aqua-tinted water below. My head spun. My breathing became shallow and labored. My stomach crawled up into my throat in a spasm of nausea. My heart thumped madly in my chest. *It's too much . . . I can't do this . . .*

*I want to jump. I do . . . I really do . . . but my body is covered in chains. I'm in a tiny cell. There's no door—only a window throwing striped shadows at my feet. I'm being held prisoner . . . by fear . . . fear of taking that step . . . that one step . . . that teensy-weensy step over the end of the board and downward into the unknown . . .*

A horn blared. I jumped back from the highway. An eighteen-wheel Mack truck rolled by and blazed north toward the Canadian border. I watched until it was gone. Then I turned my gaze south and imagined I could see home, over three hundred miles away. *My room, my very own bed . . .*

*First you will need to face your greatest fear . . .*

I looked over my shoulder and into the Tunnel of Doom. Although I couldn't see him, I knew Spencer was still there by the pitiful moans escaping from the tunnel's mouth. He was incapacitated and no longer a threat. His presence didn't factor one way or the other into my decision. I looked southward again. *If I start walking now, each step is one step closer . . .*

Gripped by the same fear that had prevented me from jumping off the high dive, I stood frozen in my tracks, unable to move forward and unwilling to go back. Was history destined to repeat itself? Or could I summon the courage, the strength, to break free from the shackles of my fear? To take a leap of—

My thoughts were interrupted by an errant wind blowing from the north—perhaps from as far away as some distant mountaintop in Canada. Roaring with the ferocity of a tornado and assuming the shape of a funnel about my height, the wind swirled down the highway, eased up directly in front of me, and perused my face in an apparent attempt to decide if it was really me. Seeming to make up its mind that I was the real McCoy, it encircled me, wrapped itself around my slender shoulders, and embraced me passionately. A gentle gust broke free from the spinning funnel and caressed my face before flying into the hollow of my ear. At first it was like listening to the sound of the ocean in a seashell.

Then a voice whispered, *Have faith.*

"Have faith?"

*Have faith.*

Summoning all my resources, I stepped boldly across the threshold and onto the highway.

Suddenly my world was filled with the deafening roar of a runaway steam locomotive barreling through the middle of my head. A flash of daylight lit up the earth. The sun rose from the eastern horizon behind me, raced across the sky, and disappeared into the west.

Utterly bewildered, I stepped back onto the dirt road. Then, appearing from over the western horizon, the sun reversed its direction, streaked over my head, plummeted toward the opposite horizon, and vanished into the east. The locomotive in my head came to a screeching halt. Once again it was nighttime.

*Have faith, Ricky . . .*

I took a deep breath and stepped forward. The noise returned. Again the sun rose from the eastern horizon, raced across the sky, and disappeared into the west. A full moon rose to its apex and came to rest directly overhead. A full day had come and gone, come and gone, and come and gone again in a matter of only a few seconds.

It's quiet . . . *mystifyingly* quiet.

Other than my breath rolling into the night in a steady flow of gentle waves, there's no sound of any kind. No crickets chirping. No owls demanding I identify myself. No four-legged creatures rustling in the brush. No ill-tempered spirits on horseback galloping through the woods. No bullfrogs croaking. No loons crying out to me from Parson's Pond. No . . . no . . . no more moans from the mouth of the tunnel. I tilt my head in that direction and stand perfectly still. I listen . . . and listen some more, but I can no longer hear Spencer. *Maybe he's crawling back to his cabin . . .*

I turn south. The moon illuminates the road at my feet. I take a step . . . and another . . . It's a miracle! There's no more pain. I proceed down the middle of the highway toward home, feeling light and free . . . as if walking on air . . .

I prance along like this for miles, encountering not a single vehicle—no eighteen-wheelers, no pickup trucks, no buses, no vans, no cars, no motorcycles—or anything else, really. Not an animal stirs. There are no lightning bugs, mosquitoes, or bats in the sky. There's not even a breath of wind. The grass and bushes and trees by the side of the road are as motionless as a Monet hanging in a gallery at the Met.

The entire world has become perfectly still . . . still and quiet . . . soothingly so . . . A shower of peace washes over me and forms little beads that roll across the blacktop and into the soil at the side of the road. As my sneakers strike the pavement, the sound resonates down the road . . . and far, far into the countryside. I imagine this sound carrying all the way to South Orange, to our redbrick house on the corner of Turrell and Grove, and finally into my mother's bedroom. She wakes with a start and knows instantly I'm coming home.

On I walk . . . and on and on and on . . . but the moon doesn't waver from its fixed position in the sky. It's as if time and all the laws of the physical universe are taking a holiday. Yet I continue merrily on my way toward home, whistling a happy tune.

I'm almost to the border of Maine and New Hampshire now. My journey is leading me through a little harbor town named Kittery. There's nothing special about Kittery, other than the fact that there are no people. None. According to the clock on the bell tower of town hall, it's two fifteen. But even at this ungodly hour, there should be *some* activity—sleepy workers reporting for the graveyard shift at the hydraulics plant on the outskirts of town, a few drunks staggering out of the local tavern, a police car patrolling the neighborhood, a street cleaner sweeping up after the annual block party, or a lone taxi wandering through downtown in search of a fare. Yet there is no activity. Kittery is a ghost town.

Since there's no traffic, I march right down the middle of the street. The bell tower frowns at me as I pass. *Killjoy.*

*Oh, well. Whatever . . .*

A split-level bridge appears up ahead. It reminds me of a bridge my father and I built in the basement with an Erector Set he gave me for my seventh birthday. The top level is for cars and trucks. It's very narrow—there's room for only two lanes of traffic. The lower level is for trains. At least a half-mile

long, the bridge passes over the Piscataqua. On the other side
of the river is the city of Portsmouth, New Hampshire.

Two steel towers rise from the middle of the bridge and
extend into the sky. They look like a pair of giant robots guard-
ing the border. Each tower is crisscrossed with metallic bars
that form dozens of triangles and squares shining brightly in
the moonlight. Beyond the towers is the boxy outline of the
Portsmouth skyline.

I'm about a block from the bridge when a gust of wind
blows into town, followed quickly by a crack of thunder that
shakes the ground under my feet. A bolt of lightning drops
from the sky and strikes the bell tower. Town hall rocks back
and forth on its foundation. The bell clangs loudly. The sky
opens up and dumps a heavy rain on Kittery. Within seconds,
I'm drenched from head to toe.

Before I can even think about looking for shelter, two
tiny pale yellow lights appear, shimmering in the pouring rain.
They're headlights. A car is approaching from the far side of
the bridge.

The roar of an engine closes in on me from behind. I jump
aside just in time to avoid being hit by a very large, top-heavy
delivery truck. Without slowing down, the truck barrels past
me and speeds toward the bridge. It's going much too fast and
accelerating. Its tires are sliding all over the slick road. It reaches
the bridge and veers into the same lane as the approaching car.
Swerving to avoid a head-on collision, the car goes over the rail
and plunges into the river.

I run to the rail. I slip on the pavement. I scramble to my
feet. I peer down into the river. The face of a little girl appears

in the car's rear window. Her eyes are wide. Her mouth opens into a gaping hole.

The river swallows the car.

I jump in. The water is dark and cold. It feels like thousands of pins and needles pricking my skin all at once. I kick against the current and follow the glowing headlights to the river's bottom, where the car has come to rest.

The backseat window on the passenger side is open just wide enough for me to squeeze through, I think. With one last kick, I reach for the window and grab it with both hands. I peek inside. The car is filling up with water. The girl is floating like a rag doll over the back seat. She has pigtails and a button nose. Her eyes are closed now. Her mother is in the driver's seat, trying to free herself from her seat belt. Her head is just barely above the rising water. She sees me and cries for help.

I slip through the window and propel myself toward the girl. She drifts into my arms. Cradling her tiny body to my chest, I return to the window and squeeze through. The current sweeps us downriver, and we rise to the surface. It's no longer raining. I open my mouth and allow the sweet night air to rush in.

Still cradling the girl in my arms, I swim to the riverbank and place her on the soft grass. Her eyes are closed, and her face is blue. I touch her skin. It's cold. Suddenly, she coughs up a stomach full of river water and takes a ragged breath. Her face turns pink.

I gaze down at her and whisper, "I'll be right back."

I sprint upriver and find the spot where the car went under. I dive in. Once again, I'm swimming against the current toward the submerged car. When I get there, I wiggle through the backseat window and discover the interior is completely filled with water. Holding her breath, the little girl's mother is still trying to escape from her seat belt's grasp. She repeatedly pounds the locking mechanism with her fist, but the belt remains strapped tightly across her chest. I reach forward between the two front seats and push the release button. Nothing happens. I push it again, and still nothing happens. I push it a third time. The mechanism clicks. The belt slips out of the buckle and drifts out of the way.

The little girl's mother is free!

She lowers her shoulder into the door. It opens just a crack, but that's all she needs. In one fluid motion, she slithers through the opening and rises to the river's surface.

I slide forward between the two front seats and start to follow her through the driver's side door. But something grabs me by the ankle and pulls me like a slingshot back into the car. I glance down. My foot is tangled in the seat belt. I attempt to pull it free, but the harder I pull, the tighter the belt's grip becomes. My lungs are aching for air. In a panic, I jerk my leg away from the tangle. Something in my knee snaps. Crying out, I swallow a mouthful of water. The door slams shut and hits me hard on the temple. My body relaxes, and my foot comes loose. Bathed in a deep sense of calm and surrender now, I float serenely toward the opening in the backseat window.

*It's okay . . . I've done what I needed to do . . .*

*Something's wrong, and together, we're going to make it right . . .*

*Make it right? But I just saved the little girl and her mother . . .*

*Something's wrong, and together, we're going to make it right, my love . . .*

The water sparkles and pops with the effervescence of an April rain shower. A pair of eyes appears—the most beautiful eyes I've ever seen. Dark and rich as chocolate, they're filled with a soft, warm brilliance that shines into my life from another world. They're the eyes of an angel.

*My angel! You're here. I've waited so long for this moment.*

*Yes, my love, I'm here. I've always been here.*

*Here*, she says, lightly touching my forehead with the tips of her translucent fingers. *And here*, she says, placing an open palm upon my chest. With her eyes fixed upon me in a loving gaze, her face fades into the sparkling bubbles that continue to surround us. When she's gone, another face appears.

*Daddy! Is it really you?*

*My dear, sweet boy . . . my beautiful son . . . my beautiful, courageous son . . . I'm so proud of you, Ricky, so very proud of the young man you've become . . . If words could only express how much I love you . . . You've come so far and accomplished so much, but your journey has only just begun . . . There's something else you need to do.*

*Something else? What, Daddy?*

*Travel into the future . . .*

*The future?*

*Your future—twenty-five years into your future—where you will meet someone in desperate need of your help.*

*Who?*

*A man—a grown man—who has lost his way. He's in pain, a lot of pain, Ricky. He believes the world has treated him unfairly. And he's angry about it . . . very angry. Consumed by rage and obsessed with revenge, he's about to carry out a plan that will have dire consequences. The lives of innocent people are at stake, Ricky. You must do everything in your power to stop him.*

*But what can I do?*

*Befriend him. Become his teacher, his guide . . .*

*Me? But I'm just a kid . . . and he's a grown man!*

*Give me your hands, Ricky.*

*Daddy, I—*

*Give them to me. Now close your eyes.*

There's a twinge in my fingertips—a twinge that flourishes into a surge of warm electricity that passes through my hands and courses up the length of my arms. It's a strange sensation—like pins and needles dancing through my veins—but not unpleasant.

My brain lights up in a kaleidoscopic burst of color. Instantly, I know everything my father knew in his lifetime and more—much more! Somehow I've become imbued not only with all his earthly knowledge but also all the wisdom and power of his eternal spirit.

Opening my eyes, I find myself in the middle of a world sparkling and popping now with the intensity of a pot of water at full boil. My father's face begins to fade into the bubbling melee. I'm no longer afraid, but I still have questions.

*Don't go yet, Daddy. How will I know this man when I see him?*

*I've given you everything you'll need. Just keep following your path. All will be revealed to you in good time. Above all, have faith! You have within you the power to change the world—the power to save humanity from itself.*

*I do?*

*Have faith, Ricky. Follow your path and have faith. Remember, we will always be with you.*

*We? Who are we? Who will always be with me, Daddy?*

*All of us. We are your truth. We are your power. We dwell deep within your heart . . . We are love.*

My father's face disappears in a flash of white light, and everything in my world turns black.

I opened my eyes and gazed upward into the face of a man about the same size, build, and age as my father. But not my father. Definitely not my father. Still, this face was somehow, somehow familiar—familiar in a strange, almost spooky kind of way. Allowing my eyes to adjust to the warm shades of amber light encircling the two of us in a cocoon-like bubble, I took a closer look.

No, Stanley. This man was not my father. But there was something, *something* in the way he knelt beside me, held my hand, and returned my gaze with a tender look of both concern and relief in azure eyes that seemed to deepen in hue with each passing second.

Instinctively, I attempted to move toward him, but my body froze up and refused to cooperate. Cold and stiff as a corpse in the throes of rigor mortis, I was lying on the shore of a body of water that was completely foreign to me. I had no idea where I was or how I'd gotten there, but I knew for certain I was not on the bank of the Piscataqua in Kittery, Maine.

Beyond the man's face, the sky gave birth to the brilliant colors of a new day. The sun peeked its head over the horizon and began its ascent, painting the heavens a spectacular shade of magenta, fading into purple, fading into violet, fading into a deep, deep, deep sapphire blue.

Again I tried to move, but it was hopeless. I was trapped—trapped in my own body, which had become a prison, a kind of purgatory between worlds. Feeling utterly helpless and panicking now, I broke into a series of furious tremors in a mad attempt to break free from the invisible constraints that prevented me from sitting up. Then, just when I was ready to give up the fight, the invisible grip relaxed its hold and released me into the arms of this man—this man with the strangely familiar face.

I sobbed. I sobbed uncontrollably, hot tears of confusion rolling down my cheeks.

*Where am I? How did I get here? Who is this kind man with the gentle embrace? The last thing I remember is banging my head against the inside of a car door . . . and . . . and the car was underwater . . . and . . . and the water was sparkling all around me . . . and . . . and . . . then there was a flash of white light, followed by darkness, only darkness.*

But there was something else—the sensation of floating upward.

Cradling me in his arms, the man sang to me, softly, soothingly. Soon my sobbing subsided. All confusion, anxiety, and fear dissolved into a vast ocean of serenity and peace. I gazed deeply into the azure eyes of this man—this man with the strangely familiar face—and smiled.

*I'm home.*

*Your journey has only just begun . . .*

# END OF FIRST BOOK IN THE HERO'S PATH SERIES

# ACKNOWLEDGMENTS

F IRST OF ALL, I'D LIKE TO EXPRESS my heartfelt thanks to Paulo Coelho and Joseph Campbell for forging the path that made *A Hero Dreams* a possibility.

Writing and publishing a book can be a daunting undertaking—especially so for a first-time indie author. The good people at Beaver's Pond Press paved the way, and then allowed me to express my vision, while seeing to it that I didn't stray too far from the pack. Thanks to Athena Currier, Lily Coyle, Laurie Flanagan-Hegge, Tom Kerber, MacKenzie McCullum, and especially to Hanna Kjeldbjerg, who faithfully carried my torch along each step of the journey.

I owe a debt of deep gratitude to Mary Logue, Nicole Helget, Rebecca Molloy, and Angela Wiechmann for their expert editorial advice and for helping me to see *A Hero Dreams* through the eyes of a potential literary audience.

Thank you to both the early and late readers of the manuscript: Tracy Dyer, Aamera Siddiqui, Stephanie Welsch Lewin,

Rob O'Neill, Gregg Johnson, Chad McKenney, Judy Healey, and David Kansas. There's a piece of each of you in *A Hero Dreams*.

A special word of thanks to fellow indie author Stephen Yoch for his mentorship, kindness, and generosity of spirit.

Thank you to Kelly Acheson, Michelle Dench, and all the folks at Abacus Wealth Partners for their very practical financial advice and for keeping the wheels turning and the lights burning.

I am indeed privileged and honored to be working with an exceptionally talented and tireless publicist, Rachel Anderson, to bring *A Hero Dreams* into the world. Thank you, Rachel. Let's go get 'em!

Throughout my writing journey, those closest to me—my family—filled my life with their love, patience, encouragement, and enduring support. As I've learned, home isn't a place, but the *people* one returns to after a long journey . . . time and time again. Thank you to Mike Ristau, Laura Ristau, David Ristau, Claire Ristau, Rip Burgwald, Larry Koll, and most of all, my mother, Susan Koll.

And finally, thank you to Cindy Fox, a real-life angel who, many years ago, performed an act of true heroism and saved a drowning boy. It is because of you that *A Hero Dreams* is now coming into the light. You will always be remembered in my heart, and perhaps in the hearts of those who will be touched, and hopefully inspired, by my story.